By Cheryl Etchison

American Valor Novels
Here and Now
Once and For All

Here and Now

AN AMERICAN VALOR NOVEL

CHERYL ETCHISON

AVONIMPULSE
An Imprint of HarperCollinsPublishers

Excerpt from *One Lucky Hero* copyright © 2016 by Codi Gary.
Excerpt from *Stirring Attraction* copyright © 2016 by Sara Jane Stone.
Excerpt from *Signs of Attraction* copyright © 2016 by Laura Brown.
Excerpt from *Smolder* copyright © 2016 by Karen Erickson.

EPub Edition JULY 2016 ISBN: 9780062471062
Print Edition ISBN: 9780062471079

10 9 8 7 6 5 4 3 2

For Mom and Dad—
Thank you for showing me happily-ever-afters do exist.
Happy 50th Anniversary.

Here and Now

Here and Now

CHERYL ETCHISON

Prologue

June 2006

EVEN THOUGH HE knew it was coming, Lucky James flinched at the first volley of gunfire. He remained steady for the next two volleys, the loud crack giving way to the mournful sound of the bugle.

During his five years with the 75th Ranger Regiment, he'd never attended a stateside service for a fallen soldier. He'd stood at attention on a tarmac halfway around the world as the American flag was lowered to half-staff and "Taps" blared from loudspeakers. He'd carried flag-draped metal coffins holding the remains of his brothers-in-arms up the ramp of the C-130 that would deliver them home. He'd knelt beside many of those coffins, placed his hand atop them, silently begging forgiveness for failing them. After all, as a Ranger medic, his number one priority was to return his fellow soldiers home to their loved ones safe and sound. Not in a box. *Never* in a box.

When the bugler finished, the honor guard lifted the American flag from Ethan Dellinger's casket and began the ceremonial folding. Everyone watched in silence as the soldiers worked in tandem, pulling the fabric taught, smoothing each crease, making each fold with precision.

It had been years since he'd last seen Ethan; his last memories of him were as a chatty middle schooler who invited himself to shoot hoops with Lucky at a nearby playground one day. Over the course of the next few years, Ethan would show up out of the blue and follow Lucky around as he worked on his car, mowed the yard, whatever he was doing. Right up until the day Lucky left for basic training.

To be completely honest, Lucky hadn't given much thought to Ethan during the past five years. After all, he was just a kid he once knew. He hadn't even known Ethan had joined the army immediately following his high school graduation. Only after arriving home on leave the day before had Lucky learned from his father that "the youngest Dellinger boy" had been killed by a roadside bomb in Iraq.

Barely three weeks into his very first deployment, Army Pfc. Ethan Dellinger died two months shy of his nineteenth birthday.

His immediate family assembled only feet away from his casket with the remaining friends and family forming a semicircle around the grave site. From where Lucky stood at the back, he could see each of their faces. Ethan's mother and father sat side by side on small folding chairs with elderly relatives, grandparents perhaps, seated next to them. The youngest of four children, Ethan's immediate family was large to begin with, and when in-laws, nieces, and nephews were thrown into the mix, it grew to massive proportions.

Despite the large gathering, his eyes were drawn to Ethan's sister, Rachel. She stood out even among her own siblings with her fiery red hair and bright blue eyes.

She and Lucky were of the same age, had attended the same schools from the time Lucky and his father moved to Durant, Oklahoma, in the middle of seventh grade. In all that time, he'd never spoken more to her than the occasional hello, goodbye, or single-word answer. And for as long as he could remember, while she'd never paid any mind to him, she'd always had his attention, despite the fact they traveled in different social circles.

But what stood out about her today he found upsetting. There she was, surrounded by all these people, all family or friends of her brother, and she stood completely alone. With her arms wrapped tight around her middle, Rachel comforted herself at a time when no one else seemed to notice or care.

It took every bit of self-restraint for him to not make a scene, march over to where she stood, and pull her into his arms. He was on the verge of saying to hell with being polite when the service ended and the crowd began to disperse. Everyone except him. He remained right where he stood, watching Rachel as she walked over to Ethan's casket, pressed a kiss to her fingertips, and laid her hand upon the polished wood.

He had only taken a few steps in her direction when

her head lifted and she caught sight of him. Much to his surprise, she stepped away from Ethan's casket and walked toward him. Her blue eyes were red and swollen, her face tearstained.

"Rachel," he began the moment she was in earshot. "I'm very sorry about Ethan. He was a great—"

Before he could finish his condolences, her palm met his cheek with a resounding crack.

"How dare you come here," she said bitterly.

The tears fell freely down her face now. Her hands shook and her body vibrated with restrained fury.

He apologized a second time for reasons unknown even to him. But judging from the expression on her face and the hurt in her eyes, the words needed to be said.

"This is your fault," she said, pointing to the hole where her brother's casket would be lowered and the adjacent pile of red dirt that would bury him deep beneath the earth's surface. "Ethan idolized you. Wanted to be you. He joined the army in hopes of following in your footsteps. Except he didn't score high enough to be a medic. Wasn't fit enough to be a Ranger. I hope you're happy."

Stunned into silence, he could do little more than watch as Rachel Dellinger turned her back on him and walked away.

Chapter One

September 2012

THEY WERE GIGGLING again.

Lucky kept his head down as he strode past the group of young coeds huddled along the sidewalk. Three weeks ago he wouldn't have thought anything of it, not even if he noticed them stealing glances as he made his way past. But now he knew better. Now he knew they were friends with his assigned lab partner. Thankfully, they kept their distance and didn't approach him or call out his name. But the giggles whenever he walked past? Not even two months into the semester and this shit was getting old.

If there was one thing he hated about college, it was the age difference between him and most of the other students, something he'd never really considered when he left the 75th Ranger Regiment. With his thirtieth birthday on the horizon and at least six years of schooling ahead of him, not counting internships, residencies, or any specialties, it was now or never. So he'd chosen not to renew his contract, separated from the military at the beginning of August, and as a result was now surrounded by packs of giggling, teenage, selfie-taking girls.

Lord help him.

A little voice in the back of his mind told him he should probably refer to them as young women instead, but with their short shorts, long ponytails, and glossy lips, he certainly didn't— couldn't—regard them as women. Sure they were of legal age to have sex, but not being able to buy their own beer was a strike against them in his book.

Damn, he sounded old.

And compared to them, he *was* old. By the time he finished his undergraduate degree he'd likely be telling incoming freshmen to get off his lawn.

Having finally reached the science building, Lucky pulled open the door and made his way inside for his last class of the week. Fridays were his long day, with an early morning English class and then his chem class right at lunchtime. Afterward, he'd head home for a nap, and get up just in time for dinner with his dad and his dad's girlfriend, Brenda, before heading into work.

And the nights he didn't work weren't much better. Usually he'd study a couple of hours, watch some television, then hit the hay early. Thank God his buddies didn't know just how sad his social life had become since he'd returned home to Oklahoma. He'd never hear the end of it.

Of course, it had never been his plan to stay in the army so long. He'd enlisted before graduating high school in spring 2001, intending to serve out his contract and use the GI Bill to pay his way through college before continuing on to medical school. Then 9/11 happened and the 75th was called upon to lead the way, first into Afghanistan and then Iraq.

Year after year he deployed with his brothers-in-arms, choosing to renew his contract more than once instead of keeping with his original plan. Medics were hard to come by and the need for 68Ws in particular was great with his unit literally taking the fight to the enemy's doorstep. Night after night, under the cover of darkness, the Rangers hunted high value targets featured on the Iraqi deck of cards and the elusive leaders of the Taliban. Finally, after a dozen years of fighting, as the Global War on Terror began to wind down and forces withdrew from the Middle East, it was time for him to go.

As much as he liked moving forward with his life plans, Lucky couldn't help but miss the military. Mostly he missed his friends and the camaraderie, but he also missed the adrenaline rush of combat, where every day was a matter of life and death. Now he was just an almost-thirty-year-old college student with a full course load and a job working as an ER tech in the local hospital.

For a man who had served as a special ops medic for over ten years, the position was far below his level of knowledge and experience. While serving his country he'd performed venous cutdowns, inserted chest tubes, and externally fixated severe limb injuries under the harshest conditions. But all that military training and experience didn't mean shit in the civilian world, so his responsibilities were now limited to starting IVs, drawing blood, and screening urine samples. Exciting stuff for sure.

But he made this choice. No one forced him into it. If he wanted to be a doctor, monotony was the price he'd have to pay for now. All part of paying his dues. In the meantime he'd have to shove all his frustration deep down inside and lock it up tight.

At the end of the hall he rounded a flight of stairs, finally reaching the chemistry lab. But instead of entering right away, Lucky took a deep breath and fortified himself. Ridiculous when one considered all he'd been through in the army. And yet, what he would face behind that door struck more fear in him than the killing season in Afghanistan's Panjwei province.

He exaggerated, but still.

From the pounding footsteps in the stairwell behind him, he knew additional classmates were on the way up and the last thing he wanted was to be caught standing all alone in an empty hallway. A few weeks earlier he'd been bored to tears in Humanities and let his mind wander. Caught staring off into space, some snot-nosed kid sitting next to him leaned over, shook his shoulder, and asked if he was having a PTSD flashback. In reality Lucky had been making a mental note to change the oil and rotate the tires on his Jeep. When he explained what he was lost in thought about, the kid laughed in relief and admitted he was on the verge of bolting from the lecture hall out of fear Lucky was about to go postal.

When his fellow classmates appeared at the top of the

stairs, Lucky reached for the door and held it open for them. He followed the last one through, finally facing his fear.

"Hi, Lucky!" His nineteen-year-old lab partner waggled her fingers at him from across the room, as if he might have forgotten his assigned table.

Brittany Jacobs was a sweet girl with long blond hair and light green eyes who chattered incessantly. She talked about some singer dude named Louis, whoever that was. Her labradoodle named Buttercup. Her red Volkswagen convertible with car lashes and black spots to make it look like a ladybug. Even about housewives and wedding dresses. Most of the time he had no idea what in the hell she was talking about. And to be completely truthful, he only really listened maybe five percent of the time.

"Wanna study this weekend? Big test coming up Tuesday."

As he settled on the stool across the table from her, Brittany leaned forward on the tabletop, the motion pressing her breasts upward and together. Based on the slight smile on her face and raised brow, it was obvious the bird's-eye view of her cleavage was more invitation than accident.

"We could grab a bite to eat Saturday night and quiz each other afterward?"

Ten years ago, he wouldn't have thought twice about sampling the wares of a pretty girl in search of a little fun. Hell, he probably would have jumped at the opportunity even five years ago, especially if he'd just returned from the sandbox and hadn't gotten laid in four months. But now? Now he couldn't help but wonder if in all that yapping she'd spoken of an older brother. And if so, what would he have to say about his baby sister making a move on someone a decade older.

"Sorry, but I'm working," he muttered before digging around in his backpack for his notebook and pen.

Her smile faltered a moment, but she quickly recovered. "Then how about Sunday evening?"

Lucky shrugged. "Can't do that either. I work third shift on the weekends. Seven p.m. to seven a.m. And when I'm not working, I'm sleeping."

That slight smile now gave way to a pout. She actually pursed her lips and pouted like a five-year-old on the verge of stomping her foot. He could only imagine she wasn't used to hearing the word *no*.

"If you're really in need of a study partner, I'm sure there's someone in here who'd take you up on it." He quickly scanned the room, then pointed at a tall, lanky, dark-haired guy with glasses. "Like him for instance."

Brittany looked to where he pointed, then quickly turned around. "Ugh. R.J.? No, thank you."

"Why not? He seems like a smart guy." And age appropriate.

"Been there, tried that. He slobbered all over my face like a dog the one time I let him kiss me."

"That must've been a long time ago, right? When was it? Eighth grade or something?"

She answered without any hint of amusement. "Last Fourth of July. And let's just say that horrific kiss was his best move."

Ouch. Even he had to admit he couldn't blame her for not wanting to "study" with good ol' R.J.

Then she reached across the table and patted his forearm, that sly smile on her face again. "Don't you worry about R.J. or your work schedule. I'll figure something out. Just leave it to me."

Before he could say anything more to deter her, class began, and he knew he was as good as fucked.

WRAPPED IN A towel with her hair dripping wet, Rachel Dellinger found herself in a race against the clock. With less than forty-five minutes to get dressed and to the hospital before her shift started, there was a good chance she'd be late clocking in. Not the best way to start off in a new department.

In need of extra cash, she left her job as a daytime floor nurse for a night shift weekend rotation in the emergency room when an opening came available. The schedule change made her boyfriend, Curtis, less than happy because that left her no time to wait around on him. What he didn't know was her reason for the schedule change. The small bump in pay would provide just enough to let her get a place of her own, permanently moving Curtis from current boyfriend to ex-boyfriend status.

Grabbing a laundry basket half-filled with clean but not folded clothes, Rachel began pulling the finished load from the dryer as she searched for her scrubs. She found the top first, then spotted the pants at the back of the dryer. Grabbing hold of one leg, she pulled it free from the pile only to find a pair of ice blue lace panties dangling from the opening of the opposite leg.

Panties that were definitely not hers.

Staring at the undergarments she held in her hand, Rachel waited for that oh-so-familiar sting of tears. This time, they never came. Just as there were no chest pains, no bile rising up her throat. Instead, her body went completely numb. A sure sign she was completely over Curtis and more than ready to move on.

Rachel calmly walked to the trash can, opened the lid, and dropped the panties inside and went on about her business.

Sadly, it wasn't the first time she'd found evidence of his cheating. She first suspected something months earlier when she overheard two of his friends talking about their weekend in Dallas. Friends he'd supposedly gone out with the Friday night before. When she finally gathered the courage to say something to Curtis in passing, he told her she must have misunderstood. That his friends had been talking about a different weekend, not "last" weekend.

With her bank account in dire straits, she didn't have the means to leave him then. So she ignored the feelings in her gut and let him convince her he was telling the truth. And for added measure, he piled on the guilt for her accusations.

Determined to be a better girlfriend, she kept the house spotless, made dinner every night even if he wasn't there to eat it, and she certainly didn't nag him about their future. She'd almost convinced herself things were going well between them until she found a wadded-up receipt in the pocket of his jeans. When confronted with the piece of paper from a nearby casino itemizing dinner for two, he tried to pass it off as a night out with his cousin.

But knowing his cousin like she did, she was damn sure that redneck wouldn't be caught dead drinking anything but Jack Daniel's or Jim Beam, much less some pink, fruity girlie drink that had probably been garnished with a tiny umbrella.

As she blew her hair dry, Rachel made a mental list in her head of things she needed to do. First things first, find a place to live. Which wasn't as easy as it sounded. Just today, she'd tried to adjust her body clock for the night shift and quickly learned apartment living wasn't conducive to a daytime sleep schedule. People tromping up the stairs. People tromping down the stairs. People tromping across the floor overhead.

Obviously her apartment building was home to a herd of elephants.

What she'd really like was a house. No shared walls with noisy neighbors. A little breathing room. Maybe a small fenced yard so she could get a dog. A really big, scary one.

Unfortunately, if she had to guess, most of the rental properties in her price range would already have been snapped up by college students. If the new place wanted first and last month's rent, plus a deposit, she'd be living on peanut butter and jelly for the next month. Throw in the utility deposits and it might be only bread and water for two months.

And so very worth it.

As the sun set, she headed out the door and hopped into the pickup truck that once belonged to her younger brother, Ethan. He'd bought it brand-new just after joining the army, and when he died he left it, along with everything else of his, to her. Much to the disappointment of their parents. So instead of using his death benefits to pay off the truck, she gave the money, along with her old car, to her financially strapped parents and went about paying for Ethan's truck herself.

More than six years later, it was just as he'd left it. An army decal stuck on the back window. His favorite CDs in a holder strapped to the sun visor. The tassel from his graduation cap hanging from the rearview mirror.

About every three months she'd tell herself she'd take it all down the next time she cleaned it out. But when the time came, she couldn't do it.

Halfway to the hospital, the cell phone rang where it sat in its hands-free holder. She pressed the speaker button and said hello.

"There's nothing to eat," Curtis said immediately.

No "Hi" or "How you doin'?" No simple courtesies at all. It was all about him. And for all she cared, Curtis could starve. The days of fixing him dinner and waiting on him hand and foot were over.

"Then go to the store. I'm on my way to work."

Even without seeing him, without him saying a word, she could picture him standing in front of the refrigerator, resting one arm on top of the door as he stared inside, and waiting for something to magically appear.

"What am I supposed to do about dinner?"

"You're a big boy. You'll figure it out. I gotta go." Rachel quickly disconnected the call as Curtis swore and sputtered on the other end.

She really wanted to tell him to have little Miss Blue Panties make his dinner, but shooting off her mouth would only hurt her in the end. If she had a place to crash temporarily, she would've said it. But Curtis was just vindictive enough he'd destroy her stuff before she'd have a chance to retrieve it.

Nope. She needed to play it cool. Avoid him at all costs and find a new place to live ASAP. Which also meant she needed to find someone to help her move out in the middle of the day when Curtis wouldn't be home.

The idea of a covert moving-day operation made her laugh. What she wouldn't give to see the look on his face when he returned home to find her stuff gone.

With only seven minutes until her shift began, Rachel whipped into the employee parking lot. And as her luck would have it, the first row was completely full. As was the second and third. Through the half light, she saw a car on the next aisle backing out and hurried to claim the spot. Without coming to a complete stop at the end of the aisle, she made a quick right and saw something flash in her headlights just before the moment of impact.

LUCKY GINGERLY PUSHED himself up to sit with one hand, instantly feeling the throb and burn of a good old-fashioned case of road rash. With his feet tangled with the frame of his bike and the cleats from one pedal digging into his calf, it took several seconds to extricate himself from the wreckage.

"Oh, my God," he heard a woman say as she came around the front of the truck and fell to her knees beside him. Although it was hard to make out her features looking into the glare of the headlights, he could see she pulled a cell phone from her pocket. "Don't move. Just give me a second to call 911."

"I'm fine," he said, reaching out to stop her from calling.

"You don't know that. Since you aren't wearing a damn helmet you could have a concussion and not really be aware of your injuries."

Who did this chick think she was? After all, *she* hit *him*. Not the other way around.

Lucky tried to get a look at her face, but the bright headlights silhouetted her so that he could only make out the color of her shoulder-length hair. Blond.

Figured.

"I promise you, I'm fine."

He must've convinced her since she shoved her phone into her pocket. She put both hands on her knees and huffed. "I'm a nurse. At least let me take a look at you."

"I think you've done enough," he mumbled under his breath.

As he rose to his feet, Lucky felt a sharp pain in his hip where he'd taken the brunt of the fall. He doubted it was anything more than a deep bruise, something he'd definitely feel for the next couple of days, but nothing that required medical attention. Thankfully, the pickup had only clipped his back wheel and sent him into the curb instead of hitting him directly. Otherwise, who knew what kind of injuries he'd have ended up with.

Again, she asked him to let her have a look.

"No need. I'll handle it," he said, waving her off. "Just pay attention next time."

With the front wheel of his mountain bike now resembling a taco, he lifted it over his shoulder and walked to the side entrance of the hospital. Outside he locked his bike to a light pole, then headed in through the automatic doors and down the hall to the ER. The desk clerk, an older woman with big hair and an even bigger smile, waved hello as she hung up the phone.

"Well, hello there, handsome," Dottie said in her southern drawl. "You're a little late tonight."

"Some idiot driver clipped my back wheel and tossed me into the curb." He showed her the giant tear and bloodstain on the sleeve of his shirt. "I need to clean myself up before clocking in."

"Sure thing, sugar. Exam room seven is open. Anything else you need? A kiss to make it all better?" she asked with a wink.

Lucky chuckled. "Another time, maybe." She was old enough to be his grandmother, but that didn't deter her from a little innocent flirting. "I could use some scrubs."

"Absolutely. We can't have you looking like that. Whatever will the ladies think?" she said with a laugh. "Give me just a minute and I'll bring you some."

Chapter Two

WHEN THE PHONE kept ringing nonstop and the desk
clerk asked her to take a set of scrubs to exam room
seven, Rachel didn't think much of it. It was, after all, an
ER and she assumed they were for a patient whose clothes
were ruined and was in need of something to wear home.
She gave a light tap on the exam room door and pushed it
opened further, expecting to find someone at least sitting
on the exam table and requiring assistance. What she
did not expect was to see a fine physical specimen, up-
right and most certainly able-bodied, whipping his shirt
off over his head in one swift fluid motion. Nor did she
expect to be greeted by strong shoulders, a broad muscular back, and narrow hips.

Holy moly.

This guy was by far the best-looking man she'd seen in
the flesh in a very long time. Maybe ever. And she hadn't
even seen his face.

She clutched the scrubs to her chest and stood silent and tongue-tied, watching, appreciating, as the muscles in his back and arms flexed and strained as he unfastened the leather belt around his waist and released the button. All those finely sculpted muscles worked in unison to create a stunning physical display of power and strength as he shoved his pants to the floor.

Wearing only white crew socks and gray boxer briefs, he turned to face her and she nearly forgot how to breathe. She thought the back was nice? The chest. The abs. The dark trail of hair that began just below his navel and disappeared beneath the waistband of his briefs.

"You could've dropped them on the table and left instead of just standing there."

Her gaze shot upward to see one corner of his mouth lifted in a half smile, and as dark brown eyes stared back at her she was immediately struck by the feeling she knew this guy. There was something so familiar about him, but she couldn't quite put her finger on it.

She swallowed hard in an effort to unstick her tongue from the roof of her mouth. "You knew I was standing here?"

Instead of answering, he simply held out his hand, his eyes flicking to the scrubs she held in a stranglehold against her chest before lifting to meet hers once again.

"How?" She relaxed her grip, felt the blood rush back to her fingertips as she placed the scrubs in his hand. "How did you know?"

"Spatial awareness," he said, taking the clothes from her and immediately tossing the shirt onto the gurney.

"That and you knocked on the door before you came in." He flashed that half smile again before stepping into the pants and tying the drawstring. "Thanks for the clothes, Rachel. I can handle it from here."

Immediately she looked down to see if he'd read the name from her badge, only to realize her crossed arms were covering her ID. Clearly, he knew her. So she looked harder this time, doing her best to ignore the chest and abs and arms and focus on his face. As she mentally stripped away the disheveled hair, the heavy scruff covering his face, the laugh lines around his eyes, the earlier feelings of lust were replaced by a sinking feeling in the pit of her stomach.

There was little doubt the man standing in front of her was the one and only Lucky James.

She swallowed around the lump in her throat. "How long have you been back in town?"

His eyes softened. "Since August."

From his tone, she knew he was thinking back to that same hot summer day, when she was angry at God and everyone but lashed out at Lucky. And the last thing she wanted to do right now was talk about it.

There was a loud knock on the door as it pushed open and in walked another man with a stethoscope dangling around his neck. Although he was about the same age, this guy was blond and wore glasses. He stopped short at the sight of her and offered his hand. "Are you Karen's replacement? We haven't met yet. I'm Chad Ferguson."

That was a name she recognized as being one of the ER doctors.

"I'm not sure who Karen is," she said, taking his hand, "but I'm Rachel Dellinger. I transferred down here from the floor. Tonight's my first night."

"It's good to have you," he said with a nod and a smile before turning his attention to Lucky.

"So, what in the hell did you do, man? I couldn't believe it when Dottie said you were in here. Thought I'd come check on you to make sure you didn't do some real damage."

It was then she noticed the fresh blood and dirt on the backside of Lucky's right arm. Which meant *he* was the guy from the parking lot.

Lucky's gaze momentarily slid to her, then back to the ER doc. "Nothing major. A little bit of road rash and that's it. Give me five minutes and I'll be outta here."

"No rush," Ferguson said as he grabbed a couple of latex gloves from the dispenser on the wall. "Not like there's anything going on out there anyway."

"You know you just jinxed it, right?"

"Hell, yes." Ferguson laughed. "You know there's nothing I hate more than a quiet ER. Now let me make sure you didn't break anything."

Rachel tried to back out of the way, but found herself hemmed in as Ferguson manipulated Lucky's arm, working it to and fro, testing the elbow and then the shoulder.

"Any pain in your wrist? Hand?"

"Nope."

Then, as if the room couldn't be any more crowded, another woman she didn't yet know poked her head in the doorway. "We've got an ambulance en route. Patient is twenties, male. Motorcycle versus pickup."

"Ask and ye shall receive," Ferguson said with a wide grin on his face. He took a moment to strip off his gloves and toss them in the hazardous-waste bin. "Things look fine, like you said. Let Rachel get you all bandaged up. But don't be too long. This could be a good one."

As the ER doc rushed out of the room, she turned to grab wound cleanser and gauze pads from the supply cart. "Without a mirror, there's no way you can see to clean it properly."

"You can go." He tugged the bottle of wound cleanser from her hands. "I can take care of this."

Rachel grabbed the bottle back from him and set it down next to the gauze pads, daring him to try that little maneuver a second time.

Once she was convinced he'd leave things well enough alone, she yanked a set of latex gloves from the dispenser and immediately pulled one on her right hand while leaning over to get a closer look. It was nothing more than a scrape, a pretty good one that had to hurt like hell. And when it started to heal and scab over, it was bound to pull and break open every time he bent his elbow.

"So you're the idiot from the parking lot."

The smile was gone from Lucky's face this time when she looked up at him. Not that she could really blame him since she hadn't really meant to say that last little bit out loud.

That's when she heard him mumble something under his breath about her driving skills. Obviously he didn't think riding around on a bicycle in the almost dark didn't play a part in their little incident in the parking lot.

She blew out a frustrated breath and pulled on the second glove, snapping the latex against her palm while reminding herself that when she became a nurse she swore she'd treat all patients with care, no matter their gender or race or rotten disposition and holier than thou attitudes.

"So, obviously you work here in the ER," she said, turning her attention to the sterile packaging she was tearing open. "What do you do? Are you a doctor?" She held her breath hoping he wasn't since she kinda hit him with her truck even though it was totally his fault. But it'd just be her luck to get fired the first night on the job.

"I'm a tech."

Rachel breathed a sigh of relief. "That's it?"

"Wow. Don't hold back from saying what you really think." He grabbed the freshly opened gauze pad from her hand. "Since I'm the lowly technician who'd normally handle this type of stuff, I'll just take care of it myself."

"Don't be ridiculous. We've been over this." She snatched the gauze four-by-four back from him, doused it with antiseptic, and pressed it to his scrape at the widest point.

"Goddammit," he said through gritted teeth.

She maybe could have used a more gentle hand, but what was done was done. "Who knew a Green Beret would be such a baby about a little scrape."

"Ranger. Not the same." He took hold of her wrist,

pulling her hand from his arm. "I promise you, I can handle this from here."

"Fine. If you say so."

She stripped off her gloves and dropped them along with the gauze in the hazardous-waste bin and marched out of the room, thankful she didn't have to spend one more minute taking care of the man.

AFTER A HELLISH night at work, all Lucky wanted to do was go home, pull his blackout curtains closed, and turn off his phone. It ended up that wrecking his bike was just the beginning of his bad night. He was pissed on, vomited on, and then there was the unfortunate patient who needed assistance removing his penis ring. For four days the poor guy had tried to remove it on his own and only came in when the swelling reached the point he couldn't pee anymore. It definitely gave a whole new meaning to blue balls and he and Chad couldn't help but wince in sympathy when they got a look at the mess.

So when the sun came up and his shift was over, Lucky was more than ready to get the hell out of there. His hip ached, his knee ached, and his elbow was wrecked enough he had to change the bandage more than once through the night. Then there was the little problem of his transportation home. Any other day, he'd heft the bike over his shoulder and haul it the two and a half miles home on foot. But today, he'd had enough. He was tapping out because he could.

Not even two full months out of regiment and already he was going soft.

For the next few minutes he chastised himself enough to feel sufficiently guilty for being so damn lazy. Was even on the verge of calling his dad back and telling him to forget about the ride when his old man pulled up to the hospital's front entrance. Lucky gave himself a pass this time, taking a silent vow this would be the one and only time he'd do this. Next time, he'd suck it up and haul himself home on his own two feet, no matter what kind of day he'd had.

"So much for the saying 'Just like riding a bike,'" Duke James said with a laugh when he got a look at Lucky's road bike. "It definitely looks like somebody forgot how."

"I didn't forget how to ride a damn bike," Lucky countered as he lifted the wrecked bike into the bed of the truck, then climbed into the passenger's side. But his mood brightened almost instantly as he was greeted with the heavenly scent of cinnamon and sugar. His stomach rumbled right on cue. "Cinnamon rolls?"

Duke answered with a smile and handed over a Tupperware container filled to the brim with sticky, gooey goodness.

God bless Brenda.

It didn't matter that he'd be home in a few minutes, he wasn't going to waste any time popping the lid off and sinking his fingers into the sweet, doughy goodness. He lifted one roll to his nose, inhaled its sweet scent so as to savor the moment much like a wine aficionado would do with a full-bodied red. Then he opened his mouth wide and shoved it in, his eyes drifting shut in pure ecstasy. There might have been inappropriate noisemaking as well. No regrets.

"Good stuff, isn't it?" his father asked.

Before Lucky had even finished the first, he was grabbing a second roll from the container. "Absolutely."

There was nothing healthy about his father's girlfriend's cooking. The woman put Paula Deen's love for butter to shame. An old school kind of cook, Brenda poured off leftover bacon grease into an empty Crisco can she kept beneath the sink. Whenever a dish lacked a little flavor, out came the can and a little helping of meat fat was added. His arteries screamed at the thought of it, but damn if her cinnamon rolls weren't a little slice of heaven worthy of a few months off his life.

"You never said how you wrecked your bike."

"Had my back wheel clipped in the parking lot and it tossed me into the median," Lucky said around of mouthful of cinnamon roll. "The front wheel is toast. Basically folded it in half."

"Someone hit you? Did they at least stop? Make sure you were okay?"

"Oh, yeah," Lucky said before taking another bite. "Funny thing about it . . . the driver was Rachel Dellinger."

"Did she know it was you? Maybe she did it on purpose," his dad said with a chuckle.

Lucky shook his head. "She didn't do it on purpose.

She didn't even recognize me at first. It wasn't intentional, it was an accident. Nothing more."

"If you say so." His father was still smiling, still amused as he pulled into the driveway and threw the truck into park. "But if I were you, I'd keep an eye out. That girl definitely does not like you."

As Lucky opened the passenger door, he looked back at his father. "Are you gonna come in?"

"Sorry. Can't today. Brenda's cousin's daughter is getting married this afternoon, so I gotta hurry back and get ready for that."

"Sounds like fun."

"Not sure I'd go that far." His father reached out and patted the back of Lucky's shoulder. "Anyhow, I'll see you later. Get some rest."

Lucky thanked his dad one last time for the ride home, then lifted his bike from the back of the truck. His dad backed out of the driveway, gave the horn a little beep and one last wave.

After watching Duke drive away, he hefted his bike over his shoulder and made his way around to the back side of the house. He climbed the steps and promptly dropped the wrecked mess on the screened back porch. Hopefully, he'd be able to find a replacement wheel in town. Otherwise, he might have to head south across the river, maybe even drive the hour or so to McKinney in order to find one. Not that he was in any rush to find a replacement because his days of riding the damn thing to work were definitely done.

Since his belly was full, he headed straight for the bathroom and turned on the shower, cranking the temperature as hot as it would go. As he stripped off his clothes, his body ached and creaked like that of an old man and in the mirror he caught sight of a dark purple bruise that had bloomed on his hip. He stripped off the wrappings and bandages covering his arm and climbed into the shower. The hot water stung his road rash like a son of a bitch, but eased the feeling in his muscles that he'd been hit by a Mack truck. He closed his eyes and turned into the hot spray and within an instant her face appeared beneath his lids. Those bright blue eyes. The full rose-colored lips. Rachel Dellinger was just as beautiful as he remembered.

Lucky remembered his father's teasing words, how she might have tried to run him over on purpose. While they both knew that wasn't true, his dad was definitely right about one thing—she did not like him. That had not changed.

But unlike the last time he saw her, he wasn't leaving town the following week. And with them working not only at the same hospital but the same shifts in the same department, running into each other wasn't just a possibility. It was a damn certainty.

EVEN THOUGH SHE was bone tired, the last thing she wanted to do was rush home and face Curtis. She was just too tired, both emotionally and physically, to deal with any of his crap this morning. Besides, if she wasted another forty-five minutes, he'd be leaving for work and she could avoid him completely.

So she drove to the one place where she always found peace. The gravel crunched beneath the truck's tires as she passed under the familiar iron archway leading into the cemetery. Rachel followed the single lane road around the perimeter, finally parking beneath a large pin oak in the back corner.

Unlike so many other times when she'd come here, there were no weed eaters or lawn mowers buzzing around, no backhoes digging another grave site. Instead, the only sounds were the wind rustling the leaves in the trees and a dog barking in the distance.

"Hello, Ethan."

She ran the palm of her hand over the smooth top of curved white granite before taking a seat in the grass.

"You won't ever believe who I saw today. Yesterday, really," she said while brushing away the dried leaves and grass the wind had piled against the base of his headstone. "Lucky James is back in town. He left the army last month. I'm actually working with him at the hospital."

Of course, if everything she was taught as a child about heaven and angels watching over us was true, he probably knew that already.

She traced the letters of Ethan's name carved into the stone, using her fingertip to clear away the dirt caught in the little crevices, and making a mental note to come back the following week with a bucket and brush to clean it properly.

"I avoided him most of the night since I almost ran

him over with your truck." She winced, hoping he'd missed that little incident. "I promise, I didn't do it on purpose."

If she were a nicer person, she would've offered Lucky a ride home well before their shift ended. After all, she was partly at fault for his bike being in the condition it was. Okay, mostly at fault. And she shouldn't have waited until she was climbing in her truck to leave work and happened to see him standing outside with his broken bicycle. She'd only just begun to consider offering him a ride when a pickup pulled up, stopped, and Lucky tossed his bike in the back.

But giving him a ride home would have meant being in close quarters with him for the ten, fifteen minutes it would take to get him to wherever he was going. And that was a really long time, especially when one considered not just their last encounter where she damn near ran him over, but the one prior to that where she slapped him.

She could practically hear her brother lecturing her.

"I know, I know. I need to apologize. Not just for yesterday but for everything else. It wasn't his fault that you died. I get that now. It's just . . ." She paused, trying to find the right words. "You know I've never been very good at apologies. At least, not when it really counted."

With the sun now fully up and the temperature rising, she pulled off her jacket and wadded it up in a ball, using it as a pillow as she lay down on the ground. Rachel reached out with one hand and placed it flat against the cold stone.

"I miss you. Every day," she whispered. "So much."

Chapter Three

RACHEL EFFECTIVELY AVOIDED him the remainder of their weekend shift. The few times their paths did cross, it was no different than when they were in school together. Nothing more than polite nods followed by one-word replies. The place where he'd felt most at home had become an emotional minefield overnight. And Lucky knew in his gut if he made one wrong move, the whole damn place would be blown to hell.

As a matter of fact, the tension during his weekend shift had become so unbearable that by the time classes rolled around on Monday, he welcomed the loud, obnoxious coeds surrounding him. Even Brittany droning on and on to him about the latest *Housewives* marathon didn't bother him.

By the time he had his regularly scheduled Thursday morning breakfast with his dad, Lucky knew there was no two ways about it. At some point in time, he and

Rachel would have to sit down like two responsible adults and hash things out between them. And when he asked his oh-so-helpful father for his advice on the situation, his old man suggested Lucky made sure their conversation did not take place in a parking lot. "Otherwise, she might just finish what she started."

Duke was still laughing at his own joke twenty minutes later.

Come Friday evening Lucky arrived early to work, stood outside the hospital entrance, and waited. Fifteen minutes before their shift began, Rachel's large pickup truck rumbled into the parking lot. When she spotted an open space at the end of the row, she jumped up and over the adjacent median as she whipped it into the empty slot.

She really was a terrible driver. Or maybe she was just terrible at parking. Either way, it looked like his dad was right and it was a damn good thing Lucky was standing near the building instead of waiting for her out in the lot.

He watched as she made her way across the parking lot, pulling and twisting her hair back from her face and securing it with an elastic band. Only as she crossed the service road that circled the building did she notice him standing there. Almost immediately she reverted to her avoidance ways, bowing her head and focusing her attention on her fingers as they fiddled with her car keys. As she stepped up onto the sidewalk, she raised her head just enough to offer a polite smile, much like one given to perfect strangers.

One of his best friends from regiment had a go-to

saying in situations like this. He could almost imagine what Calder "Bull" Magnusson would say to him. "The best way out is always through. Walking on eggshells doesn't help things."

The best way out is always through.

Lucky took a deep breath, and just as she was about to pass him by, he called her name, reaching out a hand toward her in the hopes she'd stop. "Can we talk a minute?"

She glanced at her watch, at the entrance doors, and then back to him. "We only a have a few minutes before our shift begins and I'd rather not be late."

She took another step forward and this time he was close enough to touch her. "Then maybe we can talk afterward? Go for a coffee? Breakfast?"

Rachel looked down where his hand rested on her forearm and then met his eyes. "I have a boyfriend."

As if that somehow explained everything.

The automatic doors slid open in front of her and she hurried inside, her steps longer, faster now. But he was taller, his legs longer. Not to mention he was determined to get them both past this road bump, even if he had to drag her over it kicking and screaming. He followed her through the doors and darted past her, then turned around to face her, walking backward as he spoke.

"Bring your boyfriend along if you like."

Her eyes widened and she drew to a halt. Obviously she didn't expect that.

"I'm not asking you out on a date," he quickly added. "I just want to talk things out. Hopefully make it where things aren't so tense between us. So if you'd prefer to have him there, that's fine with me."

She just stood there, wide-eyed like a deer in headlights. But after a moment the wariness in her eyes disappeared and one corner of her mouth lifted just the slightest bit. "I'd rather not. Invite him, I mean."

"Okay, then. Great," he said, finding it impossible not to smile. "I'll meet you outside after our shift is over."

He stepped aside and gave her space to go on without him. Already a weight had lifted from his shoulders, and hopefully, by this time tomorrow, his college classes would return to the top of his list of worst places to be.

JUST LIKE HE said, Lucky was waiting for her outside after their shift ended. Since "lunch" had consisted of a pack of peanut butter on cheese crackers and a Diet Coke from the vending machine, she jumped on his offer of breakfast. Even if the last thing she was hungry for at the moment was breakfast food.

She followed him in her truck to an old-time diner a little over a mile away, and as they waited for a table to be cleared, he chatted with the hostess like they were old friends. They were barely seated in a booth by the windows when their waitress appeared out of nowhere with a warm smile on her face.

"Hiya, Lucky. Brought a friend today?" She placed a glass of water in front of Rachel and a large soda and paper-wrapped straw in front of Lucky.

"This is Rachel. We work together."

"So you've brought me another third shift vampire," said the woman with Peggy on her name tag. "I suppose you aren't in the mood for breakfast food either."

Lucky leaned on the table and spoke to Rachel in a conspiratorial whisper. "Peggy knows I'm usually not in the mood for eggs and pancakes when I get off shift. So she breaks the rules and fixes me a club sandwich with French fries."

"I don't break the rules so much as bend them, darlin'," she said with a smile. "And it's not like there's a whole lot of extra effort that goes into making those club sandwiches for you." Peggy then turned to Rachel. "So what's it gonna be for you? I can get you the breakfast menu if you'd like."

She'd been craving a cheeseburger for the past hour or so, but she wasn't willing to push her luck. Anything not pancakes or eggs and toast or even a bowl of cereal was a plus in her book. "I'll just have what he's having. Thank you."

With a polite nod, Peggy was off to place their order, returning only momentarily when she brought lemon slices for Rachel's water and deposited another large Dr. Pepper in front of Lucky. With several minutes to kill before their food was ready, there was nothing left for them to do but talk. And wasn't that the reason he asked her to breakfast in the first place? She'd promised Ethan she would apologize, but she couldn't dive in headfirst. She needed to ease her way into it.

"I take it you come here often?" she asked while squeezing lemon juice into her glass.

He smiled at her question, his face more noticeably relaxed that it had been a few seconds before.

"It started out with me and my dad meeting here every Thursday for breakfast."

"You meet every week? That's nice."

"To be honest, it's a way for my dad to ease his guilt." While he talked, Lucky fiddled with the paper wrapper from his straw, twisting and untwisting it from around his index fingers. "A week before I was due to move home I got this text message saying he was moving in with his girlfriend. Which was kind of ironic seeing as the reason I was coming home to go to college was so I could spend more time with him. Try to make up for the fact I hadn't seen him much in the past twelve years."

"Well, that has to stink."

"It's not so bad. I have a free place to live all by myself," Lucky said with a shrug. Then a wicked grin spread across his face and once again he leaned across the table, narrowing the distance between them and lowering his voice so only she could hear. "At least my dad and Brenda are having sex across town instead of me hearing them go at it in the next room."

Rachel wrinkled her nose. "Ewww."

"Exactly."

He laughed then, a warm, rich sound contagious enough that soon she was laughing along with him. Which was so very welcome because she couldn't remember the last time she'd laughed. With Curtis. With people from work. With anyone.

"Anyhow, that's why my dad and I started meeting

here once a week." He paused to take a quick sip of his drink. "Then when classes started, I realized it was easier to stop here to eat when I got off work on Monday mornings than go all the way home and back to campus before my first class. Then there are times when I get off work and I know there's nothing in the fridge at home so I'll come here."

"You really do come here a lot."

Just then Peggy returned with two large platters and a ketchup bottle that was filled to the top. "Of course he does. Not just anyone can roll in here off the street and sweet-talk his way into ordering something not on the menu. Isn't that right, sugar?"

It was hard to tell because that dark scruff covered so much of his face, but it looked like Peggy had actually made Lucky James blush.

Peggy set both plates down at the same time and Rachel suddenly realized hers looked just like his, with two club sandwiches cut into triangles and a ginormous mound of fries. When she told Peggy she'd have what he was having, she didn't realize there be so much.

"Oh, my God. I had no idea I was ordering enough food for a small country."

Lucky chuckled and slid the ketchup across the table to her, "Don't worry about it. If you can't eat all of it, I'll take home the leftovers. That is unless you want it?"

"I can hardly believe you can eat this amount of food." She poured ketchup in the one tiny space she could find and passed the bottle back to him.

"Not only can I eat all of this, I'll be hungry in a couple

of hours." He shoved the contents of his plate to one side and dumped out a lake-size amount of ketchup.

Then they both dove into their food, giving them another temporary reprieve from talking about the stuff that really mattered. But three-quarters of the way through one sandwich and a dozen or so fries later, she'd reached full capacity. And a little voice was telling her it was time to get it over with.

"I owe you an apology."

Although she found the courage to say the words, she still felt like a coward, staring down at her plate instead of looking at him.

"You don't owe me an apology because you were right," he said. "I shouldn't have been riding a bike at that time of night. It's hard enough to see cars much less someone on a bicycle. Especially when you aren't expecting it."

"I didn't mean that." She dropped the fry she'd been using to draw patterns in her ketchup and lowered her hands into her lap, hiding them away from view. "I mean, I'm sorry for that, too. And I'll pay for any damages to your bike—"

"Don't worry about that."

"But what I really need to apologize for is what happened at Ethan's funeral. What I did. What I said." She rubbed her sweaty palms across the tops of her thighs. "I should never have blamed you. It wasn't your fault and I'm so very, *very* sorry I ever said that."

"Hey, Rach?" He reached across the table and rested his hand next to her plate, right in her line of sight. When she looked up at him, she realized he was waiting for her to do just that. His dark brown eyes looked back at her with such kindness. "You don't need to apologize. You were grieving. It's completely understandable. Besides, it was a long time ago."

The tears began welling in her eyes and she knew she wouldn't be able to stop them. "Sometimes it feels like it just happened." She hiccupped. "Other days it feels like he's been gone a lifetime. Or that I imagined him in the first place."

Rachel shielded her eyes from view as the tears spilled over and soaked her face. She was doing her best to not draw any attention, discreetly wiping away the tears, keeping her sniffles to a bare minimum. Then she felt a bump against her wrist and she lowered one hand to look at him.

"Here," he said, offering her a stack of napkins.

She whispered her thanks and went about drying her face, hoping that she did a good enough job she wasn't left with raccoon eyes.

"You know," Rachel said after exchanging one dampened napkin for another. "He used to talk about you all the time. Lucky this and Lucky that. Always Lucky, Lucky, Lucky." Her heart ached with the memory, but thinking of Ethan never failed to make her smile. "God. He made me crazy back then. Our brothers were so much older than him. They didn't take time to teach him a jump shot or show him how to throw a curve ball. But you did."

She looked up at him then, saw the smile on his face.

"He told you all of that?"

It was amazing the number of people that became irritated with her whenever she was overcome with sadness at her brother's death, or even wanted to talk about him at all. But apparently her reminiscing didn't bother Lucky. "Like I said, he talked about you all the time."

"Ethan was a good kid. Funny. And, considering he liked to show up at the most inopportune times, a bit of a pest. Kind of reminds me of his sister."

"Of me?" She furrowed her brows. "What are you talking about?"

"Do you recall walking in the exam room and having a good long look at my ass while my pants were on the floor and I was bleeding profusely?"

She felt her skin heat in embarrassment. "I wasn't looking at your ass," she countered. "I was admiring all those shoulder and back muscles. And you weren't bleeding profusely. You barely even had a scratch."

Lucky laughed out loud this time, a full-bodied laugh instead of just a chuckle. And then, much to her surprise, she caught herself laughing along with him for the second time since they'd sat down.

It was at that moment she knew they would become great friends. And she firmly believed that Ethan was responsible for the entire thing.

Chapter Four

RACHEL TURNED IN a slow circle, surveying the living space. While it was clean and the fixtures far newer than most of the rental properties in town, she just wasn't sure whether she could live here. Even for the short term.

For one, the location was a little . . . remote. Sure, the owner was only a quarter mile down the lane. And not sharing walls and floors and ceilings with rowdy college kids was always a plus. The quiet during the day would be lovely. But the nights she would be home, they would be the scary kind of quiet. The kind where every creak, every coyote howl, every moonlit shadow, would have her heart racing in a matter of seconds.

Then there was the fact it was a mobile home.

Having been born and raised in Oklahoma and witness to twenty-nine tornado seasons, she knew just how mobile the suckers really were. Like, pick them up and dump them in the middle of a field a mile or so away.

"There's a tornado shelter out back," the owner said as if reading her mind.

She forced a smile. "Oh, that's good to know."

Walter Culpepper, the owner of said trailer, was a standard issue good ol' boy. From the graying hair and receding hairline, she guessed he was nearing sixty if he wasn't already. He wore the ranch owner's uniform of Wrangler jeans, boots, and a plaid shirt with pearl snaps stretching over his potbelly.

"So . . . what do ya think?" With his thumbs tucked in his front pockets, he rocked back and forth on his feet, a hopeful smile on his face. Just like a little kid waiting to be told he'd "done good."

"It's nice. Quiet."

"I liked it."

"You lived here?"

His nod wasn't more than a slight dip of the chin. "Bought this place and moved it here after I got divorced in '04. My dad lived in the main house until he passed last spring."

"I'm very sorry for your loss."

He waved off her condolences. "Mean ol' coot lived to be ninety-six," he said with a chuckle. "Definitely nothing to be sorry about."

"So . . ." Rachel took one look around the empty living room, dining room, and kitchen. "Five hundred dollars a month. Is there a deposit?"

"To be real honest, I don't know anything about deposits and leases and all that. Anyways, my ex-wife's sister-in-law vouched for you, so that's enough for me."

She smiled at that. If there was one advantage to living in a small town, it was people knew each other. And desk clerk, Dottie, was her new favorite person. The only way Rachel had even found out about this place was because Dottie saw her checking rental property listings on Craigslist during her lunch break.

"Are you sure?"

"To be honest, I don't really need the money. This place is paid for, but I thought if someone wanted to rent her for a bit, then I'd use that money to haul her over to a lot on the lake. But I'm not in any hurry though. So—" Walt clapped his beefy hands together "—let's just do five hundred a month and that'll include your water and power and trash. If you want television you could hook up the satellite dish in your name. Afraid there's no cable out this way."

Finally some good fortune was coming her way.

Rachel fought to contain her excitement, just so Walter wouldn't suddenly realize he could charge her a heck of a lot more. "That's fine. How soon can I move in?"

"Anytime you want."

"I work weekend nights in the ER. So . . . next week? Would Monday be too soon?"

"Like I said, anytime you want will be just fine." Walter smiled and handed her the keys. "Just lock her up on your way out."

"Oh . . . okay. Thank you!" she called to him as he headed out the front door.

She curled her fingers around the two brass keys on a plain key ring. For the first time in her life, she would be completely on her own. Living alone, paying her own bills, answering to no one but herself. While the idea of a new beginning was exciting, it also scared the total crap out of her.

Her cell phone vibrated in her pocket for the third time in ten minutes. She didn't need to look at it to know it was Curtis. Wondering where she was, when she was coming home, whether or not she was stopping at the grocery store and bringing home breakfast.

Instantly, her previous fears vanished.

She needed to focus on the positive. Like the fact she'd crossed the first major item off her first list—find an affordable place to live. Was it her dream home? Not even close. But was it affordable enough she didn't require a roommate? Absolutely.

Now all she needed to do was find someone who didn't know Curtis and would be willing to help her move.

And she had just the man in mind.

IN THE SHORT amount of time he'd worked at the hospital, Lucky had gained quite a reputation for himself. When he saw nurses or other techs having a hard time drawing blood or starting IVs, he'd politely offer his assistance. Time and time again, he succeeded when others had failed.

It also helped working with docs like Chad Ferguson, guys who appreciated Lucky's medical training and battlefield experience. Chad knew Lucky's qualifications far exceeded the medical certification given to him by the state and so he trusted him completely to handle patients others might have found challenging. Like Mrs. Hembree, a little old lady with bad veins and suffering from dehydration. Plenty of people would have a tough time with her. But for Lucky, treating a patient under good lighting and a sterile environment was a cakewalk.

Lucky pulled back the curtain to find a tiny slip of a woman, not more than ninety pounds, curled into the fetal position on the gurney. Sitting next to the bed was the granddaughter, a heavyset woman probably not much older than him.

"My name is Lucky," he said, offering his hand to the granddaughter. "I'll be helping to take care of your grandmother."

Immediately she hopped to her feet with a smile conveying a far happier disposition than she should have considering the circumstances. Not that there were any indications that Grandma was on the verge of death or anything. But still.

"Angela." She shook his hand while simultaneously fluffing her hair with her free hand. "Are you a doctor?"

"Afraid not."

Her smile slipped and she released his hand. "Are you a nurse, then?"

"No, I'm a technician. Kind of like a paramedic."

A full-fledged scowl replaced her smile. "I want her to see a doctor."

"And she will. Dr. Ferguson will come in when he's available."

What he didn't tell her was that Chad was currently

taking a well-deserved nap in the exam room next door and had left specific instructions to only disrupt him if something critical, exciting, or unusual came in. Dehydrated little old ladies, unfortunately, didn't fall into any of those categories. It was likely Chad would only come in once all the labs were run and Mrs. Hembree was ready to be admitted upstairs.

Angela dropped back into her chair with a huff as he turned his focus to the patient.

"Mrs. Hembree," he said, taking her hand in both of his. "Since you've been running a fever for a couple of days, we're going to start with an IV. Once we get some fluids in you, we'll draw some blood and figure out what's going on here. Okay?"

The little old woman looked up at him with sad, blue eyes. "I hurt all over."

"I know, sweetheart. We'll take good care of you. I promise."

Rachel arrived with an armful of blankets from the warmer and helped change Mrs. Hembree into a hospital gown. After piling the blankets on top of her, Lucky wrapped an extra blanket around her arm to help bring her veins to the surface, all while the granddaughter watched him with an eagle eye.

As he waited for the blankets to work their magic, he did a second check of her blood pressure, pulse ox, and temperature, then reviewed the medications listed on her intake chart. Several minutes later, he unwrapped her arm and lowered it below heart level, looking for a vein.

Rachel stood behind him, careful not to block his light as she leaned over his shoulder to watch.

"If you're the nurse, why aren't you doing this?" the granddaughter asked Rachel as he began palpating the veins in the antecubital space. "I don't want my nana being used as a training dummy."

Lucky bit down on the inside of his lip to keep from saying something that'd get him fired.

Rachel must have sensed he was pissed and placed a hand on his shoulder. "I promise you, your grandmother is in excellent hands," she said with a syrupy sweet tone. "She's definitely got the best man for the job."

What this woman didn't know was that Rachel wasn't standing there to supervise, but to learn. When the triage nurse offered Rachel Mrs. Hembree's chart, she readily admitted she had a horrible time with dehydrated geriatrics. It just so happened that Doc Ferguson overheard and suggested she watch Lucky to see how he did it. After all, he'd spent a lot of time deployed to the sandbox where treating dehydrated patients was a common occurrence.

Unsatisfied with Rachel's answer, the granddaughter huffed. And kept huffing. So much so, Lucky wouldn't have been surprised if she passed out as a result. Then, with one last, dramatic huff, the woman rose from her chair and stormed out of the curtained area.

Lucky glanced back at Rachel and chuckled when she widened her eyes and whispered, "Uh-oh." They both knew what was coming next. And Lord help the person who woke Doc Ferguson from his nap for a dehydrated geriatric.

"Since she's gone, tell me exactly what you're doing. Step by step." Rachel leaned closer, the scent of her shampoo tickling his nose.

He'd dealt with all kinds of distractions over the years, but never one quite like her.

Lucky took his time, showed her how he used the 22-gauge needle and went at the vein from the side to keep it from rolling on him. "Because she's dehydrated, you have to take your time," he explained. "Otherwise, you'll blow the vein."

She watched closely as he waited for the flashback, pushed a little fluid, and secured it with tape.

"*Voilà*," he said. "Success."

Rachel offered him a polite little golf clap. "Nicely done."

Within thirty minutes, Mrs. Hembree had perked up quite a bit, although she was still running a fever. Thankfully, the granddaughter had only returned briefly during that time, then quickly excused herself to make a phone call.

Lucky closed off the IV and waited a few minutes, preparing to draw blood from her other arm.

"You remind me of my Harold." While her voice was soft and shaky, Mrs. Hembree's eyes were clear and focused.

"And who would that be?" Lucky strapped the tourniquet around her arm, formed her fingers into a fist, and held them there.

"He was my third husband."

"Third?" He inserted the butterfly needle into her arm and waited for the first collection tube to fill.

"Oh, yes. My first husband was a boy I went to school with. He lived on the farm next door so we walked to school together. And when we were older, we wandered off into the woods together to do other things." Her eyes twinkled with mischievousness. "He was killed in a tractor accident just months after we were married."

"I'm sorry to hear that."

"Me, too. But it's nice to think he'll always be young and beautiful."

"What about number two? Was he young and beautiful as well?" He removed the first tube and tipped it side to side before placing it on the tray.

"My second was a rat bastard of a man who drank our bank account dry. I wasn't sorry when the sheriff showed up on my door to tell me they'd found his truck at the bottom of a ravine." She paused. "He died."

"Really?"

"Oh, yes. Many prayers were answered that day."

Lucky could only shake his head. Never in a million years would he ever have imagined this sweet old woman would say something like that. He inserted the second collection tube into the holder and waited.

"But like I said, you remind me of my Harold. Such kind eyes." She smiled at him. "I was only twenty-four when my second husband died and in our small town rumors began to circulate that I was cursed. Men would cross to the other side of the street when they saw me leaving the market as if I had something to do with my previous husbands' deaths. Like I was a witch or something.

"I was alone for a long time until I met Harold. He fought in the war and survived being shot several times during the Battle of the Bulge, although he used a cane the remainder of his days. Despite being ten years older than me, he asked if he could walk me home one Sunday after church. Told me I was the prettiest thing he'd ever seen. We married three weeks later and had five children together. Such a smart man. Great with numbers. Sadly, he died seven years ago."

With the final tube filled, he removed the needle and replaced it with a cotton ball, taping it down to hold it in place. "Any plans to remarry?"

"Me? Heavens, no. If I were to meet anyone now I'd do just like you young kids do and live in sin."

He couldn't help but laugh at that. "That's what my father and his girlfriend are doing. Living in sin."

"Is that right?"

"Yes. They've only been living together a few months. Her husband died a few years ago and if she were to remarry she'd lose his government pension."

"Smart woman. Are you married?"

"No, ma'am."

She narrowed her eyes at him. "And why is that? You're not a rat bastard, are you?"

"I certainly hope not," he said with a chuckle. "I just don't have time to date."

"I find that hard to believe. What about that nurse that was in here earlier? She's pretty."

That was true. Instead of a sleek ponytail, today Rachel wore her hair clipped up in a twist. Fine strands that had escaped their hold framed the sides of her face. The royal blue scrub top only made her eyes looks that much bluer, despite the dark circles shadowing her eyes. A sure sign she was still trying to adjust to the vampire shift schedule. And, as always, she smelled fantastic.

"Well, I just moved home after twelve years in the military. Between working here and going to school and studying, there's no time."

"Oh, boo . . ." Mrs. Hembree said, patting his forearm. "Sounds like excuses to me."

He smiled. "Maybe."

And then, as if they'd conjured her up by speaking about her, Rachel appeared at the foot of the bed.

"Knock, knock." She smiled at Mrs. Hembree. "Sorry to interrupt, but, Lucky, there's someone at the desk to see you."

"Who is it?" he asked without turning around.

"I didn't get her name. Do you have a sister?"

"I don't have a sister."

The little old woman's eyes widened with interest.

"A girlfriend, then?" Rachel asked.

"Nope. No girlfriend either."

"Well, she asked for you specifically. She has long

blond hair. Younger. *Really* young come to think of it."

Lucky spun around on the small stool and looked her straight in the eyes. "You're joking."

When Rachel shook her head, he swore under his breath. Then remembering himself, he asked Mrs. Hembree to pardon his French. "I'll be right back."

The little old woman smiled. "Take your time, dear."

He grabbed up the chart and lab work, then yanked the curtain closed behind him.

"I've got to run these to the lab. Can't you tell whoever it is that I'm busy?"

"Sorry." Rachel bit back a smile. "I'm just the messenger. Dottie's already told her you're here and that you'll be right out. If you'd like I can take those to the lab so you can go on break. It looks like she brought you dinner."

She followed him through the emergency department wanting to see how this little melodrama played out. Dottie and the other nurses watched with bated breath. Even Ferguson was standing there, just leaning on the desk like he didn't have anything better to do. Sadly, it was the most interesting development they'd had all night.

Lucky peeked around the corner, catching a glimpse of the young blonde messing with her phone while sitting in the waiting room. He closed his eyes, leaned his head back against the wall, and pressed the heel of his hand to the bridge of his nose. "Fuck me."

"It's awfully late. Won't her daddy be mad she's breaking curfew?"

His eyes shot open and he stared down at her. "She's not . . ."

"What?" Rachel interrupted. "Your plaything? Your friend with benefits? I have to say I'm kind of hurt. What would your girlfriend think if she knew we went to breakfast together just this morning?"

"She's my lab partner. My *assigned* lab partner." He scrubbed a hand over his face. "I think she has a bit of a crush on me."

Rachel laughed. "You think? Well, good luck with that, Romeo."

She headed for the front desk to claim a front row seat, but he grabbed hold of her arm and tugged her back to stand in front of him. "Could you, please, tell her I'm not here? Tell her I went home sick. Tell her anything."

"Can't do that. Like I said, Dottie's already told her you're here."

"Rachel, please. Help me out here?" Lucky pressed his palms together and begged. "I'll owe you."

She'd swear on a stack of Bibles that a heavenly ray of light shone down when he said those three little words. "Will you help me move?"

His hopeful look was replaced with disbelief. "Are you kidding me?"

"No."

"That's blackmail."

She shrugged her shoulders in an "oh, well, tough shit" manner and turned to walk away.

"Okay," he called after her. "You win."

She turned to face him, unable to hide her triumphant smile. "See? That wasn't so hard, was it? What's the girl's name?"

"Brittany."

Rachel had to laugh. "Are you serious? Does she dot the *i* with little hearts?"

"You know what, maybe this isn't a good idea."

Good Lord, he was such a nice guy. One look in his eyes and anyone could tell he was truly concerned about this girl's feelings.

"She's a nice girl. Very smart as a matter of fact. It's just that she's very young. Very innocent."

"Oh, honey, you'd be surprised," she said, patting his arm. "She's probably not as innocent as you think."

LUCKY SHOOK HIS head in disappointment at Chad and the rest of the staff who gathered at the front desk to watch the show. Well, unlike them, he had shit to do. Like take Mrs. Hembree's blood draws to the lab for instance.

Avoiding the elevator, he headed for the stairwell at the opposite end of the hall, far from the waiting room. Typically he took the stairs two at a time, but this time he dawdled. Even chatted with the lab tech for a bit to waste a few more minutes before heading back downstairs.

By the time he returned, the group at the desk had dispersed, the show clearly over. While he waited on Mrs. Hembree's results, he decided to take lunch and just so happened to find Rachel in the break room.

"So . . ." He pulled his food from of the refrigerator and sat down at the table. "What did you say to her?"

She looked up from her magazine. "I promise I was

very nice to her. So much so I got complaints from the peanut gallery. I guess they were hoping for a catfight."

Assholes. Every last one of them. But he couldn't help but smile at the visual it painted.

"So . . ." She closed her magazine and crossed her arms atop the table. "About Monday."

"No can do," he said while stabbing a piece of cold steak onto his fork. "Have three classes and an exam. It'll have to wait until Tuesday."

"But I can't wait until Tuesday."

"What's the rush? Do you have to be out of your place by the end of the day or something?"

"Yes. No. Not really." She avoided eye contact by staring at the tabletop. "I just don't like the idea of having to spend one more night with Curtis."

"Your boyfriend?"

"Ex-boyfriend," she corrected.

"Oh. He doesn't know you're moving out."

She shook her head.

"So tell him you're picking up an extra shift and go stay somewhere else. What about staying with your parents?"

"You're joking, right?"

"Okay, a friend, then."

"My only friend who isn't married with children recently stopped returning my calls and texts. No idea as to why." She pushed back her chair and gathered her things from the table. "It'll be fine. I can tolerate him one more night, I guess. Just be ready to go first thing Tuesday. I need to have all my stuff out of there by the time he gets home from work; otherwise, he'll destroy what's left once he realizes what's going on."

"Hang on a second." Lucky called out to her before she went back to work. "If you need a place to stay, you can stay with me. I've got a spare bedroom."

"You're sure?"

"I'm sure."

"Damn," she said, smiling. "I almost feel guilty about blackmailing you into helping me."

Chapter Five

RACHEL WAS SURPRISED to learn Lucky was living in the same house he grew up in, not more than a few blocks from the playground where he played basketball with her little brother. The neighborhood was filled with homes that were nearly eighty years old, but not the historical kind with fancy stained-glass windows and architectural details that had renovation snobs frothing at the mouth. These were utilitarian, bare bone kind of structures that were nothing more than one giant square box with more boxed-off rooms inside. Located just a stone's throw from the cemetery and the railroad tracks in the run-down part of town, these homes weren't anything special when they were built and they sure as hell weren't special now.

His house, however, stood out from the others on the block. Whereas most were likely rental properties with landlords who didn't care about anything else aside from whether you paid the rent on time, this house was loved.

No peeling paint. No broken steps or railings. No half-dead trees in the yard.

She parked along the street and made her way across the stepping stones leading to the front of the house. Without warning, the door swung open before she reached the bottom step.

"So you're my girlfriend now, huh?"

"You wanted me to get rid of her," she said, not really feeling the slightest bit guilty.

Lucky folded his arms across his chest and leaned one shoulder into the door casing. He narrowed his eyes at her and attempted a whole pissed and threatening look. Instead, his expression was more faux-mad, like beneath it all he was fighting hard not to laugh.

"I take it you saw *Brittany* today?" And of course she couldn't help but raise her voice a few octaves and accentuate the syllables when saying the girl's name.

His mask cracked, finally giving into a laugh. "Sure did. As a matter of fact, she made a point to track me down after our exam."

Holding the front door open with one hand, Lucky took her duffel bag with the other, gesturing with it for her to lead the way inside. "You'll be in here," he said just before disappearing through a doorway immediately off the living room. When he returned he had her follow him as he gave a quick tour of the place. The front room, as he called it, was cozy but not cramped, with a sofa, recliner, and coffee table. They passed through the small dining room to the kitchen and past it, at the very back of the house, was the only bathroom.

"My room is there," he said, nodding at the closed door off the kitchen as he pulled open the refrigerator. "Can I get you something to drink? Tea? Bottled water? Jack Daniel's?"

He smiled at the last one and for a split second she was halfway tempted to take him up on it. Not because she was a whiskey drinker, but mostly just to see his reaction. "I'm fine, thank you."

"Okay, then, here's the deal," he said, shutting the fridge. "Glasses are in the cabinet by the sink, drinks are in the fridge. Help yourself to whatever you'd like. The lasagna will be ready in forty minutes. In the meantime, I'm going to hop in the shower."

"*You* made lasagna?"

Lucky shook his head. "Can't take the credit for that. Every once in a while I come home and find that my dad's girlfriend has stuffed all kinds of food in my freezer. Not that I'm complaining." He smiled then. "Anyway, make yourself at home."

As he headed for the bathroom, she wandered back through the small dining room, stopping briefly to look at the collection of school photos hanging on the wall. On the round oak table that seated four sat a laptop along with a stack of books. Organic Chemistry. Microbiology. Modern Humanities. Psychology.

Rachel picked up the one on top and flipped through the pages until it sent a shudder down her spine. She couldn't imagine going back to school at her age. No way. The year before she'd looked into an online master's program that would certify her as a nurse practitioner but decided against it. For one, the small salary increase wasn't enough to justify the expense. Secondly, Curtis thought any kind of higher education was stupid. Which said a lot about him.

And even more about her for dating him as long as she did.

In the living room, her cell phone chirped in her purse. Text message. If she had to guess, she'd say it was Curtis texting because he just received her note about picking up an extra shift. Which meant she wouldn't be there to wait on him hand and foot and he would have to figure out dinner on his own. Again.

A door opened and she turned just in time to see Lucky go from the bathroom to his bedroom. His hair was wet and water droplets still clung to his chest. With one hand, he held the ends of the towel together at his hip. His eyes met hers and the corner of his mouth lifted in a polite smile before he disappeared into his bedroom.

It was no big deal that he strode through his own home in a state of undress. They were both medical professionals.

Theoretically, Lucky James didn't have anything she hadn't seen before. And even if she hadn't, she'd seen quite a bit of him just the week before. But she must not have gotten a good look the first time because *holy good God* he was beautiful. A word she couldn't ever remember using to describe a man. And at the moment, she found herself a little breathless. And light-headed. She needed to sit down before she fell down, because that was not the kind of impression she wanted to make.

So she scuttled into the living room, taking a seat on the brown leather sofa. The front room was like the rest of the house: neat, clean, and very masculine, decorated in brown and beige. A brown leather recliner to match the couch. A dark wood coffee table. Only blinds on the windows, no curtains. No pillows. On the fireplace mantel there were several more frames filled with photos of Lucky, mostly with his father. The only other decor was a wall-mounted television currently tuned to ESPN.

Several minutes later, a door opened once again, followed by footsteps on the linoleum floor. The refrigerator opened and closed before the footsteps came closer. Now dressed in basketball shorts and a plain gray T-shirt, Lucky dropped into the recliner and placed an unopened bottle of water on the coffee table in front of her. "Just in case," he said.

He cracked open his bottle, tilted his head back, and drank down half in just a few swallows. Entranced by the sight of his Adam's apple working in his throat, she suddenly found herself a little . . . parched.

She reached for the bottle of water he'd brought her. "So you didn't say if Brittany was upset."

"Far from it," he scoffed. "In fact, I think she's regarding you as a challenge. She was also quick to inform me she's not looking for anything long term and only wanting a 'taste,' " he said, adding the air quotes. " 'A little fun on the side.' Something 'no one will ever have to know about.' "

"She did not."

"What am I gonna do about this girl?" He held his

hands up in surrender and all she could focus on was the snug fit of his T-shirt that was dampened in interesting places and highlighted the flex of his biceps. "She's coming at me with the full court press."

Rachel attempted to smother her laugh, but Lucky wasn't having any of it. He pointed directly at her. "It's not funny."

"It is. Kind of."

"I don't get it. Why is she chasing after me? Why do her little friends giggle every time I walk past?" He leaned forward, resting his elbows on his knees. "Explain it to me, please."

This poor guy. He really didn't have the slightest idea as to why these girls were following him around. "You're a unicorn."

He scowled, a little crease appearing between his brows. "What the hell does that mean?"

She couldn't help but laugh at him. "First off, you've got this whole mysterious vibe going. The dark hair. The beard. Then there's the fact you were in the military. And it's not like you were a file clerk or something. You were doing the kind of stuff they make movies about. You've traveled the world and haven't spent your entire life in this Podunk town."

"And that makes me a unicorn?"

A timer buzzed in the kitchen, signaling dinner was ready and ending their discussion.

In sharp contrast to her life with Curtis, and every other man she'd ever lived with, Lucky wouldn't let her help make the salad or garlic bread, saying she was a guest in his house and her only job was to eat. After badgering him for fifteen minutes, he finally relented and let her set the table. While she stood there, placing knives and forks on napkins, her phone chimed again with a text message. And again. And then a third time.

Even though leaving Curtis was the right decision, she couldn't stop that niggling of guilt for sneaking out like a thief in the night. Until she officially informed Curtis she was ending things between them, she was no better than him. She was a cheater.

For the fifth time since she'd arrived, her cell phone chimed. Rachel pulled her phone from her pocket and quickly scrolled through the messages. Out of habit she nearly sent a reply, but caught herself in time, choosing instead to delete the string of texts before setting her phone to silent.

"Someone's popular tonight," he said, trying to be funny.

But she felt anything but amused.

"Given the choice, I'd rather not be."

THINGS WERE PRETTY quiet the remainder of their dinner, which suited Lucky just fine. His friends in the 75th were always commenting on how calm and quiet he was. That an entire week could pass without some guys hearing him say a single word. His verbal thriftiness was never considered a negative though. If anything, the veterans said his quiet demeanor showed the hallmark of a great special ops medic, because when everything went to shit and someone's life was on the line, the last thing that person needed was a medic who was highly excitable.

So a quiet dinner for two wasn't something he ever considered awkward or uncomfortable. Probably because most of the meals he shared with his father while growing up were virtually silent.

But this Jekyll and Hyde thing with Rachel? It bothered him. A lot.

When she arrived at his house, she'd been her normal chatty, happy self and within a matter of minutes she spiraled into a woman who would barely speak or make eye contact.

Clearly, it had something to do with those text messages, which if he had to guess were from her ex.

No wonder she was in such a hurry to move and didn't want to spend one more night in his presence, let alone share a bed with him. Just the thought made him sick. He didn't even know the guy and he wanted to commit bodily harm.

Sure they got off to a rocky start her first day in the ER, but since they'd gone to breakfast and hashed things out, things had been far better than he expected. He liked her. He liked that she was funny and sarcastic and didn't know a stranger—that she chatted with patients like she'd known them twenty years instead of twenty minutes. He liked that she, in stark contrast to Brittany, didn't constantly talk about herself. She asked questions, she listened to the responses. Rachel was, in a word, genuine.

Who wouldn't want a woman like that? And what

kind of man was her soon-to-be ex that he could affect her in such a way with a few text messages?

When dinner was through, he didn't give her too hard of a time about wanting to help him clear the table or rinse the dishes. Instead, he politely thanked her for her help and finished things up on his own. With the dishwasher started and the trash taken out, he grabbed a couple of beers from the fridge, thinking they could both really use one right about then.

He found her standing at the fireplace mantel looking at a photo of him taken in full kit, an American flag used as a backdrop. And he couldn't help but notice she looked so, so sad.

"Admiring my younger, pimple-faced self?" he asked while offering her a longneck, hoping to lighten her spirits a bit. It worked, but only for a split second when a slight smile appeared on her face, then vanished just as quickly. If he had blinked he would have missed it altogether.

"This is how you looked back when—"

She spoke so softly as she accepted the beer from his hand and he had a hard time making out what she said. And then when he did, it took several more seconds to realize she was talking about Ethan's funeral. Rachel also happened to be right—the picture had most likely been taken the very same year.

She moved to the next photo, one of him and his father taken at his graduation from Ranger School. "Your dad looks just the same."

"Don't you dare say that to him. He's likely to dump Brenda and ask you out."

She smiled a second time, this one lingering a little longer than his previous attempt. It was a small victory, but one he'd gladly claim.

He took a seat in the recliner and she followed, settling on the sofa and tucking her feet up beneath her.

"I do wish I'd known Ethan was considering the military. I would have told him to go air force or navy. I could've suggested an MOS that was maybe a little safer, with less chance of being sent to the sandbox."

He was taking a huge risk bringing up her brother and his death. But after seeing how she looked at his army photo, his gut told him her thoughts were already on Ethan. Might as well give her an opportunity to talk about him if she wanted.

"Why?"

"Because regular army isn't like Special Forces or Ranger Regiment. We had the best training, the best equipment. Hell, in the early years, a lot of soldiers didn't have ceramic plates to go in their body armor. I probably would have told him to forego the military altogether and do almost anything else."

"That wouldn't have changed his mind. As a matter of fact, he knew all of that."

"You're certain?"

"Absolutely. Because I was the one showing him the news articles, trying to convince him to not enlist. But he wasn't the best of students and the last thing he wanted was to spend the rest of his life working odd jobs and never getting anywhere. He needed to get out of this town. The military was the obvious choice."

That was something he could relate to. But to hear her say it surprised him. "If this town's so bad, why are you still here?"

"I've asked myself the same thing thousands of times since Ethan died. Honestly, I don't know why." One corner of her mouth lifted as she pointed at his stack of textbooks on the coffee table. "You're the one taking psychology, you tell me."

"Nope. No way, gorgeous. You won't get me to touch that with a ten-foot pole."

She threw her head back and laughed, at what he said, at him.

As much as he hated to admit it, for the first time since he'd left regiment, he found something that gave him far more purpose, more fulfillment, than he could ever get from being a college student or ER tech. And that something was putting a smile on Rachel Dellinger's face.

Chapter Six

One thing Lucky had learned all those years in regiment was that moving always took far longer and required more help than most were willing to admit. What didn't look like much at the start often turned into a full day's work with several trips that in the end could have been reduced to one, if only they'd rented the largest U-Haul truck available.

Since time was of the essence and Rachel needed to have her things completely cleared out of the place before her ex arrived home from work, he'd traded vehicles with his dad for the day. That way they'd have two pickup trucks at their disposal.

He followed her through town, down University Boulevard to a newer complex on the west side. With most of the parking lot empty, she was able to back into a spot along the curb with him parking alongside her. And when she stopped in front of her apartment door that was not only downstairs but on the side closest to the parking lot, he fell to his knees in mock gratitude. "Thank God."

"Were you that worried I might live upstairs?"

"Absolutely I was," he said with a smile.

She smiled back at him, then turned the key in the dead bolt. "Here goes nothing."

The smell of stale smoke hit him the moment she opened the door. Pizza boxes, food wrappers, and empty beer cans littered the living room. On the floor next to the sofa was a cereal dish filled with cigarette butts and, next to it, a small burn in the carpet.

"Well, it looks like he didn't starve to death after all." She turned to hide her embarrassment, but not before he saw tears welling in her eyes. "I'm sorry about this. Usually it doesn't look or smell this bad. But since I started in the ER . . ."

Lucky took hold of her shoulders and made her face him, bending his knees just enough to bring his face down to her level. "Do not apologize for this. Do not. He's a grown-ass man and you are not his maid. It is not your job to clean up after him." He stared into those crystal blue eyes and waited for his pep talk to take hold. She could do this. She could leave him. She just needed a little boost of confidence, a little extra push to find her inner strength. After a few deep breaths, Rachel straightened her spine, the threat of tears now passed.

"Let's just get you out of here. Okay?"

She nodded in agreement, ready to get to work.

With the apartment having only one bed and one bath, it didn't look like she'd underestimated things.

Now he just needed to figure out what she was leaving behind and what she wanted to take with. In the living room, there was a small sectional sofa, a rickety old coffee table, and a flat-screen television on top of a glass stand. "Which big items are yours?"

"The television I bought for his birthday, so I'll leave it. Especially since he hates that I didn't buy him the one he wanted. And since he ruined the sofa, there's no point in taking it."

He headed for the bedroom next. "What about in here?" he asked.

"Just the dresser, nightstand, the floor mirror, and lamp. Then all of my clothes and stuff."

"What about the bed?"

"The mattresses, sheets, pillows, all of it he can keep."

Surprised, Lucky turned to face her. "Are you sure about that?"

"Absolutely. I don't want to sleep in that . . . that . . ." Rachel waved her hand in the bed's general direction. "Cesspool."

He chuckled at that. Couldn't help himself. Then he saw the mischievous twinkle in her eye.

Seeing a lighter on the nightstand, she picked it up and flicked it, a four-inch blue flame shooting up from between her fingers. "Maybe I should burn them?"

He shrugged. "If you don't mind going to prison for arson, sure thing. Let's fire it up."

"On second thought." She dropped the lighter on the floor.

"Probably the smart decision," he said, following her into the kitchen. "But what are you going to do about a bed in the meantime?"

"Rough it, I guess. I can sleep on the floor."

"You could, but I don't recommend it."

She folded her arms across her chest and cocked one hip. "Because I'm a girl?"

"No." He laughed. "Because it sucks."

They made quick work of the kitchen, packing things haphazardly in a short-ride-across-town fashion as opposed to the professional-move-cross-country style. A dozen black garbage bags were filled with clothes and shoes. Her bathroom items were tossed into a large box and quickly taped shut. Thankfully, she wanted to keep her womanly secrets secret and packed that box herself.

Within a matter of hours, they'd packed, loaded, and hauled her things across town. Getting her dresser up the steep steps and through her front door was a bit of a challenge, but they got it done. Of course, he practically carried it on his back up the stairs all by himself, but he wasn't keeping score. If it hadn't been for her repeated cheers of "You can do it! Almost there!" he'd likely never have reached the top step.

By late afternoon, they were starving, so she ran to pick up a pizza while he finished unloading.

Lucky was standing in the bed of the truck unloading the last two boxes when an older gentleman walking down the lane called out to him.

"Hello, there!"

Lucky waved in return and jumped down from the tailgate, dust pluming around his feet when they hit the ground. "Lucky James," he said, extending his hand.

"Walter Culpepper." For an older man, he had a firm grip and shook his hand vigorously. "Are you related to Ms. Dellinger?"

"No, sir. We work together at the hospital. I'm just helping her move."

"How many more trips do you have? I only saw you come past the house once."

That made him feel a bit better, knowing that Rachel's landlord paid attention and knew who was coming and going from his property.

"That's it. She doesn't have much stuff. Left most of it behind, if you know what I mean."

Walter nodded. "I was afraid of that. She seemed like she was in a pretty big hurry to move in."

As if on cue, Rachel returned, and as they both turned to watch her come up the drive, he patted Lucky's shoulder. "Not to worry. I'll keep an eye out for her."

She hopped out of her truck, pizza in one hand, six-pack in the other, and a huge smile on her face. "Hello, Mr. Culpepper. Would you care to join us?"

"No, but thank you. Just wanted to stop by, see if you were all settled."

"Almost there," she answered with a big smile on her face. "I just have a few things I need to buy."

Hearing Lucky chuckle at the understatement, she cut her eyes at him, before turning back to Culpepper.

"Sounds good." The old man gave a short wave and ambled off down the lane back to his place.

Lucky grabbed the last two boxes from the truck and followed her inside. Foregoing bar stools for fresh air, they headed out to the large back deck, where they sat on the steps facing the open fields, the pizza and beer between them.

She tore a paper towel from the roll and handed him one. "Who needs plates or furniture when you have a view like this?"

He couldn't help but to smile back at her. She didn't have anything to sleep on, anything to sit on, and most of her possessions were crammed into garbage bags, but she was happy and relaxed. At least for the moment.

And she wasn't wrong about the view. Low rolling pastures dotted with the occasional elm or maple tree, cattle grazing in the distance, and about a hundred yards off the deck a good-size pond.

"Did your landlord say whether or not that thing is stocked?"

"The pond?" she asked around a bite of pizza. "You wouldn't really eat something out of there, would you?"

"Depends on what's in there."

She wrinkled her nose and did a full body shiver, mumbling something under her breath along the lines of how gross fish were.

"I think you should get a dog." He pulled a second slice of pepperoni from the box. "A really big one. Maybe even two dogs."

"I've thought about it. But I'd hate they'd be locked up for so long on the weekends."

"Are you sure you don't want to stay a few more nights at my place? At least until you have a bed?"

"I'll be fine. I'll make a run to Walmart and grab one of those big air mattresses and a few pillows. That will work until I can buy something else." She studied him while taking a drink of her beer and he knew those little wheels in her head were turning. "Where's the worst place you ever slept?"

"That's easy. New Orleans."

"That's your worst?"

"Were you expecting me to say Iraq or Afghanistan?"

She shrugged one shoulder. "I sure wouldn't have guessed New Orleans. Was it for work or for fun?"

"Oh, definitely fun. I'd turned twenty-one a few months before and a bunch of us decided to spend part of our block leave there. The problem was there weren't many rooms available and the rooms we could find were expensive. We wanted to spend most of our money on booze, not a place to sleep. So we got one double room and crammed nine guys into it. Guys slept on the floor, in the chairs. One slept in the bathtub. We drew straws for the beds."

"Where did you end up?"

"I got a bed."

"How is that your worst if you got a bed?"

"Nine guys who'd been drinking heavily and eating nothing but Cajun sausage and fried food all day sharing a confined space with no air circulation? Yeah, it was pretty awful. Give me the desert any day."

Their shared laughter gave way to the peace and quiet of the country. Once again, they sat in comfortable silence, drinking their beer as the sun sunk below the horizon, setting the clouds afire against the dark blue sky.

"Do you miss the army?"

"Way more than I thought I would." He finished the remainder of his beer and tossed it in the empty pizza box. "I guess I shouldn't be surprised though. It was my life for twelve years."

"What do you miss most?"

"The guys. The camaraderie. Being surrounded by people who've got your back no matter what."

"Sounds nice." She wrapped her arms around legs, resting her chin on her knees. "I don't know that I've ever had anyone in my life like that."

"Well, now you do." He leaned over, bumping her shoulder with his. "If you need someone, I've got your back. No matter what."

LUCK, IN ADDITION to a man named Lucky, was on her side that afternoon. The fact she got all of her things out of the apartment before Curtis came home from work, thus avoiding a face-to-face confrontation, was nothing short of a miracle.

Now she stood in her own place, as empty as it was, and felt like she could breathe for the first time in months. It didn't matter she didn't have a sofa or a bed or a television. She could eat her meals at the breakfast bar since there were two bar stools. She didn't have to haul her clothes to the laundromat since the trailer came with a washer and dryer. And if the weather stayed nice and she felt like cooking out, there was a small gas grill on the back deck, along with one helluva view. It was more than a lot of people had and it wasn't as if she would be without the other things for very long.

Since Mr. Culpepper didn't make her pay the last month's rent or deposits on the utilities, she'd be able to buy new furniture come payday. Nothing fancy. Certainly nothing custom ordered. But she'd have enough to buy new instead of scouring the ads on Craigslist. Heck, she might even find a furniture store that would deliver it for her. Of course, if they didn't deliver she knew exactly who to call.

In high school, Lucky James was one of the nice guys. The teachers liked him because he was smart. The coaches liked him because he was a team player. The guys wanted to be friends with him and the girls wanted to date him.

And much to her surprise, he hadn't changed one bit. He was still smart. Still nice. A real white knight kind of guy she could fall for so easily if she weren't careful. But she would be careful because she'd learned her lesson this time. Especially since once upon a time Curtis had been a nice guy, too.

They'd met at a Super Bowl party thrown by mutual friends. At the time, she was sleeping on her friend's sofa, having moved in only weeks before after she found out her previous boyfriend was stealing money from her. But Curtis was different than other men she'd dated. He had recently moved to Durant, working as security at the casino. He had never been married, didn't have any kids. Their friends said he was a great catch who'd never found the right girl.

In the beginning, he brought little things each time he saw her—a single rose, her favorite kind of candy. Each gesture practically sweeping her off her feet. He was straightforward with his feelings, told her he wanted to be with her, only her, for the rest of their lives because from the moment he laid eyes on her he knew she was "the one." Within a matter of weeks she moved in with him and by the month's end he began to change. He wanted to know everywhere she went, who she was going to be with, and how long she'd be gone. If a trip to the grocery store ended up taking longer than he determined to be an appropriate length of time, he'd call her.

For too long she ignored her gut feelings. It didn't help that her friends were convinced he was just a romantic. They thought his possessiveness showed how much he cared and they often wished their boyfriends and husbands bothered half as much as Curtis did. But as time went on, he became more controlling than caring, more manipulative than romantic.

Then, as if she conjured him by merely thinking his name, her phone chimed with a new text message.

You stupid bitch.

Who the hell do you think you are?

I should have you arrested for theft.

Her heart pounded in her chest as the messages came fast and furious to her phone. But she swallowed down her fear, determined to stand up to him one last time. With trembling fingers she texted her reply.

I didn't take anything of yours.

I'm sorry but it's over.

Please stop texting me.

Even as she hit send she knew it wouldn't be as easy as asking him to leave her alone.

I'm sorry for calling you a bitch.

I love you.

I don't understand why you left.

Please come back home.

There it was, a prime example of the up-and-down roller coaster he'd kept her on for nine months.

She opened the contacts, scrolled to his name, and selected the option to block, then did the same on her Facebook, Twitter, and Instagram accounts. Then she finished strong by deleting every picture of him from her photo gallery, effectively erasing him from her past.

But the text messages she kept, a perfect reminder of a mistake she didn't want to repeat.

Chapter Seven

_____

LUCKY ALWAYS LOOKED forward to his Thursday morning breakfasts with his dad. It was a chance for the two of them to talk and catch up about things they typically didn't talk about in the company of others. Like his mother or his time in the 75th. For Lucky, this one-on-one time with his dad was the best kind of therapy session, a time when he could say anything without someone passing judgment or twisting it into a political argument. His dad just listened. And if there were times when Lucky couldn't find the right words or needed to change the subject, his father happily took the lead.

But this morning, the conversation was light as they sat in their regular booth against the front windows. His father was looking to buy a RV, something he and Brenda could use for travel since she had a fear of flying. While she thought a small trailer that could be hitched to their truck would suffice, he was looking at something bigger. Something more along the lines of a luxury motorcoach.

"You do realize you could buy a couple vacation homes for the cost of one of those?"

His dad smiled and shook his head in disbelief. "You're starting to sound like Brenda."

Lucky was taking a drink of his coffee when the bell on the front door jingled and a flash of red caught his eye over the rim of his cup. At first he thought his eyes were deceiving him, that it wasn't really her at all. Then Rachel pushed her sunglasses onto the top of her head and smiled a polite smile at the woman standing behind the register.

"Dad, would you mind if I . . ." He watched as the hostess grabbed a single menu and led her to an empty seat at the counter. Before he finished asking the question and before his father could even answer, Lucky was waving his hand in the air.

Duke twisted around in his seat. "Is that the Dellinger girl?"

"It sure is. You don't mind, do you?"

His father might have answered, he didn't know, didn't care, because Rachel smiled the moment she saw him. Lucky rose from his seat, watching as she made her way through the maze of tables.

"Dad, you remember Ethan Dellinger? This is his sister, Rachel."

His father slid from the bench seat and held out his hand. "Duke James. Nice to meet you."

"Nice to meet you, too," she said, shaking his hand.

"I'm sorry to interrupt your breakfast, but I wanted to thank your son again for helping me move."

Lucky avoided his father's eyes, knowing that he was secretly having a heyday about that little piece of information. Especially since he had avoided telling his dad exactly why he needed to borrow his truck.

"Well, look at the time." His father pulled his wallet from his back pocket and tossed a twenty-dollar bill on the table. "Rachel." He gave a slight nod of his head. "It's nice to meet you. Good luck with your new place." And then he turned to Lucky. "I'll be seeing ya." He gave a quick pat to his shoulder and headed out, leaving them standing in the aisle.

She watched his father leave, then turned back to him. "Are you on your way out, too?"

"I've got another hour before I have to leave for class if you want to sit down."

She slid in across from him and Peggy quickly arrived, clearing away his father's dishes. Rachel spent the next few minutes perusing the breakfast menu, talking to herself, maybe to him, as she discussed the finer points of both pancakes and waffles. This amused him because, really, weren't they the same damn thing? But he liked watching her chew on her bottom lip, fiddle with her hair, tap her finger against the menu.

When Peggy returned to take her order, he waited in almost breathless anticipation to see which breakfast she would ultimately choose: pancakes or waffles? And the answer was . . . a ham and cheese omelet with fresh fruit and a double side of bacon.

Satisfied with her decision, Rachel tucked a strand of her now reddish blond hair behind her ear and blew across the surface of her coffee, a slight smile on her face.

"Your dad has the best name," she said out of the blue.

Whiplash.

This woman gave him conversational whiplash since he could never predict just what she might say next. It was a trait that reminded him of his friend Gibby. Only she was far prettier and smelled a helluva lot nicer.

"Duke is a nickname. His real name is John Wayne James."

"Huh." She narrowed her eyes at him while taking a careful sip of her coffee. "Now I have to ask—is Lucky a nickname or your real name?"

"Real name."

"Really?"

"Yep. Named for my grandfather."

The waitress returned with Rachel's breakfast and Lucky drank the last of his coffee, watching in silent fascination as she drowned her eggs in Tabasco. "How was your first night?"

"Quiet. A little creepy, I have to admit," she answered between bites. "I slept with the bathroom light on like a little kid."

"It'll be better once you get some furniture."

"You'll be happy to hear I actually have some furniture now," she said, waving her fork in the air. "After you left, I went to Walmart. I was wandering around in there eleven o'clock at night intending to only buy sheets, pillows, and an air mattress, but I ended up buying a television and two camping chairs, too."

"Camping chairs, huh?"

"You know the kind that come in their own little bag? They're hot pink and have a built-in drink holder." She tore a piece of bacon in half as she spoke. "I bought two in the event I have a guest. That way they'll now have a place to sit besides the bar stools."

Peggy was back, topping off his cup of coffee.

"What classes do you have today?"

"Modern Humanities and Freshman Comp."

"Sounds . . . exciting." When he didn't react, she quickly added, "That was sarcasm by the way."

"I was hoping it was."

"Do you have to write a research paper?" When he nodded, she asked, "What's your topic?"

"Women in combat."

"Should be an easy A for you. And what are your thoughts on the subject, Mr. James?"

"It's a research paper, not an opinion piece. I'm just listing the facts."

"For instance . . ."

"That a dozen of our allies have had women in combat roles for over a decade or even longer. Sweden. Canada. Germany. Israel, of course. The US already has women out there in the middle of it, but they're classified as 'enablers' and attached to combat divisions rather than assigned to combat divisions to skirt the whole ban on . . ."

Catching himself in mid-diatribe, he stopped. "I don't really want to talk about this."

"Okay, then. Talk about something else."

"You changed your hair." It wasn't quite the fiery red-orange color of her youth, but the bleached look was gone. "Did you get that at Walmart, too?"

A pink flush crept across her cheeks as she smiled, her hands immediately going to her hair and smoothing over the long strands. "I did it yesterday, between unpacking and loads of laundry."

"It looks nice."

"I like it. Far more than I did the blond. Curtis would always tell me I was beautiful, but that I would be even more beautiful as a blonde. So I changed it to make him happy." And like before, her smile disappeared and her demeanor changed in a heartbeat as she spoke about him. "But then he'd find something else to change. He even told me he didn't like women who talked too much, so . . ." She dropped the fork on her plate and scooted the plate a few inches away from her. "Pathetic, now that I think about it. Embarrassing, really. I shouldn't even be telling you all of this."

The more she talked about this guy he'd never met— this . . . asshole—the more he wanted to go back to that apartment and pound his face in. "Have you heard from him?"

Just give me one good reason. . .

"He texted me a few times last night. Nothing major."

Out of habit, he twisted his neck, trying to relieve the growing tension in his spine and shoulders.

"Okay. Here's the deal." He leaned his forearms on the table and lowered his voice so only she could hear. "I need you to be completely honest with me, for my own peace of mind at least. I need to know how much of an asshole this guy is. Is he a 'get a restraining order' kind of asshole or a proximity asshole?"

She mimicked his posture and whispered, "What on earth is a proximity asshole?"

"The kind of guy who is an asshole whenever you're around or easily accessible via phone or text, but is too fucking lazy to actually go out of his way to be an asshole."

Here he was being serious and the corner of her mouth lifted as if she were on the verge of laughing. "I'm pretty sure he's not the restraining order kind."

"So . . . no chance of him showing up at the hospital or following you home from work?"

She shook her head slowly. "No. Like you said, he's too lazy. I think he'll move on to someone else pretty quickly."

"You're sure?"

"Why? What were you planning to do?"

"Become your personal bodyguard. Drive you to and from work. Spend the nights sleeping on your living room sofa with a loaded gun."

Now she didn't even bother trying to hide her smile. "But I don't have a sofa, remember?"

"I would have bought one."

And that made her laugh, which made him feel like a superhero of sorts. Especially after the head games this guy had obviously played on her.

Without warning, she reached across the table and touched his wrist. "What time is it?"

Damn. He had about twenty minutes to get to class when he could easily spend another hour just talking to her. Hell, he'd be happy to just sit there and listen to her talk the entire time. "Unfortunately, it's time for me to go."

When the waitress brought the check, he insisted she let him pay; after all, she had kept him company until it was time to go to class. They walked out of the diner together, stopping just outside the doors when they realized they were parked in opposite ends of the lot.

"Any classes with Brittany today?"

"Not today. Thank God."

She smiled at him while slipping on her sunglasses. "Well, if you're ever in need of a bodyguard, feel free to give me a call."

Then, with one last goodbye and a little wave from her, they went their separate ways. And he knew he'd be counting the minutes until he saw her again.

AFTER HER UNEXPECTED run-in with Lucky at the diner, Rachel found herself singing along with the radio as she drove to her parents' house. She couldn't remember the last time she was in such a good mood.

There was just so much to like about the guy. For one, he was nice. Two, he was protective without being controlling or overbearing. Three, well . . . he was really good looking without even trying. His dark hair was a little long and could use a trim, but it worked with the not-quite-a-beard thing he had going on. And then there were those hypnotic dark brown eyes. During breakfast, she had to make a conscious effort to not just sit and stare at him the entire time.

But as good looking as Lucky was, as nice as he was, she'd made a promise to herself to not immediately jump into another relationship and she was going to stick to it this time. Of course, it wasn't like he was offering anything aside from friendship to begin with.

Just before noon, Rachel pulled into the driveway of her childhood home just blocks from Lucky's house. Hidden from the street behind a row of cedars, the hundred-year-old two-story was worlds apart from his when it came to appearance. At first glance, most people would assume it was abandoned. The paint had peeled years ago. Cardboard and duct tape covered the cracked windows. The chain-link fence that bordered the property gaped and sagged in places, rendering it completely useless. In the yard there was a collection of rusted-out vehicles her father had hauled home over the years with the intention of fixing them up and selling them. Of course, that would have required him to be home to actually work on them or have money to buy the necessary parts.

Once Ethan joined the army, life should've been easier for her parents with no extra mouths to feed, except her father injured his back while working on one of his many cars. Now, with both of them having a host of medical problems, between the doctor's visits and their prescriptions, her parents were in a financial rut from which they'd never escape.

With plastic grocery bags dangling from her fingertips, Rachel climbed the dilapidated front porch, careful to avoid the rotted boards. She knocked twice on the front door of her parents' home and waited a moment before shouldering it open and going inside. Instantly she was greeted by the smell of stale cigarette smoke and a blaring television. She wasn't surprised to find her father sitting only feet away in his broken-down recliner, his attention held by the local news station's fishing report.

"Hi, Dad. How are you feeling today?"

Her father tore his gaze away from the television for only the briefest of moments to look at her, then went back to watching without saying a word.

Some would consider Rachel a glutton for punishment coming here week after week, caring for a father who did his best to ignore her and a mother who often had her walking on eggshells. But as the only child still living within shouting distance, not to mention being the only daughter, the responsibility naturally fell upon her shoulders.

"I picked up your prescription along with some other things I thought you might like."

She settled the bags on the small kitchen table and couldn't stop herself from holding her breath while listening for a response. Again, nothing.

"Just so you know, I'm not living with Curtis anymore," she told him, even knowing her father didn't care one iota. "I've moved out on my own. I'm renting a place off old Highway 70. It's a mobile home, but it's nice and fairly new." After putting everything away she stepped back into the living room. "It's not in a trailer park, it's . . ."

The chair where her father had been sitting was now empty and the door to her parents' bedroom closed.

Rachel could only shake her head in wonder.

For as long as she could remember, there had been an underlying tension in their home. Rachel always assumed it had to do with money, how her father was always going from job to job, sometimes being gone for weeks or months at a time. Meanwhile her mother worked odd jobs all around town in an effort to keep the electricity on and food in the cabinets.

When she was young, her older brothers were often left in charge while their parents were away at work. But by the time she turned ten and both of her older brothers were working part-time, it became Rachel's job to clean the house, cook the meals, and keep an eye on her younger brother. Her mother's moods ran hot and cold; sometimes she was a joy to be around and then there were times Rachel couldn't wait to leave the house. For the most part things were fine, until her mother returned home from work earlier than expected one day and caught Rachel making out with an older boy on the couch. The boy, of course, rose to his feet and immediately scuttled out the front door, leaving Rachel to face her mother alone.

"Don't believe what that boy tells you. He's only using you for one thing," her mother had said. "The sooner you learn that love doesn't last, the better."

Desperate to prove her mother wrong, Rachel ran out the door and caught up with her boyfriend. Then, at her request, he drove her out to the lake where he divested her of her virginity in the backseat of his Pontiac Sunbird. He was her first serious boyfriend and at the time she believed they'd be together forever, mostly because he told her they would be. Except he proved her mother right and broke up with her the following week.

Rachel climbed the narrow staircase to the second floor, the wood treads creaking beneath her weight. The top floor consisted of two bedrooms separated by the thinnest of walls. The ceilings sloped lower than she remembered. The bedrooms seemed smaller. Her old room was completely barren, just the way she left it the day she moved out. From there she wandered into Ethan's room, the one he didn't have all to himself until both of their older brothers had moved out. She sat down on the edge of one bed and looked around his mostly empty room, trying to remember how it looked the last time she was in this space. A few newspaper clippings and photos were taped to the wall, some participation medals hung from a nail.

He had always been hers to care for, to dote on. She taught him his colors and letters and how to tie his shoes. Instead of leaving like her older brothers, she applied to a nursing program at a small college thirty miles away and paid for it with grants and financial aid. When she wasn't at school she worked part-time, if only to buy things for Ethan that her parents couldn't afford. When he needed new cleats, she bought them for him. When he asked a girl to the prom, she rented his tuxedo and paid for his date's corsage. She went to his football games and baseball games because their parents didn't. She helped him with algebra and biology because they wouldn't.

The day Ethan left for basic training at Fort Jackson was the day she moved out. Unable to afford rent on her own, she moved in with her boyfriend at the time, who shared a house with two of his friends. And so began the cycle of going from one relationship to another, always hoping the next time would be different, that this would be the time she would find her happily-ever-after.

Fifteen years had passed since that afternoon she followed her boyfriend out of the house in search of a love that would last forever, and she still hadn't found it.

Chapter Eight

FOR IT BEING the last weekend of October, the weather was surprisingly warm with no sign of autumn arriving anytime soon. Not that Rachel was complaining. Minus a few exceptions, the leaves on the trees were still green. The wildflowers were still blooming. And the migratory birds weren't in any hurry to head south.

She wiggled her toes in her flip-flops and grabbed a second beer from the cooler as the sun rose higher in the sky, warming the morning air. "What time are we supposed to be at your dad and Brenda's?"

"Couple hours." Lucky stood at the edge of the pond, patiently watching the end of his fishing line. "I told him we can't stay much later than twelve-thirty; otherwise, we won't have enough time to sleep before work." He reeled in the line, then cast it to another area of the pond.

Over the last several weeks, this had become their routine. On Saturday and Sunday mornings after their shifts at the hospital had ended, they'd hang out a few hours before going their separate ways to sleep. Sometimes they'd go to his house for whatever Brenda had left in his refrigerator that week and watch a movie since she still only had camping chairs for living room furniture. Sometimes, they'd come back to her place, drag those pink chairs out onto the back deck, and cook something on the grill. If the weather was nice and the winds were calm, Lucky would break out the fishing pole he'd stashed in her laundry room.

He'd been at it for over a month and still hadn't caught a damn thing.

During the week, if he wasn't studying for an exam and she wasn't picking up an extra shift, they'd hang out. Sometimes she'd tag along on his workouts, other times he'd tolerate running a shorter distance than usual. They laughed a lot when they were together and sent random texts to each other when they were apart. She still found him to be attractive and was pretty sure the feeling was mutual, but for now, there were no games. They were simply friends with no pressure to become something more.

"Where did I leave off?" she asked before taking a sip of her beer.

Lucky hung his head. "Not again. It's my birthday. I shouldn't have to play twenty questions on my birthday."

She laughed. "But what better way to celebrate your thirtieth?"

The man liked to pretend he was all quiet and mysterious, but truth be told, he was quite the Chatty Cathy once you got him started. Even more so if she got a drink or two in him.

"Who did you lose your virginity to?"

Lucky shook his head and reeled in his line. "I'm not answering that."

"Oh, come on. Tell me."

"Why does it matter?"

"Because I'd find it hard to believe that you didn't lose your virginity to someone we went to school with. And I'm dying to know who it was!"

"Still not answering."

"Come on. Give me something."

"Okay. I'll tell you this much. It wasn't someone we graduated with."

"Oooh . . ." Rachel rubbed her hands together, excited to make some progress. "Was it someone older than us? Was she a virgin, too, or did she show you the ropes?"

"As a matter of fact . . ." He smiled when his phone buzzed in his pocket. "Saved by the bell. Sorry, but I have to take this."

"You're not getting off that easy!"

He laughed, handing her the fishing pole before heading down a narrow path worn in the grass that followed the edge of the pond. When he was almost out of earshot she heard him say, "Hi, Mom," and nearly choked on a swallow of beer.

Not once in the past six weeks had he ever mentioned his mother. There were plenty of pictures of him and Duke on display around the house, but she couldn't recall seeing any photos with someone who could be his mother.

And now, the curiosity was killing her.

She watched as he stood at the water's edge, and as far as she could tell, he wasn't doing much talking. Occasionally, he'd lean down to pick up a rock or stick and chuck it into the water until he finally said goodbye about ten minutes later and ended the call.

"My mom," he said, shoving his phone back into his pocket.

"So I heard."

He plopped down onto the blanket next to her as if nothing unusual had just happened.

"And what did *Mom* have to say?"

"Happy Birthday, of course, and talked about how busy she was with the kids and stuff."

"Kids?"

"Yeah."

He laid back on the blanket and closed his eyes as if he were going to take a nap, his legs crossed at the ankles, his arms crossed over his chest. But no way in hell was she going to let him just drop a bomb like that and not say anything more. The fact that out there somewhere, Lucky James had a mother and siblings and hadn't once mentioned them? Crazy. Especially since she'd always assumed his mother was dead.

"Come on. This conversation is like pulling teeth. Spill," she ordered, giving his shoulder a little shove. "Or no cupcakes for you."

He turned his head toward her, one brow raising above the frame of his sunglasses. "Are cupcakes a euphemism for something else?"

"No."

Lucky shrugged his shoulders. "No sweat off my brow. I'm sure Brenda will make me all the birthday cupcakes I want."

"Oh, come on."

"Fine. But I'm gonna need another beer for this." He sat up and reached into the cooler, grabbing a bottle from where it was buried in ice. He popped the top off his longneck and took a long pull before he began.

Like a kindergartner at story time, she sat crisscross applesauce on the blanket and waited for his story to begin.

"My mom is eleven years younger than my dad. She worked at a little convenience store in McAlester. At the time my dad was working on a road construction crew and he and a couple other guys would stop in almost every day for lunch. He asked her out and she said yes. She was only eighteen when she got pregnant and they got married. By the time she turned twenty-five, she was tired of being both a wife and mother."

"Just like that?"

"Yeah. She wanted to go see the world, not be stuck in Oklahoma her whole life. So she left. She lives in California now."

"Because that's not cliché or anything." She snorted. "Sorry. I shouldn't have said that."

"Why? It's the truth."

"I do have to say while it's shitty that your mother abandoned you, it was pretty brave for her to pack her things and move across the country all by herself. To start all over in a new place. I don't think I could do it. Did she ever remarry?"

"Her husband is a golf pro, has a couple of kids from another marriage. But he and my mom have two boys who are thirteen and eleven."

"And I thought the twelve-year age gap between Adam and Ethan was wide. You're practically old enough to be their dad."

"I try not to think about that."

He took another long pull from his beer while she picked at the label of hers. "Do you get to see them much?"

Lucky shook his head. "After I joined regiment, she started emailing me a lot, especially when I was deployed overseas. That's actually when we communicated the most. I guess that's when she worried about me the most. And she'd always say how much she missed me and how much she wanted to see me, so I decided to go visit her one leave. I flew out to San Jose, rented a car, and drove south to Monterey. When I got to my hotel I called her to let her know I'd arrived. That's when she got all weird, saying the boys were sick and then her husband was sick and that I shouldn't come to their house because she didn't want me to get sick on my vacation. We met for lunch the next day and that was it."

"What do you mean that's it?"

"That's it. It was awkward and uncomfortable. I think we both realized our relationship worked better on a pen pal kind of level. So I changed my flight and went home two days early. She calls on my birthday, I call on hers. She sends a card at Christmas, but that's it. We've never discussed seeing each other again."

"What did your dad say?"

"We don't talk about it much. He blames himself for her leaving, but all he ever did was love her. A lot of people kept telling him to file for divorce, to move on with his life and find someone else. But he held out hope she'd change her mind and come back home one day. By the time they actually divorced, they'd officially been married sixteen years even though she'd been gone for almost a decade."

"Wow. And I thought my family was screwed up."

He held the neck of his bottle out toward hers. "To family."

She smiled, tapped the neck of her bottle to his before they each took a drink.

And in that moment they were more than coworkers or friends. Instead, they were more like kindred spirits.

IF GIVEN THE choice, he'd rather spend the remainder of his birthday just hanging out with Rachel, even if it meant more prying questions regarding his mother or the loss of his virginity. But Brenda and his dad really wanted to have him over for his birthday, and to make sure he didn't have a reason to refuse, Brenda invited Rachel as well. Not that he minded at all.

When they pulled into the driveway, his father was standing in the middle of their large yard, an ax in one hand, the handle resting on his shoulder.

"What is he doing with the ax?" Rachel whispered.

"You really don't want to know."

Duke waved hello and made his way across the grass to them. "How's my birthday boy?" he asked, one arm stretched out wide to embrace him.

"I'd be doing a lot better if you put the ax down."

Duke chuckled as he placed the ax on the ground. "I can do that." Not one to settle for a polite, manly handshake, Duke wrapped his arms around Lucky and gave a few hearty thwacks to the middle of his back before letting him go. "So tell me, how does thirty feel?"

"It feels a lot like twenty-nine to tell you the truth."

His father then made his way to a smiling Rachel, greeting her with a kiss on the cheek. "Rachel, it's good to see you again."

"Same here." She held up the covered Tupperware bowl in her hands. "Is Brenda inside?"

"She sure is. Just head on in there. You know the way."

Lucky watched as she made her way up the front walk until she disappeared around the corner. Only then did he realize his father had been watching him watch her.

"You two seem to be spending a lot of time together."

"A product of circumstances, I guess," he said with a shrug. "It's not like there's an abundance of people our age to hang out with."

"Mmm-hmm . . ." His father looked skeptical, but

wandered back onto the lawn anyway, the ax once again resting on his shoulder, his eyes scanning the grass in front of him for any movement.

Lucky followed. "Got moles again?"

"Brenda came out this morning and noticed a bunch of her annuals were sitting all cockeyed. Little sucker ran a tunnel from the tree to right underneath them last night."

Since his father moved in, he'd become the mole hunter. Having tried traps, poisons, and just about everything else out there on the internet, he decided to try something a little more low-tech. Armed with a shovel and an ax, he'd spend a few minutes tromping down the tunnels the moles had made and the next few hours watching the grass, waiting for it to shiver. Then he'd start chopping away at the soil in the hopes of getting his mole.

At first, he thought his old man was nuts. Come to find out, he'd been pretty successful.

"So you two aren't dating or hooking up or whatever you kids call it these days?"

Lucky shoved his hands into his pockets and shook his head. "Jesus, Dad."

"I'm just looking out for you. I really like Rachel, but the girl has spent her whole life in this town."

"And?"

"For most people that wouldn't be a problem. But you're like your mother, not that it's a bad thing. You're smart and adventurous. Definitely just as pretty."

"Will you stop with that?"

"Every time after we see you, Brenda is always going

on about those long, dark lashes of yours. How it's a crying shame that God gave a man such eyelashes." His dad laughed and smacked the middle of Lucky's back.

"Jesus. I can't take anymore."

He was on the verge of heading inside and hanging with the womenfolk. Anything to get away from this conversation.

"Now hang on. Before you run off, listen to me for a second because this is important. Like I said, you're just like your mother. You're willing to go wherever the wind blows you and if the wind doesn't blow hard enough, you'll get there on your own. But Rachel, her roots are dug deep and I doubt she's going anywhere."

"We're strictly friends. Neither of us are looking for a relationship because we both have other things going on at the moment."

"I hear ya. But I also know that things change sometimes. Especially when you're a . . . what did you call it? A product of circumstances."

Lucky nodded, knowing his dad was right. As attracted to Rachel as he was, as much as they enjoyed spending time with one another, what chance could they really have? His plan was to go on to medical school. After that, could he see himself coming back to Durant to practice medicine? Not really. Only hours earlier, when they were talking about his mother, Rachel said she couldn't see herself starting over someplace new.

Just like his mom and dad, he and Rachel were on the same path for now, but it was only a matter of time before they would be headed in opposite directions.

"Hang on a minute. I have one more thing for you." In a flash she was slamming the passenger door shut and bounding up the front steps to her trailer.

To ensure he didn't stay too long, he left the engine running. Otherwise, ten minutes would turn into an hour and one hour would easily become two before he headed home. That's just how it was when he spent time with Rachel. He never wanted to leave her.

Lucky got out of his car when the storm door flew open and she ran down the stairs with a big smile on her face. Rachel handed him a striped gift bag with red tissue paper poking out of the top, practically giddy with anticipation. A sure sign she was not to be trusted.

He narrowed his eyes at her. "You shouldn't have."

She waved off his words with a *pfft* as he dug through the tissue paper and pulled out a rolled up T-shirt. Always helpful, she took the bag, giving him both hands to hold it up and read the front.

Always be yourself, unless you can be a unicorn. Then always be a unicorn.

"Dear God."

"Isn't it great?" She clapped her hands and laughed. "I think you should wear it to class Monday morning. I'd bet money Brittany would love it."

"And that's reason enough for me to never wear it." He refolded the shirt before his eyes met hers. "Thank you for a great birthday."

"Well, you only turn thirty once, right?" As she looked back at him with those crystal blue eyes, her smile slipped. She lifted her hand and pressed the back of it to his forehead, then moved her palm to his cheek. "Are you sure you're okay? You were quiet all through lunch."

There was a moment between them, like neither were really sure what to do next. He'd never had a female friend before. But just walking away seemed like the wrong decision.

He covered her hand with his, then pressed a kiss to her palm. Before he could second-guess himself, he leaned over and wrapped his arms around her waist, hugging her tight and lifting her feet from the ground at the same time. It felt so good to hold her in his arms, to feel her body pressed against his. And with the way her arms wrapped around his shoulders and she sighed against his neck, he had to believe she felt the same way, too.

But his dad was right. He didn't have any plans to stay here for the long term. Two, maybe three years at the most. And Rachel wasn't the kind to leave. So it was best for both of them to let sleeping dogs lie.

As much as he hated to, he put her feet back on the ground and brushed his lips across her forehead.

"Thanks again, Rach. I'll see you later."

And before he did something he wouldn't really regret, he climbed in his Jeep and drove home.

Chapter Nine

IF HE HAD things his way, Lucky would already be out on the road, his feet pounding the pavement. He'd run at that six-minute-mile pace he'd become accustomed to during his dozen years in regiment, push his body to the point of exhaustion so he'd be too tired to think about his problems.

But he promised Rachel he'd wait and run with her. Which, to be completely honest, meant it wouldn't be much of a run at all. More like a trot. And since she was one of the problems he didn't want to think about, well, that made shit just a whole lot worse.

Since he was stuck waiting, he decided to fire up his laptop, check his email, do a little homework. At the very least he needed to be somewhat productive. In his in-box he found the review from his English Comp critique partner, who happened to be even younger than his chem lab partner. This one was merely eighteen.

He opened the attached document and found bright red text splattering the pages. Punctuation errors. Grammatical errors. Several places were highlighted and marked as *repetitive* or *redundant*. Then there were whole paragraphs struck out and rewritten because, he could only assume, he was such a terrible writer that his paper was incomprehensible. But when he read the new and improved paragraphs, they didn't make any damn sense.

Then, at the very bottom of the page, was the suggestion he get a tutor since he hadn't been in school in, like, forever.

Followed by a smiley face, of course.

It took every ounce of self-restraint to not slam the lid shut on his laptop and send it flying across the room.

Luckily for his laptop, a Skype window popped up in the corner, and in an instant, Lucky's mood changed.

"Gibby! What the hell's up?"

Definitely a sight for sore eyes, Lucky smiled when Jeff Gibson's ugly mug filled his screen.

"Just kicking back. Didn't have shit to do aside from laundry, so I thought I'd call and wish you a happy birthday. A day late, of course."

"I'm touched, man. Can't believe you actually keep track of stuff like that."

"I only remember yours because it's the same day as my mother's, asshole."

Lucky first met Jeff Gibson just minutes after reporting to 1st Batt at Hunter Army Airfield more than a decade earlier, but they didn't become friends until after they faced off in hand-to-hand combat. Gibby kicked his ass, then offered a hand to help Lucky up from the dirt afterward.

Of course, being close friends more than ten years now, Gibby liked to take it one step further and tell strangers, family, anyone who would listen, really, that it was love at first prod, dating back to the moment Lucky shoved his finger up Gibby's ass. Which then meant Lucky spent the next ten minutes explaining that rectal exams were an unfortunate but required part of their battlefield medical training.

"Anyway, I thought it was a good excuse to give you a call. See how things are going out in the real world." Gibby laughed. "Ready to come back?"

Only Lucky didn't find it all that funny. "Not the best of times to ask."

That got Gibby's attention, his expression turning serious as he leaned closer to the webcam. "You can *always* come back."

"Don't tempt me." Anxious to not dig too deep into the topic, Lucky quickly changed the subject. "You guys heading out soon?"

"Yeah, but let's not talk about that. How's college life? Banging your way through the sorority houses?"

"Jesus, Gibby. That's not even funny. If you saw how young these girls are . . ."

Gibby leaned back in his chair, laced his fingers behind his head, and kicked his feet up on the desk. "As long as they're legal. That's all that matters."

Lucky couldn't help but laugh. "And here I thought you didn't have any standards at all."

They spent the next several minutes catching up, talking about Gibby's recent vacation, his family, his notoriously bad golf game. Then there were a few stories of how Gibby found himself in some crazy-ass situation that only happened to guys like him. By the time they were done, Lucky was caught up on all the guys—Bull, Soup, T-Rod, and the MacGregor brothers.

And he was missing every last one of them.

Rachel knocked a couple of times on the front door and let herself in, a habit that had developed over the past several weeks. As she walked inside, she pushed her sunglasses to the top of her head, her red hair swept up into a ponytail. "Hey, there. Sorry it took me so long, but I had to throw a load of towels in the wash before I left. And then Walter caught me on the way out. He says 'hello' by the way."

Lucky looked back to the screen. "Hey, Gib? I gotta go."

"Oops," she whispered, not realizing until he spoke that he was in the middle of a conversation.

"Hold up just a second. I heard a female voice. You're holding out on me. Who's there? Did your little lab partner come to visit?" Gibby, being Gibby, laughed at his own joke.

"Just a friend from work."

"What kind of friend? The kind you bang?"

Overhearing his comment, Rachel raised an eyebrow in question.

"You do realize she can hear you, right?" Lucky asked.

"She must be ugly, then," Gibby countered.

"I'm not having this discussion with you."

"Then I'll have it with her. Put her on."

"No fucking way, Gibby. Not doing it."

"Come on, man. Let me have a little fun."

"I'll talk to him." Rachel elbowed him in the shoulder, forcing him to scooch over a bit. She had the biggest smile on her face when she plopped down on the sofa, her face appearing on the laptop. "Hello."

Immediately, Gibby's feet dropped from the tabletop and he leaned closer to the monitor. "Well, hello, sweetheart. Jeff Gibson here. Your ex-husband to be."

"Is that so?"

"Damn straight. What's your name, beautiful?"

"Rachel."

"Nice name. And how do you know my boy, Rachel?"

"We work together at the hospital."

"Are you a nurse?"

"Yes."

"Nice. If you ever need a little anatomy refresher, I'm your man."

Rachel tilted her head and with a sweet smile said, "Emphasis on the 'little,' I would assume?"

Gibby barked out a laugh. "Hardly, sweetheart. And Lucky can attest to that."

Lucky threw his hands in the air. "Leave me out of this, Gib."

"Aw, hell, I can do it myself." Gibby rose to his feet, brought his lower half into view of the webcam, and began unbuttoning his pants.

"Whoa. Whoa! WHOA! Hold on there, Gibby! Do. Not. Do. That!"

Laughing, Gibby dropped back into his desk chair. "You're right. I need to save that all for my girl, Rachel, here. Send me a text, sweetheart, and I'll send you back a picture of something special," he said, adding a wink.

"I can only imagine." She turned to Lucky. "I'm gonna fill up my water bottles."

"Wait, wait, wait," Gibby pleaded until Rachel sat back down on the couch. "Listen here, beautiful. Obviously my boy doesn't know a good thing when he sees one. I'll make you a very happy woman. Just say the word and I can have you on a plane to Savannah and us married by the end of the week. Then," he said with a sweeping motion along the sides of his body, "all of this will be yours."

"Hmm . . . tempting. I'll have to think about it."

"You do that. But don't wait too long. I'm a real prize!"

She waggled her fingers at the computer as she stood to her feet. "It was lovely chatting with you, Jeff Gibson."

"Sweet dreams, my love," Gibby said as she walked away. And when her backside crossed in front of the webcam, Gibby whispered in admiration, "Goddamn that ass."

Rachel was still laughing as she made her way to the kitchen and Lucky turned the computer toward him.

"I need to go. It was good talking to you. Tell the guys I said hello. And if I don't talk to you again before you leave, keep your head down over there."

"Sure thing, Luck. Take it easy."

The screen went dark. But before he even closed his laptop, his cell phone buzzed with a text message.

Fuck dude she is HOT.
Why aren't you hitting that?
She put you in the friend zone didn't she?
I'm coming to Oklahoma when I get back.
Tell her to wait for me
Gonna show you how it's done.
Lucky laughed and then sent one last reply.
Bye, Gibby.

Rachel returned as he tossed his phone onto the coffee table. "Your friend is funny."

"That he is."

But he didn't really want to talk about Gibby. Because that would only lead to talking about the life he left behind. And with the way that he was feeling at the moment, it was best he didn't think about it at all.

He pulled open the front door and held it open for her. "Ready to go?"

She took a deep breath and sighed, then nodded.

Why she was putting herself through this workout was beyond him, because she looked fantastic. But several weeks ago she'd read some Oprah type stuff about making over her whole life, and in addition to reading and meditating and eating healthy, it also included a regular exercise routine. Much to her dislike.

As he pulled the front door shut, she stepped onto the front lawn and began to stretch her hamstrings. And just like good ol' Gibby, Lucky couldn't help but admire her ass.

And in that moment, he wondered what he'd done to the universe to be tormented this way.

Thankfully, she turned around to face him as she pulled back one foot to stretch her quad. "Do you miss it?"

"I don't miss the rules and regulations so much as the adrenaline rush. And of course I miss the guys. Aside from my dad, they're the closest thing I've ever had to family."

And his family would be deploying to Afghanistan for another rotation within a matter of days.

Instead of being with them, he was writing pointless research papers, taking pointless exams, and working in a pointless job.

"Do you ever think about going back?"

"I try not to."

Which was the truth, because he was afraid if he thought long and hard about it, he'd find himself packing his bags and heading to Georgia before he knew it.

SOMETHING WAS OFF.

Rachel wasn't the type of runner that bothered with running apps or pedometers that monitored her pace or distance. She kept things simple. Lucky led and she followed. But she'd bet money that he was going at a far faster pace than normal.

Usually she ran about four or five steps behind him for several reasons. One, where she would always start out too fast, Lucky kept a perfect pace. Two, she didn't like running side by side on the two-lane country roads that didn't have a shoulder. It just wasn't safe. Three, the view. Watching Lucky James from the back was the best kind of motivation to keep up. But unlike all those other times, he hadn't looked back to check on her once. It was as if he was in his own little world and didn't remember her at all.

She did her best to keep up, but it wasn't long before she had a stitch in her side. Instead of complaining, she tried to suck it up and breathe through the pain, the distance between them growing and growing. Finally, she couldn't take anymore.

"Can we stop a second?" she asked between stabs of pain. "Take a break a sec?"

Only then did he stop and look at her. "What's the problem?"

"I didn't know you were going to try and kill me today."

She braced her hands on her knees and tried to catch her breath, meanwhile he wasn't even breathing hard. Instead, he looked like he was just out for a Sunday stroll. She took a sip from her water bottle and returned it to the holster strapped around her waist.

Lucky rested his hands on his hips, not even attempting to hide the irritation on his face.

That was not like him. The only time she'd seen him even close to being in a bad mood was that night in the parking lot where she kinda ran him off the road and caused him to wreck his bicycle. But even then, he didn't look this grumpy.

"Can we go now?"

He didn't wait for a response. Just turned around

and took off, his strides longer, his pace even faster than before.

"Lucky. Come on! Can't you take it easy?"

This time he turned around and stalked back toward her. "*You* wanted to come running with *me*. I didn't invite you to keep me company." His eyes swept over her, down her legs to her feet, and slowly made their way back to her face. "I sure as hell warned you I don't do cutesy little trots around town to show off my latest running outfit."

Oh, hell, no. No way was she going to take the shit he was in the mood to dish out.

"Hey! I like my new outfit."

He turned his back as he mumbled and swore under his breath, about her, about her clothes.

She caught up with him. Gave him a healthy shove in the back of his shoulder. "Hey!"

This time he spun around and yelled back. "What?"

"You're being an asshole! Knock it off!" He winced at the accusation, but didn't argue the point. "You haven't been yourself since yesterday. Are you okay? Are you having a midlife crisis a little early?"

"I'm fine."

She laughed at his answer because it sounded like something she would say. And she knew there was no way in hell he was *fine*.

"You just don't seem like yourself."

Finally. Finally, that calm, cool, controlled exterior that he had so carefully maintained for the past several weeks began to crack. His biceps flexed and strained as he scrubbed both hands over his face and growled in frustration.

"Maybe it's because I realized I'm thirty years old and taking writing critiques from an eighteen-year-old kid! That I'm living in my dad's house! That I'm in a job that's going nowhere!"

Now, it all made sense. "But this is what you have to do."

"Is it?"

"If you want to go to medical school it is. Is that what you want to do?"

"Fuck if I know anymore." He threw his hands helplessly into the air. "I feel like I'm just spinning my wheels here and getting nowhere fast."

"If it makes you feel any better, I feel the same way at times."

"Why would you? You have your degree, a career. You don't live with your parents."

"Are you kidding? I have hot pink camping chairs for living room furniture. If you had asked me when I graduated high school what my life would be like at thirty, I would have told you I'd be married, living in a big house, with one kid and a second on the way. I'd be driving a sporty SUV because I would never be caught dead driving a minivan. My husband would be good looking, make lots of money, and I'd be the envy of every girl in high school who dared to call me white trash."

His hands clinched into fists. "Who the hell called you trash?"

And just like that, protective Lucky was back, always willing to defend her honor.

"That's beside the point, Lucky. When was the last time you went out?"

"We are out, right now. See?" He pointed to the sky. "Blue sky. Sunshine."

Smart ass.

"I mean with people aside from your dad and Brenda. Aside from school. Aside from work. You need to get out and let your hair down. Blow off some steam. Get laid."

His eyes widened and immediately Rachel wanted to take the words back. She and Lucky were friends, but not the kind that discussed their sex lives—or lack thereof. She felt her skin heat, knowing with certainty her face was the color of a beet.

"You know what I mean," she said, waving her hand like it was no big deal.

The corner of his mouth lifted. "The same could be said for you."

"Me? Nooo." Rachel shook her head. "I'm taking a break from men, remember? Just call me Miss Independent."

"Nope. We're in this together." Lucky folded his arms over his chest and closed the space between them. "So what exactly did you have in mind?"

Chapter Ten

FOR THE FIRST time in a long, long time, she was going out. To a bar. Not as part of a couple, but as a single woman.

Lord help her.

Rachel had no romantic notions about how the evening would go. She would not find the love of her life in a hole-in-the-wall bar located in the backwoods of southern Oklahoma. Hell, she might have difficulty finding someone to dance with. But Lucky was right when he told her to follow her own advice. They both needed to get out of the house and have some fun and it just so happened that Halloween provided the best of excuses to do just that.

She checked her reflection one last time in the rearview mirror before climbing out of the truck. As she walked up the front steps to Lucky's house, the porch light flickered on and the door swung open.

"What the hell are you supposed to be?" he asked as she made her way inside.

Really? How on earth did he not know who she was? Her costume was perfect. From her berry red curls to her berry high heels. And the bodice of her dress made her boobs look fantastic, if she thought so herself. Pushed up just high enough to look bigger than they actually were, but not shoved up so high she had to worry about falling out.

"I'm Strawberry Shortcake."

He stared at her with a blank look.

"Come on. The cartoon? Strawberry Shortcake, Angel Cake, and Blueberry Pie. How do you not know this?"

"Because . . . I'm a guy?" His eyes started at her shoes and traveled upward until they hung up on her chest for a hot second. By the time his eyes reached hers, he had a huge grin on his face. "I'm gonna go out on a limb here and say you don't quite look like the cartoon; otherwise, every guy on the planet would have had the same dirty, boyhood fantasies about Strawberry Shortcake that they did about Wonder Woman and Jessica Rabbit."

She couldn't help but laugh at his blatant honesty. "You're such a pervert."

"Maybe. But I'm an honest pervert."

Speaking of fantasies, the man always looked good rocking battered jeans and T-shirt, but as far as costumes go, his was lacking.

"Is that what you're wearing?"

Lucky glanced down at the front of his T-shirt as if

he'd forgotten what he'd pulled on. "You've got something against Superman?"

"Would it have killed you to put forth a little more effort?" Determined to rectify the situation, she headed straight for his bedroom. "Do you have a button down and a tie at least?"

"We're going to the Red Dawg," he called after her. "Not some fancy Halloween party at the casino."

"Doesn't matter," she yelled back just before she found herself frozen in place. She was in his room, standing at the foot end of his neatly made bed. Then, before she knew it, he was standing beside her. Both of them. Alone. In his bedroom.

She swallowed hard and tried to remember what the hell she went in there for.

"My dress shirts are in the closet."

Oh, yes, that's why she was there. She was improving his costume, absolutely not thinking about how long it had been since she'd had sex or that the underlying scent she always smelled when he was around was stronger here in this room.

She forced her feet to move and continued to the small closet, pulling open the door. "Are you kidding me? You have neatly pressed shirts just ready to go and hanging in the closet?"

"Where else would they be?"

From the look on his face he was genuinely dumbfounded by her question.

"But I've never even seen you wear any of these shirts. Do you always have to be so prompt and neat? Can't you be like all the rest of us and be less than perfect on the occasion?"

That made him smile. She didn't even have to look at him to know he was doing it. She could just feel his smugness radiate around the room.

Rachel removed a light blue button-down from its hanger and chose a crimson tie from the small rack hanging on the back of the door. "Put these on," she said, handing him both. "Over the T-shirt."

"But I'll get too hot in the bar."

She waved off his complaint and marched into the kitchen, immediately helping herself to an ice cold glass of water. Maybe it was her imagination but the temperature in his bedroom seemed to skyrocket in a matter of seconds.

The thump of his heavy boots and creak of floorboards signaled his movements and she turned just in time to see him reemerge from the bedroom. Since turnabout was fair play, she motioned for him to do a little twirl and took a slow perusal herself, starting at his feet and working her way up as she sipped from her glass. When he was done, he wore a cocky grin on his face to go along with the dress shirt neatly tucked into his jeans. And, of course, the cuffs were buttoned and tie perfectly knotted.

"Close, but not quite." She handed him her water glass and stepped in close, mere inches separating them. Beginning with his empty hand, she unbuttoned the cuff and turned it up a couple of times, revealing the strong muscles and tendons of his forearms. Then, after shifting her water glass from his left to his right, completed the other side, too.

"I can dress myself you know. I've been doing it since I was five." His words whispered across her skin as she wrapped her arms around his middle and, starting at the back, pulled the shirt tails free from the waist of his jeans.

"Just . . . be quiet." She tugged on the knot of his tie to loosen it and stumbled on her high heels. Immediately his empty hand went to her hip, steadying her. After taking a second to catch her breath, she turned the tie slightly askew and began releasing the buttons on his shirt, revealing the Superman logo beneath bit by bit.

"Why did you have me put all this on if you were just going to undo it all?"

"Hush."

He needed to stop talking to her in low whispers. It was too distracting, too intimate. She was already having a difficult time mentally blocking out the weight of his hand on her hip or the heat from it seeping through the fabric. Then there was his warm scent that tickled her nose with the slightest movement. She kept her head ducked down, hoping he couldn't see her pulse thrumming in her throat or how she struggled to regulate her breathing.

"Are you about done?"

"Done." She released the final button and quickly backed away to break free from his spell. "You need just one more thing. Give me a second." She rushed out to the front room where she had dropped her purse on the coffee table.

"What the hell do you carry in that thing? I swear you have more shit in there than I carried in my rucksack. And that's saying something."

She cut her eyes at him, then went about digging. Finally finding what she needed in the bottom of her bag, she opened the soft case and pulled out a pair of black Wayfarer-style frames with clear lenses. "Put these on."

"I'm not ruining my eyesight for a damn Halloween costume."

Ignoring his protests, she shoved them on his face. "They aren't prescription."

Reluctantly he looked at her, then over her head at something across the room, then glanced at the watch on his wrist.

"Why the hell would anyone wear glasses when they don't need them?"

"Because it looks good," she said while tossing her handbag over her shoulder. "It's called style, Lucky. Clearly something Uncle Sam never taught you."

LUCKY HAD SPENT a lot of time in shitholes over the past decade and he was pretty comfortable with saying the Red Dawg easily made his top five list. Despite his rating, the place was packed with a mixture of college students, locals, and anyone else in a twenty-mile radius who didn't want to hang with the over-fifty crowd at the casino. And much to his surprise, there were quite a few faces he recognized from the hospital.

Leaving Rachel to chat with their coworkers, he

pushed his way through to the lone bar at the back of the building. He waited patiently, trying to make eye contact with one of the bartenders who were, much to his misfortune, both men. Odds were with the number of women crowding the bar he was in for a wait.

Lucky leaned against the bar, his eyes scanning the crowded room only to find Rachel standing just where he'd left her. Except she was now chatting with a man he didn't recognize, one who looked like he'd just walked off the course at the local country club.

What the hell was a prepster like that doing in a place like this? Because he knew damn well that wasn't a costume he was wearing.

Lucky could only watch as this guy leaned in close and got an eyeful of Rachel's cleavage as he spoke to her. And when a smile spread across Rachel's face, good old-fashioned jealousy burned in Lucky's gut.

He didn't like this. Not one bit.

And while he thought Rachel looked hot as hell in her costume, he sure didn't care for all the other men in the place checking her out.

But he had to remind himself they weren't dating. He had no claim on her whatsoever. They were friends. Only friends. And just days before his friend had suggested he get laid. In turn, he suggested the same for her.

What a fucking idiot he was.

He turned back to the bar and rested one arm on the stainless steel counter top with a twenty in his hand, doing everything short of waving it in the air to get the bartender's attention. If he was going to get through this night, he was going to need something stronger than beer.

Lucky was on the verge of whistling at one of the bartenders when she placed her hand upon his arm. In that split second, relief washed over him as he thought she'd finally ditched that idiot and joined him at the bar.

"You buying?"

But the voice didn't belong to Rachel.

It must have been one hell of a look he shot the mystery woman wearing little black cat ears and a black pleather catsuit because she immediately removed her hand from his arm.

"I'm sorry, Lucky," she said, lowering her eyes. "I was just joking and obviously you don't recognize me, so . . . sorry."

She turned to leave and the bartender shouted across the wood counter.

"What'll it be?"

In true male fashion, Catwoman had captured the bartender's attention. The mystery woman, however, directed him to Lucky. "He was here first."

Well, damn. The least he could do was buy her a drink now. "What are you drinking?"

Catwoman smiled. "A beer is fine."

He ordered three beers and took another long look. "I'm terrible with names, but I have to say you do look familiar. Do you work at the hospital?"

Her smile returned. "I'm Krista. We have Psychology together."

Shit. Another classmate.

Immediately he wondered if she used a fake ID to get in the place or if they'd bothered to card her at all. And the last thing he needed was to be busted for contributing to the delinquency of a minor.

He narrowed his eyes at her when the bartender slid three longnecks across the bar to him. "Are you old enough to be in here?"

"I'm twenty-three." She reached into the top of her black catsuit and pulled out her driver's license, apologizing for her lack of pockets as she handed him her ID. "See for yourself."

It was impossible to read her license in the dim light of the bar, so he could only assume she was telling the truth.

"I realize I'm older than most of our classmates," she said as he returned her license. "That's because I work full-time at the casino and pick up classes when the schedules allow. It might take me ten years to get my degree, but at least I won't be in debt when I'm done."

He thought it funny she considered herself older than their classmates. Which was true in theory. But twenty-three was still pretty young in his book.

Lucky handed her one of the beers and picked up the other two. "Are you here by yourself?"

"For the moment," she answered. "My friends are running late."

Being a nice guy, he invited her to join their group so she wouldn't be alone, and they worked their way back across the bar. As they arrived at the table, Rachel and preppy boy were each tossing back a test tube shot.

"Oh, hey, you're back," she said, tossing the empty plastic tube on the table. "And you brought a friend."

After introducing Krista to Rachel, he handed her a longneck. "Looks like you found a new friend as well."

"This is Rich Hamilton," she said, placing her hand upon his shoulder. "He's the new interim doc in the ER."

Even though he didn't want to, he offered his hand. Because he was a nice guy and that's how he was raised. "Lucky James. Good to meet you."

The guy looked from Rachel to him, sizing Lucky up before accepting his handshake. His grip was a little over the top. And since Lucky wasn't one to back down from a pissing match, he squeezed a little harder than usual until the jackass pulled his hand free.

When his eyes met Rachel's narrowed ones, Lucky knew she was pissed, but wasn't exactly sure as to why.

He tipped back his longneck and drank down most of it in a single swallow. Then, remembering Krista was there, he asked if she'd like to dance. They abandoned their drinks on the table before he took her by the hand and led her out onto the dance floor. It'd been a hell of a long time since he'd done any two-stepping, but he'd be damned if he was going to stand around and watch Rachel flirt with the man who would likely become her next boyfriend.

From the dance floor he kept a watchful eye on Rachel as he and Krista made small talk as they danced. It soon became clear preppy boy mustn't know how to two-step since they never attempted going out onto the floor. Instead, the jackass plied her with test tube shots, later advancing to tequila shots, ordering so many that Lucky lost count of how many Rachel drank.

Which meant he was laying off the beer the rest of the night, because no way in hell would he let that jackass get Rachel drunk and take advantage of the situation. Not on his watch. If she went out with the guy another night, well, then, that was out of his hands. But tonight they'd come to the bar together and they were leaving the bar together. End of story.

RACHEL LICKED THE salt from the back of her hand and lifted the shot glass to her mouth. After taking a deep breath, she tossed back the tequila, feeling the slow burn of alcohol down her throat, into her belly, and finally reaching the tips of her toes.

Richie Rich stared at her with a smug grin on his face. "Another?"

"Sure. Why not?" The words had barely left her lips when he rushed off for the bar, disappearing into a sea of Halloween costumes.

She wasn't a fool. She knew what was going on here. The good doctor determined she was an easy lay as long as he got her good and drunk, and if she were completely truthful, there were worse ways to spend her evening.

After all, Lucky seemed to have taken her advice to heart and found a prospect of his own. They hadn't been here ten minutes before he was leading a gorgeous brunette around the dance floor. To be sure, she was young, but beautiful as well. And she rocked the hell out of her Catwoman costume.

At the thought of him taking her home, Rachel decided Richie Rich could serve a purpose, a distraction of sorts at least for tonight. Because the last thing she wanted was to lie in bed, all alone, and have her imagination running wild with thoughts of Lucky and his brunette.

Just to make matters worse, an hour earlier she'd spotted Curtis cozying up with her dear old friend Tamara. Which should have made her furious. Instead, she couldn't really be bothered.

Once again, Lucky and Krista passed by on the dance floor and her stomach twisted. She wanted to be the one in his arms, her body pressed against his with that familiar weight of his hand on her hip. She wanted to get drunk on his scent, learn the taste of his lips, his tongue. She wanted to be consumed by the feel of him wrapped around her, on top of her, inside her.

It wasn't tequila or jealousy or anything else talking. Just the simple fact she could no longer deny wanting the man who'd become her best friend.

Chapter Eleven

LUCKY WAS ABOUT to put Krista into a spin when he glanced in Rachel's direction and saw a man who was not the ER doc towering over her. As they worked their way around the dance floor, Lucky kept trying to catch a glimpse through the sea of moving cowboy hats. From what he could see, the guy was probably about his height, but definitely thicker around the middle. And the look on Rachel's face was one he'd seen before, usually when she was talking about how her ex treated her. In a matter of seconds, she went from a woman relaxed and having fun, to one who was practically curling in on herself.

Although the song wasn't anywhere near finished, Lucky was on the verge of making an excuse when he saw another woman come along, grab the guy by the arm, and tow him through the bar toward the exit. Lucky breathed a sigh of relief knowing the confrontation was over. At least until he saw a flash of strawberry red heading after them.

Oh, goddammit. What the hell was running through that head of hers?

Tequila, if he had to hazard a guess.

He stopped them in their tracks and spoke directly into Krista's ear. "Sorry, but I gotta go." He thumbed in the direction of the door. "My ride is leaving."

She looked up at him with dark eyes. "I'd be more than happy to give you a ride home."

"Thanks, but . . ." He threw up a hand and waved, not wanting to waste time talking when Rachel had a head start on him.

He pushed his way through to the exit, his ears ringing from the loud music the moment he stepped outside into the cool night air. Although there was no sign of Rachel, her truck was right where they'd left it. Then he heard the distinct sound of her voice coming from the side of the building.

"Asshole!"

Just as he rounded the corner he saw Rachel pick up a large piece of gravel—a rock, really—from the makeshift parking lot and chuck it in the general direction of a man and woman, neither whom he recognized.

The man looked over his shoulder, laughing at her, mocking her. "You stupid bitch! You couldn't hit the broadside of a damn barn."

Unfortunately, Lucky had to agree with the asshole, whoever he was. About her throwing capabilities, not the bitch part. He would intervene, but knowing Rachel like he did, it was best to stay out of it; otherwise, he'd become her next target. Lucky crossed his arms and watched in amusement as she leaned over and picked up another rock. Again, her aim was way off, striking an old farm truck about fifteen feet to the left of her target.

Then the woman decided to take a turn yelling at Rachel. "I didn't believe Curtis at first, but you really are crazy! I can't believe I was ever friends with you!"

Ah, yes. Just as he'd suspected. This particular asshole was *the* asshole. No wonder Rachel was lobbing rocks.

"Some friend you are," Rachel yelled back. "You know what they say . . . 'With friends like you . . . !' "

The ex-friend seized the opportunity to take another verbal shot. "Curtis deserves so much better than a crazy bitch who was a lousy lay."

Lucky winced. He'd seen his share of catfights over the years and he knew damn well that chick's last comment was the lowest of blows. Never criticize a woman's sexual prowess. That's along the same lines as a woman telling a guy he had a Vienna Sausage for a dick.

"I'll show you," Rachel muttered as she swiped the synthetic bright red hair from her face. She leaned over and grabbed one last rock from the parking lot as her asshole ex turned his back and continued on to his car. With a soft grunt, she heaved the golf-ball-size rock as far as she could. Lucky lost track of it in the dimly lit parking lot, at least until Curtis grabbed at the back of his shoulder, a stream of curse words flying from his mouth.

"Oh, shit," Rachel and Lucky said in unison, both shocked she actually struck her target.

She turned to Lucky, knowing damn well she was about to have her ass handed to her if she just stood there. Wasting no time, he grabbed her by the arm and slung her over his right shoulder since he knew she wouldn't be able to run in those damn shoes she was wearing. Thankful her truck was parked in the opposite direction of her ex, he took off running. When they reached her truck, he swung open the driver's door and tossed her inside on the bench seat. The engine roared to life and he wasted no time throwing it into drive, immediately stomping on the gas and leaving Curtis standing in a cloud of dust.

Rachel turned in the seat and peered out the back window into the darkness. "You don't think I really hurt him, do you?"

At worst her ex would be sporting a bruise tomorrow. Considering the distance she threw it and the rate of speed, it probably wouldn't leave a mark at all. Instead, her little rock chucking was more like waving a flag in front of a Brahma bull.

"No, you didn't hurt him," he barked. "Now turn around and put your seat belt on."

She obliged, nearly cowering in her seat as she pulled the belt and latched it. "Are you angry at me?"

"I'm only angry that you took off into the parking lot all by yourself. What if I hadn't seen you leave? What would you have done then?" He shook his head in disbelief. "What the hell were you thinking?"

She was quiet as she tugged the seat belt across her body and latched it in the buckle.

"I wasn't, I guess," her reply soft and words a little

slurred. "I just wanted someone to feel as bad as I did at the moment."

Well, if that didn't make him feel like shit for jumping down her throat. Plenty of times he'd seen his friends do the stupidest shit when they encountered their exes out with someone new. Why would Rachel be any different? But his friends usually preferred to drown their sorrows and lose themselves in the bed of a willing woman. And in Savannah, there had been plenty who were willing, especially when it came to military guys.

But throwing rocks at your ex? He'd never seen anything like that and a part of him couldn't wait to tell the guys all about it.

Lucky chuckled to himself as the memory replayed in his mind. "I can't believe you actually hit him."

"I know, right?" She smothered her laughter at first, but then unable or unwilling to contain it, she let it go. A full-bellied, musical sound that quickly had him laughing right along with her. But it wasn't long before their laughter died down and her tone softened. "Remember when you asked if there was a friend I could stay with until I moved out, and I told you she'd just fallen off the radar? Wasn't returning my texts or phone calls and I had no idea as to why? Well, now I do."

"The woman with him was your friend?" Rachel nodded. "But that was weeks ago. That doesn't mean they were hooking up then."

"Maybe not. But I found a pair of underwear in the wash that weren't mine. That doesn't happen by accident. A woman doesn't sleep with a guy and walk out of his

place not remembering whether or not she had underwear on when she arrived."

He couldn't tell how hurt she was by the discovery.
From past conversations they'd had about her ex, it may
have been the straw that broke the camel's back. The
reason she needed to leave him for good. And while she
was better off without the jerk, he couldn't imagine how
she felt now, learning it was her best friend screwing her
boyfriend not only behind her back, but in her home.

"Rachel . . ."

She waved him off, clearly not wanting any sympathy
as she turned to look out the passenger window, hiding
her face from view.

When they reached the edge of town, she placed her
hand on his forearm. "I don't want to go home yet. It's
still early."

Stopped at a red light, he seized the opportunity to
take in her costume. The strawberry red wig, the laced-
up bodice, and extremely short puffy skirt definitely put
the sexy in Strawberry Shortcake. Not to mention the
stripped socks that stopped just above her knees, leaving
her thighs bare. "It's nearly two. Most places will be shutting down for the night."

"It's just . . ."

She cut herself off, once again turning so he couldn't
see her face. But he needed to know what was running
through that head of hers.

"It's just what?"

"I just don't want to go home." She lifted one shoulder
and let it drop. "It's lonely sometimes."

He should have known that was it. She was such an extrovert, a social butterfly. She loved being around people and chatting incessantly. Of course it made sense that there'd be times when the quiet of her place would get to her. Hell, he had led a relatively quiet, solitary life when he wasn't living in the barracks or deployed overseas and the isolation of her place would likely make him crazy.

He reached across the truck cab and took hold of her hand. Finally, she looked over at him, the red glow from the stoplight highlighting her sad smile. "That's an easy fix," he said, giving her hand a little squeeze. "You can stay at my house tonight."

WHILE HER NEWFOUND independence was exhilarating at times, it also had its occasional drawbacks. So tonight she'd gladly settle for the next best thing—sleeping in Lucky's spare bedroom.

He parked her truck in the driveway, and before she even opened the passenger door he was there, helping her out of the truck. Always the gentleman, he kept a steady arm around her shoulders as she stumbled her way across the yard and up the porch steps.

"I think it's safe to say those shoes and tequila don't mix."

"But I like my shoes."

If it hadn't been for the smile on his face, she'd have thought he was angry. "I never said I didn't like them." He dug his keys from his pocket, unlocked the door, then steered her inside. "Just a dangerous combination, that's all."

After settling her in the recliner, he knelt at her feet, mumbling stuff about broken necks as he worked to remove her shoes. The moment his hand circled her ankle, lifting her foot so he could get a better look at the small buckle of her high heeled Mary Jane, her imagination began to run wild. She could practically feel the heat from his hand as it skimmed along the inside of her leg, his fingers raking along the soft skin of her thighs. His head bowed closer to press a kiss between—

"Are you okay?"

Startled from her fantasy, she met his gaze. "I'm perfectly fine. Why?"

His dark eyes studied her intently. "You groaned like you were going to be sick or something. I wanted to make sure you weren't going to puke on my head."

Lovely. His mind was obviously not in the gutter.

"You spent a lot of time on the dance floor," she asked, hoping to avoid another trip to wonderland as he tugged on the tiny buckle of her shoe. "Did you have fun?"

"It was good to get out of the house. Just like you'd said." He raised her foot higher to get a closer look at the tiny buckle. "These little things are a pain in the ass."

After a few more tries he finally won the battle and lowered her foot to the ground.

"Are you going to ask that girl out?"

Lucky shook his head and took hold of her other shoe. "She's too young for me. Nice girl though. What about you and the good doctor?"

The good doctor?

"Oh, shit!" she said, smacking herself in the forehead.

"What's wrong?" With the second buckle undone, he removed her other shoe and placed it neatly against the other.

"He had gone to the bar for more shots when I followed Curtis and Tamara out to the parking lot. I didn't tell him I was leaving."

The idea of Richie Rich wandering around the bar looking for his sure thing made them both laugh to the point of tears. When their laughter died down, Lucky did an impersonation of the guy returning to the table only to find her gone and then they laughed some more.

Rachel held her head in her hands. "Oh, God. My head hurts already."

"Come on," Lucky said as he tugged her to her feet. "Let's get you some water and then to bed."

"Would you mind if I take a shower first?"

"Only if you promise not to drown."

She rolled her eyes and immediately regretted doing it for two reasons. One, it sent a stabbing pain to the top of her head, and two, he didn't even see her do it. What a waste.

Rachel grabbed her purse and followed Lucky into the kitchen, then continued on to the bathroom. As she switched on the shower to let it warm, he went to find something for her to change into.

As she stood in front of the mirror, she slid the strawberry colored wig off her head, revealing the sweaty mess of hair beneath. She removed the false eyelashes

and washed away her heavy makeup. When she finished, Rachel took one final look in the mirror and was
surprised to see him standing behind her, just patiently
waiting for her to finish. The tie and button-down were
both gone, along with the Superman shirt that had been
replaced with a simple white tee.

She spun around to face him. "What is it?"

He smiled, shrugged his shoulders. "Nothing. Just
watching." He shoved a stack of clothes and towels in her
direction. "Here ya go. Do you need anything else?"

"As a matter of fact . . ." Rachel turned her back to him
and drew her hair up off her shoulders with one hand. "I
can't get the zipper undone. I think it's stuck."

She held her breath and waited.

It seemed like an eternity before he finally touched
her. His first effort was nothing more than a gentle tug
on the zipper, then perhaps realizing she wasn't making
it all up, he tried again, this time pulling in earnest. He
crowded behind her, his fingertips ghosting across her
skin as they dipped beneath the fabric and took hold.

"It looks like it's caught in the fabric."

He stood so close now the warm breath of his words
sent a shiver down her spine. After several tries, the zipper
finally broke free and he immediately stepped away.

"All good, Shortcake."

Her eyes met his smiling reflection in the mirror. "Is
that what you're going to call me now?"

"I think so. I kinda like it."

Then, before she could say anything else, he eased the
door shut between them.

"GET A HOLD of yourself, man."

Lucky pulled a frying pan from the cabinet and tossed it upon the stove, desperately in need of a distraction. The woman needed some food in her belly if she was going to minimize her hangover. Something greasy. Something with bacon.

That he could handle.

He yanked open the refrigerator door and stared inside, letting the cool air wash over his heated skin. It had taken every ounce of self-control to walk away from her just then. When the zipper had finally given way, revealing the snowy white strapless bra and matching baby-doll panties she wore, his fingers itched to remove the rest of her clothing as well.

And he wasn't even going to think about the fact she was using his shower right now. Or what she might look like with soap bubbles and water droplets streaming down her naked body.

Lucky shook his head, trying to rid his brain of the image he'd painted.

Bacon.

That's why he was standing there with the refrigerator door wide open, cooling the whole damn house, as his father used to say.

When the bacon was halfway done, he heard the shower shut off. Once again, he was hit with a barrage of images. Of her toweling off. Of her massaging lotion into her skin. It didn't matter that he knew for a fact he didn't own a bottle of lotion since she probably carried one around in that freaking suitcase she called a purse.

To further distract himself he tossed bread in the toaster and reached for a tomato. If wielding a knife didn't get him to focus on what he was doing, he was bound to lose a damn finger. And explaining that to his coworkers in the ER would be just tons of fun.

"You made bacon? You are a god."

He turned to see her leaning against the small island, her damp red hair piled in a bun on top of her head. Her cheeks were flushed from the heat of the shower, making her even more beautiful than when she was completely done up. Not to mention, she looked hot as hell wearing his old gray ARMY T-shirt.

But why, oh, why, did he give her his old black PT shorts to wear?

Unless he was mistaken, she'd rolled the waistband a few times making them even shorter, like they weren't short enough to begin with. Thank God the silky running shorts came with built-in underwear; otherwise, he really wouldn't be getting any sleep at all tonight. Knowing she would be sleeping only feet away would make things hard enough.

He was hard enough already.

Lucky poured a glass of water for her, then one for himself since he clearly needed to cool off.

"Hydrate," he said, handing her one of the glasses.

After the toaster popped, he went about making their BLT sandwiches, adding cheese to both and leaving off the lettuce on hers. Instead of sitting at the table, they stood side by side, hovering over the small island as they ate their sandwiches in silence. When she was finished, he cleared away their plates and loaded them in the dishwasher.

"I've got one last thing for you." Lucky grabbed a bottle of ibuprofen from a nearby cabinet and shook out two tablets into his palm. "Better to be safe than sorry."

With a nod and a weak smile, she took them from his hand and peered over the rim of the glass with those hypnotic bright blue eyes as she swallowed them down.

And just like that he was transported back to the first time he saw her after transferring in the middle of seventh grade. How those blue eyes stared up at the new kid as he shuffled past her desk to reach an empty seat in the back. Every day, he would wait until the very last minute to arrive for math class, just to see if he could get her to look at him that way again.

Then, without any warning, she rose up on her toes and pressed a kiss to his mouth. At first he took it as a simple thank you, nothing more than a friendly gesture, until she grew bolder, taking his head in her hands and guiding his face down to hers.

Her lips were chilled from the water she'd just drank, but warmed almost instantly as they kissed. Her tongue tasted of bacon with an underlying hint of tequila. But none of that mattered because, dear God, how he'd wanted this for weeks, years even, if he were completely honest.

Lucky wrapped his arms around her middle, pulling her body flush with his, neither of them holding anything back as they kissed. When he grew light-headed and desperately needed oxygen, he trailed his mouth across her cheek to her ear, down the column of her throat. Clearly she was just as affected, her chest rising and falling in heavy pants, a soft gasp escaping her lips when he nipped at a particularly sensitive spot beneath her ear. Her hands roamed over his chest, down his stomach until she reached the bottom of his shirt where they snuck beneath the cotton fabric, her fingertips skimming across his bare skin, then edging beneath the waistband of his jeans.

The first tug on his button snapped him from his delirium.

They had to stop. He needed to stop this.

Using every ounce of willpower, he took hold of her wrists and stepped back, putting space between them. "We can't do this, Rach. I'm sorry but . . ."

A few seconds passed as her initial confusion gave way to understanding.

"You're right. I'm sorry. I shouldn't have done that."

"That's not what I meant."

Before he had a chance to explain, she rushed from the kitchen to the guest room, but not before he saw the hurt in her eyes.

It wasn't that he didn't want her, because he did. So goddamn much.

But just an hour before, she was upset from seeing her ex with her best friend. He refused to be the stand-in, the rebound guy, the one to help her temporarily forget, despite the fact his body was so very willing to oblige her. Then there was the little matter of just how much she drank.

All he knew was it couldn't happen like this. He wouldn't let it happen like this.

If a time came when they did cross that line, he'd make damn certain she was of clear mind and heart because the last thing he wanted to be was a regret.

Chapter Twelve

WHEN SHE WOKE the following morning, Lucky's house was quiet. Despite her throbbing head, she eased out of bed and made her way into the kitchen. The clock on the stove told her it was nearly ten and on the small kitchen island, next to a bottle of red Gatorade and ibuprofen, was a note from Lucky.

Meeting Dad for breakfast, then off to class. Have a project due tomorrow so it's going to be a long day.

Great. He'd essentially left her a polite but firm brush-off for the entire day.

Rachel gathered her things and pulled the locked door shut behind her, choosing to wear his clothes instead of changing back into her costume for the short drive back to her house. But even after she returned home, she stayed in the T-shirt and shorts he gave her, telling herself it was so she could finish all of her laundry in a single day.

It had absolutely nothing to do with the fact she liked

being surrounded by the scent of him or could lift his shirt to her nose anytime she wanted throughout the day and have a sniff. Of course each time she did so, it brought to mind a different memory from the night before, each one more embarrassing than the last. How he threw her over his shoulder and hauled her across the parking lot after she threw rocks at her ex. How her fantasies ran wild as he helped her out of her shoes. How she completely threw herself at him and he turned her down.

Lucky was by far the best friend she'd had in a very long time and in a single night she'd succeeded in screwing it all up. All because she'd gotten drunk and lost her head.

She didn't hear from him at all that day or the next. She was even more surprised when she arrived at work on Friday night only to find out he'd called in sick. During her lunch break she tried calling him a couple of times, with each one going straight to voice mail. She also sent a few text messages during that same time. And another as she walked out the doors at the end of her shift. So either he was really sick or something terrible had happened.

Twenty minutes after leaving work, she stood on the front step of her parents' house, knocking on the glass storm door, delivering yet another of her mother's prescriptions. Her current plan was to get in and out as quickly as possible and then drop by Lucky's house to check in on him.

A stiff breeze blew from the northwest, sending a shiver down her spine and signaling winter was on its way. She knocked a second time, the action stinging her knuckles because of the cold. Rachel wrapped her arms around herself trying to stay warm, and as she stood there freezing her butt off, she couldn't help but wonder if her brothers would bother to knock on the door of their parents' home or if they would have just walked right on inside.

She'd lifted her hand, ready to knock a third time, when the wooden door opened up, bringing her face-to-face with her father. "Hi, Dad."

Still, he made no motion to open the door or invite her inside.

"What are you doing here?" he asked through the cracked glass.

She held up the small pharmacy bag. "Mom needed a prescription refilled so I stopped and picked it up this morning."

His frown deepened as his eyes shifted to the paper bag, then back to her. "She's not here."

Finally, he pushed the storm door open just wide enough to reach through the gap and take the bag from her hand. Then he promptly turned his back and shut the door in her face.

"Great to see you, too, Dad," she said to the closed door before turning on her heel and going back to her truck.

For as long as she could remember he'd treated her this way. Not anyone else in the family, only her. At least with her mother Rachel could look to a specific moment in time and know exactly why her mother quit speaking to her. But her dad? She didn't have a concrete reason as to why. In the past, whenever she broached the subject with one of her siblings, the answer was always the same. They didn't know why he treated her differently. Or worse, they changed the subject and pretend like she never asked the question to begin with.

What angered her most was the fact his actions still had a way of burrowing beneath her skin after all of these years. No matter how much she tried to brush it off.

Then it was like déjà vu a few minutes later, when she found herself knocking on another front door waiting for someone to answer. Any other time she would have walked right into Lucky's place, but after what happened the other night and not knowing what he was thinking about things, well, it was probably for the best she didn't just barge right in.

She knocked a second time and a third since his Jeep was in the driveway. Finally, she saw shadowed movement through the door's pane of leaded glass just before it flung open. He looked like hell, his eyes red and swollen, and despite the cold front moving in, he wore only a pair of basketball shorts.

"I've tried getting ahold of you all night. Dottie said you called in sick. Are you okay?" she asked through the screen door. And then she spotted the bottle of Jack Daniel's dangling from his fingertips.

He stood there dazed for a moment before stumbling back to the couch, but at least he didn't shut the door in her face. She yanked open the screen door and invited herself in. Then, as she closed the front door behind her, took a better look at him. And what she saw scared her.

Lucky was a man who was always in control. She'd never seen him drink more than the occasional beer and now he was drinking whiskey straight from the bottle like it was water.

"Why don't I make you something to eat?" Rachel dropped her purse on the coffee table and was on her way to the kitchen when he finally spoke.

"Always the caretaker," he said, his words cold and hardened.

What he said was true about her, but his tone implied it was some sort of character flaw.

She was halfway tempted to pick up her purse and go, leave him there to wallow in his misery all alone. She'd spent enough of her life being one guy or another's verbal punching bag and she wasn't really in the mood for his crap. But she couldn't shake the idea that something had happened, something terrible.

"You know what, to hell with the food." Rachel took a seat on the coffee table, putting herself directly in front of him. "Why don't you tell me what's going on?"

Instead of answering her, he tipped the bottle of Jack to his lips, staring blearily at her as he took another long drink of whiskey.

"Is it your dad or Brenda? Are they okay?" If she hadn't just come off shift, she would've thought it a possibility. By the way he squeezed his eyes shut when he shook his head, the pained look on his face, all of it led her to believe she was on the right track.

"Your mom? Half brothers?"

Again, another shake. It was as if that was the only movement he could muster.

She took the bottle from his hand and placed it on the table next to her. "Lucky, you're scaring me. Please tell me what's going on."

He pointed to the open laptop next to her and she ran her finger across the mousepad to wake up the computer. After a brief flash or two, a news article appeared on the screen.

The Department of Defense announced today the deaths of four soldiers who were supporting Operation Enduring Freedom. All four were assigned to the 1st Battalion, 75th Ranger Regiment at Hunter Army Airfield in Savannah, Georgia.

The names listed weren't ones she recalled hearing him talk about, but with all the nicknames he used, they could have been. But whether or not it was guys he spoke often about hardly mattered since he'd always said his military unit was like family to him.

"Are these guys you served with? Your friends?"

He nodded. "Three others are hanging on by a thread."

She moved to sit next to him, turning sideways so she could cradle his face in both of her hands. At first he tried to refuse her comfort, to push her away, but she only clung tighter to him. "I'm so sorry, Lucky. So sorry."

His chest heaved while he stared at the names on the

computer screen. "I should've been there with them. If I'd been there, maybe I could've . . ."

Rachel covered his mouth with her fingers. "Don't do this. Don't. It's not your fault. I promise it's not."

Lucky squeezed his eyes shut and grasped her wrist in his hand, trying to pull her hand away as if her touch physically pained him. But she refused to move away, to give him space. When Ethan died, she would have given anything to have someone comfort her, to just hold her hand. Instead, she was left to suffer through her grief all alone and she'd be damned if she let him do the same.

Even though he tried to push her away, she fought him tooth and nail. He finally gave up the fight, first leaning into her, crying against her shoulder, his arms loosely draped around her waist. But in time, he tightened his hold, banding his arms tight around her middle, even dragging her into his lap as he buried his face in the curve of her neck and cried.

They remained that way for what seemed an eternity, until his breathing evened out and he lifted his head to look at her through bleary eyes and dark, damp lashes. She caressed his cheeks with her thumbs, wiped away the lingering wetness from his tears, before leaning forward and placing a kiss to one cheek and then the other. Then, as she stroked his jaw with her fingertips, she pressed a gentle kiss to his mouth.

His body went tense beneath her, and when she drew back, those dark brown eyes stared at her with an unreadable expression.

Her first thought was that just like Halloween night she'd gone too far.

Rachel whispered an apology as she attempted to climb off his lap; instead, his hands tightened around her waist.

"Don't leave me." He lifted one hand to push the hair back from her face, tangling his fingers in the long strands and twisting it around his fist. "I need you, Rachel. Please." Tugging on her hair, he drew her closer until her forehead rested upon his. "Please."

She knew what he was asking. Knew he wanted more, needed more from her than a hand to hold or a shoulder to cry on. A little voice in the back of her mind said she shouldn't do this. That he'd drank far too much, was far too vulnerable and upset. That she was only taking advantage of the situation.

But Lucky didn't wait for her to respond with an answer. Instead, he initiated their second kiss, with a series of gentle nips to her lips, the heavy scruff on his upper lip tickling her as he drew his mouth to hers. And without any regard to her heart, she dove in headfirst.

He might have been the one asking please, but really, she needed him just as much. Needed someone to drown out the sound of her father's voice on repeat in her head. Needed someone to make her feel needed for even the shortest amount of time. To hell with her parents, her family. To hell with everything. She only needed this one thing. She needed *him*.

Rachel took hold of her scrub top and lifted it up and off her body. As she pressed her body against his, she was surprised by the chill of his skin. He pulled her closer, soaking up her warmth as he kissed her mouth with unbelievable tenderness. His lips and tongue tasted of whiskey, his hands felt rough and callused as they moved against her skin. She thought it might be all he needed, to be connected to someone, to steal the heat from her body.

But his kisses turned frantic, desperate. His fingers pulled at the few clothes she still wore while his mouth moved over her face and body in unpredictable movements. In one second he was kissing her lips, the next, he was pulling the lace cups of her bra downward, his mouth latching on to one breast, sucking and biting her nipple until he moved to the other and repeated his actions. All the while he blindly tugged at the drawstring of her pants, then hooked both of his thumbs into the waistband and shoved them down, along with her panties, as far as he could.

Rachel raised up on her knees, finishing what he started and pulling the pants free from her legs. Meanwhile, he'd freed himself from his shorts and in an instant was thrusting upward at the same time he pulled her down onto his erection, a harsh cry escaping his lips as he buried himself deep within her. He wrapped his arms tightly around her, holding her to him as if his very life depended upon it.

"It's okay," she whispered as her own tears now fell upon his skin. Her fingers skimmed the length of his spine, stroked his nape, raked through his disheveled hair. "I've got you. I promise."

They remained that way for several moments, until

the tension reached a point she had to move. She raised up on her knees, only to slowly sink back down upon him, the motion eliciting a sound from him that was more pain than ecstasy. She continued to move slowly over him, giving him her care, her love. She would give him whatever he needed so he knew he was not alone.

Then, without any warning, he flipped them so she was now flat on her back, his arms and shoulders pressing her legs higher and further apart as he drove deeper, harder, into her body. She grasped hold of his shoulders, dug her fingernails deep into his flesh. The tension built and coiled low in her belly, bringing her to the very edge as he cried out his release. When he finished, he collapsed on top of her, his body limp from both the physical and emotional exhaustion.

She pressed kisses to his temple, smoothed her hands over the muscular planes of his back and arms, lightly dragging her nails against his skin. He relaxed further and further into her until her hips ached from the weight of him.

"Lucky . . . my hip. I need to get up."

He withdrew from her body and sat back on his heels, swearing under his breath as he tucked himself back into his shorts. At first she'd thought she'd heard wrong as he stared down at her partially clothed body. Then he swore again, this time as he scrubbed a hand over his face.

His regret came far sooner than she expected.

And while she'd been thinking her first time with Lucky hadn't been exactly what she'd imagined all these months, she didn't regret having sex with him. At least, not until this very moment.

Her stomach roiled as she sat up and tried to put herself to rights. With trembling fingers she repositioned her bra and pulled on her shirt, then rolled off the couch and hurriedly stepped into her pants.

"I'm sorry," he said, his words thick and liquor-laden.

She shook her head, a heavy lock of hair falling free from her clip. "No big deal." She couldn't look at him. If she did she'd completely fall apart and she couldn't let him see that. Wouldn't let him see that. "I gotta go."

"Wait. What?"

She scrambled around the front room to gather her things. She needed to get out of there before she was sick.

"Rach. Rach. Don't leave."

"No, I really have to go. I forgot I have to be somewhere."

Inside her heart was breaking with such force she wondered if he could hear it.

Lucky was still calling after her as she raced out the front door for her truck. She hurriedly backed out of the driveway and headed home with four little words on repeat in her head.

What had she done? What had she done?

SINCE HE'D SPENT the past twenty-four hours swimming in a bottle of Jack, he couldn't do much more than stare out the front window and watch her drive away. Getting in his Jeep and chasing after her could only make a bad situation worse. As if it wasn't bad enough already.

He'd wanted her from the moment their paths had crossed months ago. He'd dreamed of being with her when he was asleep. He fantasized about her when he was awake. But not even his worst nightmares could have predicted it would happen like this. That he would use her that way. Hurt her so badly that she couldn't get away fast enough.

He stumbled to the couch, collapsing into the cushions.

The almost-empty bottle of Jack sat on the coffee table in front of him, mocking him for losing his control in such spectacular fashion. Lucky grabbed it by the neck and slung it at the fireplace mantel, at the pictures of the man he used to be. The bottle exploded on impact, raining shards of glass and liquor down upon the room.

How did this happen. This couldn't be his life. It just couldn't.

Lucky fell back onto the couch and closed his eyes, hoping that when he woke up this all would be nothing more than a bad dream.

HE FINALLY WOKE around three the following morning, having slept off most of his hangover. And most of his work shift as well. He rolled off the couch and stepped into a blazing hot shower where he decided the first order of business was to apologize to Rachel.

He was waiting on her front steps when she arrived home from work, and from the look on her face, he was thankful to be sitting about five feet off the ground. Otherwise, she might have been tempted to take another run at him with her truck. Finish the job this time.

She threw the vehicle into park, climbed out, and slammed the driver's side door with such force the truck rocked from side to side. "You forgot to call in sick," she said as she stomped past him on the stairs. "Don't worry. I covered for you."

"Thank you for that." He gathered the various bags he'd brought and rose to his feet, trailing along behind her. "I brought you breakfast."

"I don't like breakfast food after a night shift."

Rachel jammed her key into the lock and turned the bolt as she continued grumbling about him under her breath. The only word he caught for certain was "asshole." And if that didn't make him feel like shit, because he'd now been successfully lumped in with all the jerks from her past and he had only himself to blame.

After she shouldered the door open, Rachel did as she always did and dropped her purse and keys onto a small table near the entry. Since she didn't tell him to get lost or slam the door in his face, he took the open door as an invitation. As she disappeared into the bedroom, he made his way into the kitchen and settled the grocery bags on the counter.

They'd gone through these same motions so many other times after work, but it sure didn't feel the same. If anything, it reminded him of that first weekend they worked together where they spent all their time dancing on eggshells. When he finally put Bull's advice to good use the following weekend, everything worked out just as he hoped.

Unfortunately, Lucky wasn't so optimistic this time.

"Still here?"

She was all piss and vinegar this morning, not that he could blame her.

"Did you expect me to drop the food and leave?"

Rachel climbed onto one of the bar stools as if waiting for him to serve her. "A girl can only hope, right?"

Do not engage, he told himself. Do. Not. Engage.

"So what did you bring me?"

Lucky held up a white and orange bag in each hand. "In this hand," he said, shaking the bag, "is a Whataburger with cheese, extra pickles, no onions, and French fries." He set the first bag down in front of her and watched closely for her reaction. Her right eye twitched just the faintest bit, which he took as a good sign. "And I know you don't like breakfast food when you get off work, but there's always that one exception." Her eyes widened ever so slightly and he let the anticipation build as he set the second bag down in front of her. "Biscuits and gravy with an extra biscuit."

And just as he suspected, she went for the biscuits and gravy, wasting no time opening the Styrofoam container and digging in.

He picked up the other bag, and since her mouth was already full, she shot him a look that said without words, *Get your hands off my food.*

"I'll put this in the refrigerator so you can have it later."

That must have been an acceptable solution since she went back to eating instead of vaulting over the breakfast bar at him. Now came the tricky part.

"I realize it's a little late to ask this, but are you on the pill? IUD? Anything?"

She paused midbite and just from the expression on her face he knew what the answer was going to be before she even spoke.

"Unfortunately, not at the moment."

"Well, aren't we just a couple of responsible medical professionals." He was trying to make her laugh, smile, anything to lighten the mood even though nothing about the discussion was very funny but she wasn't having any of it.

"But after I take a shower and change, I was going to drive to Sherman and pick up some Plan B." She lowered her fork, resting it on the edge of the container. "I didn't want to ask someone for a script and I doubt any place around town has it on the shelves."

He placed the small pharmacy bag on the counter next to her. "I had to drive all the way to McKinney before I found a store with it on the shelves," he said as she opened the bag and found the box of Plan B. "At least I saved you a trip."

"I really was going to go after work. If I'd been thinking straight yesterday . . ." Rachel popped the single pill from the blister pack. "I'll pay you for this," she said before swallowing it down with a drink of orange juice.

"Don't worry about it."

She kept her head down, her attention focused on the

fork she used to push around her food. "It was good that you weren't at work last night. It gave me time to think about things without you around."

He leaned back against her kitchen counter, using every bit of his self-discipline to remain calm and in control. "And what were you thinking about?"

"How I didn't hear from you for two days after I kissed you in your kitchen. How miserable I've felt for the past twenty-four hours."

His gut told him this was going to go one of two ways: badly or really badly. After what happened the day before, since he hurt her, the decision of where they went from here was completely up to her. "So what do you think we should do? Where do we go from here?"

Rachel took a deep breath, held it a couple of seconds before letting it all go. "I think . . . we should forget it ever happened."

"Which part of it?"

She lifted her head then, looking him directly in the eye. "All of it."

Chapter Thirteen

FOR THE SECOND weekend in a row, Lucky watched the new interim ER doc monopolize Rachel's time for their entire shift. Every patient Rich Hamilton saw, she saw. They took lunch at the same time and hung out in the break room together. She laughed at his jokes while he ogled her rack.

And apparently he wasn't the only one to notice.

Lucky was eating leftover cold pizza and studying for an upcoming psychology test when Dottie came into the break room on her lunch break.

"How are you today, darlin'?"

"Not too bad," he replied while consolidating his piles of handwritten notecards, making room so she could join him at his table. "How's your evening going?"

She dropped into the chair opposite him, a little sigh escaping her mouth as she took a load off her feet. "Probably better than yours."

He huffed a laugh. "I definitely hope so."

Already this evening he'd had three pukers, screaming twin toddlers, and a Code Brown. Of course, he had Dr. Hamilton to thank for assigning him all the shit jobs.

If Doctor Dick happened to see Rachel talking with Lucky, patient related or not, he'd call her away for a "consult," then tell Lucky he needed to wipe down a bed or clean an exam room. The man was clearly trying to mark his territory while sending Lucky a message at the same time.

Dottie was quiet through most of her lunch, not wanting to disrupt his studying. While she ate her sandwich and chips, she scrolled through her Facebook and Pinterest and Tumblr accounts, occasionally stopping to show him a gif or meme that had tickled her funny bone.

"I don't think I've ever seen you in here all by yourself," she said once she'd finished her lunch.

"No?"

Dottie shook her head. "When you first started here, I remember you and Dr. Ferguson would eat together a lot of the time."

Which was true. He and Chad spent most of their spare time talking about battlefield medicine. Or more accurately, Chad asked a million questions and Lucky answered based on his personal experiences. Questions like how difficult it was to treat patients, both military and civilian, in such extreme conditions. He wanted to know the kinds of equipment medical personnel had available to them in the field and how medical protocols varied between the military world and the civilian world.

It wasn't long until Doc Ferguson admitted to Lucky that at one time he'd seriously considered joining the military to become a pararescueman. But he'd been married for a few years by then, and didn't think it would be fair to his wife since she hadn't signed up to be a military wife.

"Then, once Rachel started, the two of you usually had lunch together." Dottie opened up her polka-dot lunch pail and pulled out a small bag filled with Oreos. "I have to say, I thought for the longest time you and Rachel made the cutest couple."

Then she handed him a cookie. One he readily accepted.

"We never were a couple. Just friends," he said, the words leaving a bitter taste in his mouth as he pulled his cookie apart.

"If you say so." She rose from her chair and gave his shoulder a little pat. "I'd better get back out there. Don't want people to start thinkin' I'm replaceable."

He ate his cookie while she packed up her things; then, not long after she made her way out the door, he reluctantly began to do the same.

Three months ago, he looked forward to work and enjoyed being part of the team here. And once he and Rachel got past that first awkward weekend of working together, things were really good. But since Chad Ferguson left for a more exciting position in the city and Rich Hamilton had replaced him in the interim, not only had the shine worn off his job, but he was starting to dread coming to work. There was a world of difference between working with the two men. One respected Lucky's medical training and battlefield experience while the other . . . didn't.

This job's only saving grace—working with Rachel.

With less than an hour left of his shift, Lucky was cleaning what he hoped would be his last exam room of the night when Rachel popped her head in the door. "Diner, today? I'm dying for a club sandwich and a chocolate milkshake."

"Sure. I can do that."

The words were barely out of his mouth when he heard Dr. Hamilton call her by name. Rachel made a silly face, rolling her eyes and sticking out her tongue, before disappearing into the hallway.

He had to hand it to her. She was trying really hard to make him happy with this agreement of theirs, pretending nothing happened between them.

Two weeks earlier, when tears filled her eyes as she talked about their friendship, how it meant more to her than almost everything else in her life, he would've agreed to just about anything to keep her from walking away.

So he let her make the rules.

No talking about their kiss in his kitchen. No talking about having sex on his couch. If they were going to go on as friends, they'd both have to act like it never even happened. No inappropriate touching, no sexual innuendo, no talk of something more.

She believed they'd put their friendship at risk and came so very close to ruining everything, and the only way they could avoid repeating history was to follow the rules.

When he arrived at the diner, Rachel was already seated in what had become their booth, chatting with Peggy about who knows what. Both were laughing like old friends by the time he reached the table.

Peggy slid a menu in front of him as he sat down. "Long night, sugar? You look tired."

"I've been better."

She gave him a little pat on his shoulder and told him she'd be right back with his drink.

Lucky fought the desire to lay his head right down on the table and close his eyes, but he propped his head up on his hand instead. The view was better this way.

"She's right, you know. You're not looking your best." Rachel reached across the table and pressed the back of her hand to his forehead. "Are you feeling okay?"

If it had been anybody else, he would have torn their hand off for being so patronizing. But Rachel, well . . . he'd let her do about anything to him. He was just happy she was touching him, even if it fell well within the rule guidelines. Her hand skimmed across his temple, down his cheek, and he fought the urge to cover her hand with his just so he could keep her there.

Then, all too quickly, she drew back her hand when Peggy returned with their drinks.

"You should have said you didn't feel well. I would've survived eating a club sandwich and chocolate milkshake by myself."

"I'll be better once I get some food in me."

Her smile was so sweet. He didn't have the heart to tell her he agreed partially because he feared she'd ask Doctor Dick to come in his place. And the thought of that jerk taking his seat in their booth? Well, not gonna happen.

In the meantime, he needed to keep up his side of the conversation or else.

"I forgot to tell you I got an email from Bull's mom yesterday. They transferred him from Germany to Walter Reed a week ago."

She was fiddling with her hair as he spoke, freeing it from its clip and twisting it back up. He might have been imagining it, but it was even redder than it was a couple of weeks ago. It had more fire to it now.

"So that's good news, right?"

"He's lost both legs at the knee, but at least he's alive. Thought I might go visit him when finals are over."

She smiled again. "I'm sure he'd like that."

Peggy returned with their sandwiches, a single order of sandwiches and fries for each of them this time, along with Rachel's off-menu chocolate shake.

Immediately she shoved a straw into it and took a drink.

"Look who's getting the special treatment now."

She smiled wide around the straw held between her teeth. "What can I say? She loves me."

Then, just as he always did, he offered her the ketchup first so she could make her little puddle. And then she passed it back so he could make a pond for his fries.

"Would you want to go with me? My treat."

Her eyes widened and she shielded her mouth to answer since he'd caught her midbite. "To Washington, D.C.?"

"Have you been there?"

She laughed. "Uh, no. You know I haven't."

They'd had this conversation more than once, about how he'd traveled all over the world and she'd never been anywhere, really. She'd never been on a plane. Had never seen the ocean. Had never really traveled further than a three-hour drive from her hometown.

"Would we drive or fly?" The little crinkle between her brows gave away her nervousness.

"Fly, of course," he said with total confidence. "We can drive to Dallas, fly out on a Monday afternoon, come back Thursday evening and still have a chance to rest up before our shift on Friday."

Her smile widened. "You've really thought about this."

"Sure." He could feel his own excitement growing. "I think it'd be fun."

And then, without any warning, her smile dropped and she suddenly found the remains on her plate very interesting. Lucky's gut told him there was a bomb about to be dropped.

"There's a reason I wanted us to have breakfast together. I need to tell you something and I don't want you to hear it from anyone else first."

Holy shit. This wasn't just going to be bad, but really bad.

When she looked up at him, there were no remnants of the smile that had just been there. "Rich asked me out. On a date."

"Rich Hamilton."

"Yes."

"Doctor Dick asked you out." He could actually feel the blood pounding in his skull he was so pissed off.

"Please don't call him that," she begged. "I only agreed to it because I thought it might be best to get back in the dating pool."

There was little doubt God was trying his patience today. "What happened to Miss Independent?"

"She's still here!" Her face said she needed to convince herself as much as she was trying to convince him. "I've been thinking a lot for the past two weeks. Ever since we made our little . . . agreement. I thought maybe we shouldn't spend so much time together."

He leaned his forearms on the table and stared directly at her, not even trying to hide his frustration. "I thought the agreement was so we could still be friends? Because our friendship was so important that you never wanted to lose it?"

"That is true!"

"So why are you going out with him of all people?" he said, tossing his hands in the air. "Do you not see the bullshit he pulls with me just because he can? He's at the top of the food chain and I'm just a bottom feeder as far as he's concerned. And he's taking great satisfaction in proving that." He jammed his index finger into the tabletop. "Every. Damn. Day."

Lucky scrubbed a hand over his face. He needed to regain control of his emotions, because arguing with Rachel wasn't going to help matters. If anything he might succeed in just pushing her further away.

She reached across the table and touched his arm, and when he looked up, that sweet smile had returned. But there was worry in her eyes, too.

"Maybe you should do the same thing? Ask someone out on a date. Like Catwoman."

Lucky shook his head, having no idea who she was talking about.

"The woman from the bar. You have a class with her. I can't remember her name."

"Krista."

Rachel forced a smile. "That's it. She's pretty. And she seemed nice the little bit I talked to her."

He could tell that smile was less than genuine, even if she couldn't. Rachel wasn't any happier about the idea of him going out with Krista than he was about her going out with Doctor Dick. And it was her idea to begin with.

"I hope you can understand why I'm doing this." This time she took hold of his hand, twining her fingers between his. "You have all these plans. Getting your degree. Going to medical school. You're going to leave this town a second time and move on with your life and I'll still be here."

"Rach." He tightened his fingers around hers. "Come on. That's years away."

"I know. But if I spend all of my time with you for the next two years and then you leave? I'll have no one."

He wanted to tell her she could have him forever, but that would be breaking their agreement.

Rachel pulled back her hands, sliding them over the tabletop until they disappeared in her lap. "I'm sorry," she said, "but I have to get going. I have to go to the grocery store and get some things for my mom on my way home."

When she went to pull money from her wallet, he told her breakfast was on him.

"Thank you," she whispered as she slid out of their booth. "I'll see you tonight. Get some rest."

Rachel waved goodbye to Peggy as she headed out through the front doors, then Lucky watched her cross the parking lot and climb into her dead brother's truck.

He could take her to Dallas. He could take her to Washington, D.C. He could take her anywhere in the world and she'd probably come back to this place. He knew she could leave this town and do just fine. There was no reason for her to be scared of the world outside the bubble she'd created for herself. As much as he'd like to have something far more than friendship with Rachel, his gut told him it would never work. Not until she figured out she could survive beyond the limits of this town. And that she would have to figure it out on her own.

He had two years to wait her out. He only hoped she'd come to her senses sooner rather than later.

Chapter Fourteen

FOR THE FIRST time in almost a year, she was going out on a first date. She was surprised to find herself a little nervous, a little excited, and if she were completely honest, slightly disappointed it wasn't with Lucky. She slipped on her high heeled boots, wore her nice bra, and curled her lashes, hoping the good doctor would see a noticeable difference from her everyday nurse look.

Instead of Rich picking her up, she met him in the hospital parking lot. After all, she didn't know him all that well and it was better to be safe than sorry.

And it just so happened Lucky suggested she meet him in a public place.

Knowing the kind of car Rich drove, she pulled up alongside him, and when he turned to see her pulling in next to him, she gave a little wave.

He got out of his car to greet her and as she made her way toward him, he asked, "You drive a truck?"

She looked back at it, trying to see it from his perspective. It wasn't anything fancy. No bells and whistles and certainly nothing like the car he drove. But it was clean and she hadn't had any mechanical problems with it whatsoever so there was no reason to get rid of it. Not that she'd consider it even if it did have problems. "It was my brother's."

Rich shook his head. "I've never known a woman who drove a truck. Come to think of it, I don't know many guys who drive trucks. At least, not like that one."

At least he had some manners as he walked her around to the passenger's side of his black BMW. He paused just before opening the door.

"You're wearing heels."

She looked down at her four-inch heeled boots and back to his face, realizing only then they'd brought her eye to eye with him. Actually, more like her eyes to his forehead. Oops.

"We're just going out to eat, right? It's not like we're going for a long hike in the woods," she said in hopes of a laugh and lightening the mood a bit, but that didn't happen.

Lucky would've laughed.

So she lowered herself into his car and wriggled her butt on the leather seat. She'd never considered herself a materialistic person; her childhood broke her of any such ideas. But even she had to admit his car was really nice. The all black interior. Dark tinted windows. New car smell. He climbed in the driver's side and slid what she could only assume were some high dollar sunglasses onto his face and started the car.

As the engine roared to life, the car radio blared out the latest maudlin song from Coldplay. Only after the first song finished and another began, and then another, did she realize this wasn't some random emo college station programming they were listening to, but rather a conscious musical selection made by him.

Not that there was anything wrong with Coldplay. She'd just never known a man who purposely listened to them.

She laughed to herself, making a mental note to tell Lucky later on.

"Something funny?" he asked, his tone almost accusatory.

"No, sorry. I was just thinking of something a friend told me." She bit down on the inside of her lip and stared out the window, forcing her brain to find a new train of thought as they drove to the south side of town.

"I hope you like Italian," he said after lowering the radio volume a bit. "Everyone was suggesting this new restaurant that just opened near the casino. Thought we'd try it out."

"Sounds good."

"I'm glad you think so, although I'm not sure how good it can really be in a town like this."

Great. He was one of those big city people that believed nothing in a small town could ever compare to stuff in the big city. Like only highfalutin restaurants with fancy names and valet parking and celebrity owners were the only places worth eating.

Despite the throng of people waiting for a table just inside the front door, they were seated quickly since they were only a party of two. Considering every table in the place was taken, she wasn't surprised a few minutes passed before their waitress greeted them. But when Rich's voice took on a short, snippy tone with their waitress as she handed over their menus, Rachel's gut told her this evening probably wouldn't end well. She'd seen him take the same tone with Lucky a couple of times at the hospital. In the past she chalked it up to him being exhausted or having a rough day. It happened. Everyone had moments like that. It didn't automatically mean that Rich was an asshole. But now, she began to wonder if he was only nice to people he had to be nice to.

Whereas Lucky's default setting was nice.

It didn't matter if the person was rich or poor, the busboy or the owner. The waitresses at the diner obviously adored him and gave him preferential treatment as a result. Now that she thought about it, she couldn't imagine Rich ever stepping foot in the diner.

When the waitress returned to take the order, he took it upon himself to order the dinner-for-two special. Rachel told herself it was fine that he ordered for her. He probably thought she'd find it romantic. But what if she'd been allergic? What if she didn't like mushrooms? It would have been nice if he'd at least asked her first if she even liked mushroom-stuffed ravioli.

Lucky would have asked.

Dammit.

She needed to stop. It wasn't fair to be constantly comparing Rich or anyone else she might go out with in the future to Lucky. The opportunity to have something more with him had already came and went. They agreed to be friends—admittedly it was mostly her decision—and for her own benefit she needed to move on.

While they waited on their food, Rich spent the next several minutes talking about himself—where he went to school, the neighborhood where he grew up. And since she'd never heard of Highland Park, Texas, and wasn't sufficiently impressed, he said that just went to show how little she knew about anything. He talked about the multi-million-dollar mansions. He name-dropped the famous people who lived around the corner or whose kids he went to school with. And when that wasn't enough, he moved on to the subject of the prestigious university and medical school where he attended, his successful and important fraternity brothers. All things she didn't know much of or care at all about.

Not once did he stop to ask anything about her.

He did, however, compliment her. The good doctor told her she was by far the most beautiful woman he'd seen in this godforsaken town. Such lovely words . . . all spoken to her chest.

And that was just another thing Lucky never did.

Oh, he totally ogled her on the occasion, like when she was wearing her Strawberry Shortcake costume or one of her "cutesy little workout tops" as he liked to call them. But it was always more flirtatious, more playful. And the good Lord knew she could give as good as she could get in that regard. But whenever they spent time facing each other from opposite sides of a dining room table or restaurant booth, he looked her in the eyes. Often with such intensity it felt like he knew all of her secrets and fears without her ever saying a word.

She was taking a drink of her water with lemon when the sound of glass meeting glass caught her attention. Her head shot up just in time to see the good doctor getting a better grip on his drink. Her first thought was that his water glass had slipped from his hand and smacked the tabletop. But then his face pinched as he stared off in the direction of one of the waitstaff.

"How long do I have to wait to get a water refill?"

This time she watched in horror as he purposely banged his drinking glass on top of the glass tabletop a second time.

"You're going to break the table," she said in a harsh whisper.

"It would serve them right," he replied without looking at her. "The help here is terrible."

After the third glass-banging, their waitress rushed over to him, deeply apologetic for the wait as she quickly refilled both their glasses. From there on out, their glasses were kept full, their food arrived quickly, likely with the belief the sooner they ate, the sooner they would be gone. At least Rich stopped talking about himself while they ate and it just so happened she very much enjoyed the mushroom ravioli.

Rachel was counting down the moments until their

nightmare date was over when the waitress appeared once more. "Would you like to see the dessert menu?"

She looked across the table and noticed, just seconds before, Rich had taken the last bite of food from his plate. But before he could answer for the both of them, his cell phone rang in his pocket. He held up one finger, signaling for the waitress to wait as he answered his phone. "Dr. Hamilton."

Good Lord. He really was a pretentious ass.

The waitress attempted to excuse herself so she could greet a family just seated in her section, but Rich took hold of her wrist. "We need the check."

No *please*. No *thank you*.

She nodded in understanding and then rushed over to the new table, explaining she'd be right with them.

"Sorry about that," he said after finishing his call and tucking his phone into his pocket. "But I'm afraid I'll have to cut this short. The hospital needs me to come in. I guess Dr. Roush has a family emergency of some sort and needs to leave. And since I'm on call, I have to cover his shift."

Rachel could hardly contain her excitement.

In ten short minutes, after he left a measly five-dollar tip on a sixty-five-dollar tab, they were back in the hospital parking lot. Although there was an empty slot next to her truck, he instead chose to park at the far end of the lot, angling across two spots so no one could ding the paint.

He walked her to her car, something Rachel now believe he did only because it was on his way inside instead of manners. As she stopped to pull her keys from her handbag, he leaned in close. "I'm sorry things were cut short. I was really looking forward to later."

She looked up at him. "Later?"

He smiled at her. Not the sexy, panty-melting type of smile she'd become accustomed to from her best friend. No, this smile was more of the dirty old man variety. A shiver of disgust ran down her spine just as he took hold of her head and kissed her. And by taking her by surprise, he took advantage, shoving his tongue into her mouth with such ferocity she could only assume he was attempting to lick her tonsils.

Finally, he pulled away, his smile now one of smug satisfaction. As for her, well, she was quite thankful she didn't lose her mushroom ravioli on his shoes.

"We'll do this again real soon." And with that he turned and walked away.

She'd never been so happy to see the back of someone.

Rachel climbed into the security of her truck and rested her head on the steering wheel for a moment, so very thankful the date was over. But that didn't mean she wanted to go home to an empty house where she'd have nothing to do but replay the past hour's events over and over again in her mind.

Whether it was out of habit or a need to be around someone else who could put a positive spin on the evening, she turned onto Lucky's street when she reached it. No big deal. Just a last-minute drive-by. If he wasn't there, no harm, no foul. But if he was there, then she'd pop in since it was still early, absolutely certain he wouldn't mind at all.

Just as she hoped, his Jeep was in the driveway, so she parked along the street and made her way up the front walk. She knocked once, waited a few seconds, and then knocked a second time since ESPN was blaring on the television and it was likely difficult to hear much of anything. Then, through the etched glass in the front door, she saw his shadowy figure coming to answer.

What she hadn't been able to tell from his silhouette was that he was fresh from the shower and wore only a towel around his waist.

"I thought you had a date?" With a look of concern on his face, Lucky pushed the door wider in silent invitation.

"I did. It's over already."

His look of concern was quickly replaced by amusement. "That bad, huh?"

Yes, it was, she wanted to tell him. But she stopped herself.

"No. He was called in to work."

That managed to shut him up and wipe the arrogant grin off his face.

"Grab something from the kitchen if you want. I'm gonna go . . ." He lifted his hand and thumbed in the direction of his room.

Even though her date could be easily filed under "Dates from Hell," she just couldn't bring herself to tell Lucky all about it. Not that she was trying to protect Rich's reputation at the hospital. It had more to do with the fact Lucky already had a glimpse into her last relationship and she really didn't want him to know she'd succeeded in attracting yet another asshole. In her mind, who she agreed to go out on dates with said more about her than it did the men who paid for dinner.

As she pulled a bottled water from the refrigerator, the thought crossed her mind that maybe she was judging Rich too harshly. Maybe he was really nervous and that's why he talked about himself almost the entire time. The only way she'd find out is if she ignored her gut and went out on a second date just to make certain.

The initial thought made her kind of queasy, so she took a tentative sip of her water. He seemed nice enough at work, most people liked him. And at least he made great money and didn't ask her to pay her share of the bill. That had to count for something. Besides, it wasn't like he'd be around town for the long term. There wouldn't be any expectation of a long-term relationship from either of them.

But that would likely mean he'd kiss her again. Another shiver raced down her spine.

Lucky's bedroom door opened and he made his way into the kitchen, the towel replaced with his standard at-home uniform of basketball shorts and a plain T-shirt. His hair was still mostly wet, but in places the ends were starting to dry and curl. He really needed a trim, but on the other hand, his hair was just the right length to run her fingers through.

Dammit. She really needed to stop watching him so closely. It only led to thoughts she shouldn't be having about her best friend.

"So, you never said—what happened at the end of the date?"

"He drove me back to my truck. I took your suggestion and met him at the hospital." She smiled, thinking it would make him happy to hear she'd followed his advice.

But his expression was blank, completely unreadable. "And then what?"

She shrugged, unsure of what answer he was really after. "He parked his car, walked me to my truck. He said he'd like to go out again." It wasn't exactly what Rich had said or even implied, but it felt better to sugarcoat it a smidge.

"Did it end with a wave? A handshake? A hug? How did you two leave it?" He leaned back against the counter, his hands resting on its edge, his feet crossed at the ankles. A picture of calm and tranquility.

"We kissed."

More like he kissed her. Rachel took another drink of water to suppress the bile rising in her throat.

She really wanted to ask him if what she experienced could be classified as a kiss since it felt more like a tongue probing. Like when a frog snatches his meal right out of midair. Or one of those alien movies when they use their big lizard-like tongue to—

"So you're going out with him again?"

"I haven't decided. It's nice to have someone to go out with instead of just sitting home night after night."

"But you're not alone night after night. You go out with me."

"It's not the same. I'd like to go out with someone I could—"

She stopped herself short and took a quick drink of

water. The last thing she should do was bring up kissing or sex. Or lack thereof. Especially since the person she'd most recently done both with was the man standing in front of her.

Yeah. The amphibian attack didn't count in her book.

He folded his arms across his chest. "I can't quite believe this. Are you really just looking for a hookup? With Doctor Dick of all people?"

She shot him a disapproving look.

"Okay, I won't call him that." Lucky held up both hands in front of him. "How about Richie Rich instead? After all that's what you used to call him."

"Maybe I should just go. You're clearly in a mood." She replaced the cap on her half-empty bottle and tossed it into the trash. She'd just turned to leave when he took hold of her elbow and spun her back around to face him.

"You didn't answer my question."

Rachel tugged on her arm, attempting to pull herself free from his grip. "I don't even remember what the question was at this point. What the hell is wrong with you?"

The words weren't even out of her mouth when suddenly both of his hands were on her, sliding up her arms to her shoulders.

"Are you even attracted to him? Or are you planning on a second date just to torture me?"

She couldn't think when he was standing so close, smelling so good. Her eyes drifted shut, her body warmed beneath his hands. Why was he touching her? They'd made a deal. They'd agreed it was better for them to just be friends.

"Rach." He gave her a light shake. "Answer the question."

She shook her head as her words came out in a rush. "I don't know. I don't know. I don't . . . think so?" Her eyes snapped open. "Maybe?"

Then one of his hands moved to her face and Lucky was lifting her chin, turning her face upward to his. Those dark brown eyes stared down at her with such intensity it scared her and thrilled her at the same time. Only then did she realize her hands had settled on his chest, and his heart pounded beneath her palms.

"What are you doing?" she whispered.

He smiled at her then. That sexy, panty-melting smile she'd come to love.

"Breaking our agreement."

Chapter Fifteen

FOR NEARLY THREE weeks, he'd thought about this moment, what he would do, would say. How if given another chance he would take his time with her to make up for everything that happened the afternoon on his couch. He'd thought about it so much in fact he'd nearly driven himself to the point of insanity.

Just this afternoon, he'd laced up his shoes and hit the road as he tried to outrun the images of Rachel fixing her hair and smoothing color on her lips, of her talking with that other guy and laughing at his stupid stories. And then there were the unwanted images of what could happen after, of him driving her home, of him in her bed, of his hands and mouth on her body.

But by some miracle of fate she was here with him now, staring up at him with those gorgeous blue eyes and a slight smile on her face.

He lowered his head to kiss her, but hesitated, his

mouth hovering over hers while he second-guessed himself.

"What are you waiting for?" she whispered, their mouths so close he felt her words on his lips.

He pulled back so he could study her. "Have you been drinking?"

Her eyes crinkled and the corners of her mouth lifted. "No."

"Are you upset about how your date went?"

That slight smile was replaced with little crease between her brows. "God, no. Why are you asking—"

"I need to make sure this is what you want. Not just now, but tomorrow." Even now as he questioned her, he couldn't stop touching her, couldn't let her go. He buried one hand in her hair and wrapped his other arm low around her body, lifting her onto her toes, pulling her flush against him. "I don't want you to regret this tomorrow. Or next week."

Her smile returned. "I won't."

Lucky lowered his head, traced her neck from shoulder to ear and back again with the tip of his nose. He could get drunk just on her scent alone. "I want you to be sure because I won't be able to go back to being just friends. I won't be able to pretend anymore that nothing happened between us."

Rachel had to be absolutely certain. Because if things didn't work out, he'd have to pack his things and get the hell out of Dodge. No way would he be able to stay in this town much less be around her every day, hear her laugh, see her smile, and not call her his.

She wrapped her arms around his neck, her fingers raking through his hair until she tightened her grip and gave a slight tug, lifting his head. "I promise, Lucky. No regrets."

And then she pressed her lips to his.

Their kisses were soft, unrushed at the start, until her hands snuck beneath the fabric of his shirt and skimmed upward over his stomach and chest and back again, dipping lower than where they originally started. He lost what little grip he had on his self-control, and before she could protest, he lifted her from the ground and tossed her over his shoulder, hauling her to his bedroom like a fucking caveman. She was still laughing when he grabbed a box of condoms from the top drawer of his dresser along the way and dropped her in the middle of his bed.

"That's a pretty big box," she said, eyeing the box he tossed on the comforter next to her. "Whatever do you have planned for me?"

He fought to hide his smile as he unzipped the first of her boots. "Plenty." Only after dropping it to the floor did he lift his eyes to look at her lounging on his bed.

Rachel raised an eyebrow. "And do you plan on utilizing the entire box this evening?"

He took hold of her other boot, heard himself laugh as he removed it. "If I told you my plans, you might take off running."

The second boot joined the first on the floor with a dull thud.

"That won't happen." She slid off the bed and stood

directly in front of him. "You know better than anyone how much I hate running."

"For someone who hates it so much, you sure do an awful lot of it."

Her hands went to the bottom of his shirt and he raised his arms so she could tug it off over his head. "I only do it because the view is amazing." She placed her hands on his shoulders, then watched as they slid over his skin. "But this view is even better."

His view wasn't so bad either. He liked watching her chew on her full bottom lip as her hands explored the shape of his body. He liked how her eyes widened in surprise as his muscles twitched involuntarily beneath her touch, how she smiled in amusement as her thumb brushed across his nipple, inciting a hiss from his lips. How her eyebrows quirked and immediately he knew where she was headed next. The woman was so damned predictable.

"That's enough." He took hold of her hands, stopping her exploration just as she reached the waistband of his shorts. "I've let you have your fun."

"Is something wrong?"

He smiled at her now, hoping to erase the worried look on her face.

"Nothing's wrong." He brushed his lips against hers. "I just don't think there's a need to rush. And you have a distinct plan of attack."

He began with her shirt, slipping each button from its restraint, and continued from there, running both hands over her body, even kneeling at her feet as he unbuttoned, unfastened, and removed every piece of cotton, satin, and lace. Once she was completely bare, he took a step back to admire her porcelain skin, her pale pink nipples, the triangles of skin that were even paler than the rest of her.

"Just one last thing."

He stepped close enough the tips of her breasts brushed against his chest as he reached around to tug free the elastic band that secured her ponytail. With her hair loose, he combed his fingers through the long, fiery strands, the ends curling just above her breasts.

"God. You are beautiful."

Her eyes drifted shut beneath his touch as he traced the length of her neck, dipped into the hollow of her throat with the very tip of his finger. Her breath quickened as he trailed his finger down one breast and circled her nipple, the flesh darkening to a deep rose color as it tightened into a bud. Needing to taste her, he replaced finger with tongue, tracing lazy circles on her skin, before finally taking her nipple fully into his mouth. Her first gasp came when he tested the bud between his teeth, and then a second time when his fingers found the tender flesh between her legs.

He backed her against the edge of the mattress and lifted one leg over his shoulder, making his intentions clear as she lay back on the bed.

"You don't have to do that."

Lucky laughed at that. "Oh, yes, I do. I've been dreaming about this forever."

As Lucky slid two fingers inside her, he wondered

about the guys from her past, if any had ever taken the time to please her, to worship her.

Her hands immediately went to his hair as he suckled her clit, her fingers tugging hard enough he felt little pinpricks of pain across his scalp. As the tension built within her, she was alternately pushing him away and pulling him closer until she cried out his name. Unwilling to ease off, he kept at her with hands and lips and tongue until her skin flushed a deeper pink and her muscles tensed, coming even harder the second time.

"Oh, my God," she said, dramatically draping her arm across her face, hiding her eyes from view.

"Hey now." Lucky playfully smacked her thigh. "We aren't done here yet."

Unable to deny himself any longer, he tore open the new box of condoms with such force, foil packets scattered to the four winds. Rachel laughed as she grabbed the one that landed between her breasts and tore it open for him.

As he rolled the condom on, his hands shook in anticipation. "I hate to say it, Rach, but this might be quick."

"Oh, no. That's completely unacceptable." She poked him in the thigh with her big toe and laughed. "I want nothing but your absolute best."

Which made him laugh. "Whatever you say, ma'am." He grabbed her legs and tugged her to the edge of the bed, entering her in one hard thrust. Her body arched as she gasped in surprise, and was quickly followed by a contented sigh and a smile on her face as he set a smooth, steady rhythm.

What a sight she was with her red hair splayed across his bed, her lower lip trapped between her teeth, her delicate fingers clutching his comforter. Beauty personified.

And so he did just as she ordered and gave her his absolute best. He leaned over her, changing the angle as he grasped her hands in his. She stared up at him with those bright blue eyes and raised her head enough to capture his lower lip in her teeth. Rachel gave it a playful tug before he covered her mouth with his own, his tongue delving deep, stroking against hers until they were breathless.

She clutched his hands tighter, to the point her dull nails scored the backs of his hands. "Harder," she chanted over and over.

He pushed their hands higher over her head, using his arms to press her knees higher, wider, allowing him to drive deeper, harder. He would spend a lifetime of giving her what she wanted just to prove how much she meant to him. A fine sheen of sweat pooled at the hollow of her throat. Her eyes drifted shut as her body arched and her head tipped back in a silent cry. As her body tightened around his, he chased his own release and within seconds followed her over the edge.

Completely spent, he fell to his knees and rested his head against her thigh. Not until his heart rate slowed did he go throw away the condom. When he returned from the bathroom, she was smothering a giggle with her hand. Lucky climbed onto the bed and caged her head between his hands. "What's so funny?"

Rachel smiled as she ran a hand down his throat, past

his collarbones, and stopping in the center of his chest. "Nothing's funny."

"Then why were you laughing?"

She shrugged her shoulders. "Because I'm happy."

"That's it?"

"That's it."

Lucky collapsed on the bed beside her and pulled her close to his body, deciding right then and there he never wanted to let her go.

THE EARLY MORNING sun had found the narrowest of gaps in his blackout curtains, lighting the room just enough she could make out his face. She couldn't help but stare at this sleepy, rumpled Lucky, with hair sticking up in every direction, pillow creases on his face, and those thick, dark lashes that women would kill for. She watched the rhythmic rise and fall of his chest, heard the sound of his breath as it escaped him in little huffs. She loved seeing him this way, completely at rest since he always seemed to be in perpetual motion.

The fact she was wide awake before him was a surprise even to her since she wasn't much of a morning person. Even with the lack of sleep, she felt more rested than she had in months. And she couldn't help but think it was because of him. The nights she slept in his guest room couldn't compare to the security of his arms.

But it wouldn't be the first time she'd told herself that.

Almost every relationship she'd been in started out with her feeling the same way. After spending that first magical night together just sitting up for hours and talking, they'd spend the next few weeks unable to get enough of each other. And each time she was convinced this guy was "the one."

Then she'd spend the next days, weeks, months— however long the relationship lasted—telling herself just that. Doing her best to convince herself that *this guy* was different from all the rest even long after he'd proved to be just like all the others.

While she didn't think Lucky was like all the guys from her past, and that this thing between them *was* different from all the rest, she knew she couldn't trust herself to make that call.

So it was best to not romanticize things with Lucky or to get ahead of herself. Because in a couple of years, when he finished his undergraduate degree, he'd be moving on to medical school. And the last time she checked, Durant didn't have one of those. Odds were when he finished medical school and residency and all of that, he'd be like Chad Ferguson, a doctor who wanted more of a challenge, more excitement in his ER than this small town could provide. That would mean Lucky wouldn't be returning. Sure, they might agree to the long-distance thing at first, but sooner or later he'd be too busy to come back here. And she'd still be too scared to leave.

They had barely started and were doomed already.

"Don't you know it's not nice to stare at people when they're trying to sleep?" his voice rumbled.

"How did—"

His eyes eased opened. "Spatial awareness."

Since waking him was no longer a worry, Rachel cupped his cheek with her hand, her fingers raking through the heavy scruff on his face. His eyes drifted shut and he jutted out his chin in the same way a cat does when it welcomes a good scratch.

"To be honest, I'm surprised to find you lying here next to me. I would've thought you had already been up for three hours and ran twenty miles."

"Any other day I probably would have," he said without opening his eyes. "But I'm going to count last night as my workout instead."

She felt her skin heat in a blush as she thought back to the night before. How after the first round of sex they had laughed and talked and teased each other. Which led to the second round of sex. Afterward, as they laid there in each other's arms, his stomach rumbled. So he pulled on his shorts and tugged the T-shirt he'd worn over her head and led her into the kitchen. They stood in his darkened kitchen, the only light coming from within the refrigerator as they shared the last bit of a casserole Brenda had made, followed by eating ice cream from the container. Then someone found a nearly empty Hershey's syrup bottle and things got a bit silly and a lot messy, which led to them showering together. But since the tub space was small and a little too slippery, they resorted to lots of kissing and inappropriate touching. Or should that be appropriate touching, since they both were smiling and satisfied by the time the water ran cold.

She knew without a doubt the next few days would be more of the same. They'd spend today and tomorrow and the next day in each other's pockets. They'd smile at each other's reflections in the mirror as they stood side by side in front of his small sink and brushed their teeth. And each night they'd climb into his bed and he'd pull her close as they burrowed beneath the covers. They wouldn't be able to get enough of each other.

But what would happen when they left their little bubble and ventured out into the real world? What would happen when they returned to work on Friday?

Rachel didn't realize she was frowning until Lucky stroked the crease between her brows with his finger. "Penny for your thoughts," he whispered.

She stacked her fists on his chest and rested her chin atop both so she could meet his eyes. "I'm just wondering about work."

His fingers tangled in her hair as he pushed the strands back from her face and tucked them behind her ear. "What about work?"

Surely he wasn't this dense. Just twelve hours earlier she went on a date with one of their coworkers. Just another item on a long list of stupid decisions she'd made in her life.

"I think we should keep things quiet at work. I don't want everyone to start talking about us."

The words were barely out of her mouth when Lucky dropped his hand so that he wasn't touching her. "You mean you don't want Hamilton to find out."

"I just want to avoid confrontation."

And she really wanted him to continue touching her. Without any warning he pushed himself up to a sitting position. He leaned back against the headboard and crossed his arms over his chest. "What about when he asks you out again? Because you and I both know he'll do just that."

With her resting place disrupted, Rachel had no choice but to follow his lead, sitting up in the bed and folding her legs beneath her. "I'll handle him. But I need you to let me do it, okay?"

He shook his head, unhappy with the decision but willing to let her have her way. "Sure thing. What else?"

"Why would you think there's anything else?"

"Because I know you. What other rules are you wanting to set?"

"No spending the night."

He took a deep breath and vehemently shook his head. "Nope. Nope. Nope. I won't agree to it. We're both grown adults who aren't committed to other people. Why shouldn't we spend the night together? I want to spend the night with you. I like having you in my bed. And I want to be with you in your bed. Give me one good reason for that rule."

The way things were going she might set a record this time and ruin this relationship inside the twenty-four-hour marker. She needed to diffuse the situation. Quickly.

"Okay, then, how about no talk of moving in together," she said, hoping he'd understand her reasons behind this rule. "We each keep our own place and there's a standing invitation to stay the night. But neither of us are obligated."

"Fine."

"And no talking about the long term. I want to just enjoy this. Here and now. Us. No getting ahead of ourselves."

"Fine."

He was doing his best to portray that calm, cool, and collected demeanor of his, but she could see that his jaw was clenched tight. So much so that she wondered how it was possible he hadn't cracked any teeth yet.

"You're mad at me."

"No."

"You're pouting."

Lucky shook his head. "I'm definitely not pouting. I'm just irritated."

Rachel leaned forward and placed her hand on his forearms. "What can I do to make things better?"

"Not a thing."

"Sure about that?" In one fluid motion, she threw back the covers and straddled his hips. "What about this? Better?" she asked while slowly rocking her body over his.

"Hmm. Maybe."

The tension in his jaw disappeared but was replaced with a different type of tension in his face.

"Okay, then. How about—" Rachel grasped the hem of her shirt and pulled it off over her head. "Better now?"

She loved watching his gaze lower to her breasts, how his eyes widened like those of a starving man who'd just had a fat, juicy Porterhouse steak placed in front of him. She also loved that he was still acting disinterested, still playing hard to get despite the fact she could feel him hardening beneath her.

Rachel wanted to see him crack. But if there was one thing she knew about Lucky James, it was that the man had an iron will. He called it determination. She called it good old-fashioned stubbornness.

Taking one of his hands in each of hers, she lifted them to her breasts, using her fingers to manipulate his, making his hands cup and caress her breasts. Rolling her hips, she ground down on his erection a little harder.

"I could probably come like this."

"Is that right?" He closed his eyes and faked a yawn, pretending to be bored by what was happening. She nearly laughed out loud because the man was a damn liar. His breathing was faster than before. His hands were burning hot against her skin and his pulse was pounding in the hollow of his throat. And yet, he still pretended to be completely unaffected.

Screw it. Whether he gave in first or not no longer mattered. As far as she was concerned this was a win-win for her either way. Her eyes drifted close as she concentrated on the tension building within her body. Earlier, she'd been halfway joking when she said she could come this way, but now it was more truth than lie. She used his hands to roughly grip her breasts, the pleasure bordering on pain as she rocked her body against his, chasing her release with a single-focus intensity.

"There you go, Shortcake." His words were low and rough. "Take it. It's yours."

And with his words her body strained tight as she went over the edge and rode out the last of her orgasm, finally collapsing on top of him. She was still trying to catch her breath when he rolled her over onto her back and grabbed one of several foil packets from the nightstand.

"I thought you were mad at me," she said, half laughing at the same time.

Lucky chuckled as he quickly rolled the condom on. "I could never be mad at you."

And as he slid into her in one smooth thrust, she knew this was exactly what she wanted. The two of them just living in the moment. Not getting ahead of themselves. Because here and now, things between them were very, very good.

Chapter Sixteen

LUCKY HOVERED SOMEWHERE between the living room and the kitchen, caught in the no-man's-land between those who watched Thanksgiving football and those who cooked Thanksgiving dinner. If he had his way, he'd be in the kitchen, standing right beside Rachel as she chatted with Brenda and mixed whipped cream or something like it in a bowl. But Brenda had chased him out of there not ten minutes before, stating that her kitchen wasn't big enough for a peanut gallery and he was only in the way.

So he settled for watching Rachel from a distance as she dipped her finger in the mixture and stuck it in her mouth. Her eyes drifted up to meet his and she smiled around the end of her index finger as she pulled it free from her lips.

Tease.

She must have read his thoughts, because she laughed, shook her head, then went back to what she was doing.

The group watching football erupted behind him and Lucky turned to see one of Brenda's sons and a grandson on their feet, high-fiving each other, obviously cheering for the Texans who had just scored. His own father was doing his best impersonation of a referee, waving his arms wildly as if the play would be called back. Meanwhile the rest sat and watched the whole sideshow in amusement.

All of Brenda's family had made it in for the long holiday weekend, so her house was stuffed to the gills with her three children, their spouses, and their children. When he and Rachel were added to the mix, they brought the total to fifteen.

With kids of all ages running around, it was quite a different scene from his Thanksgiving the year before where he celebrated the holiday with his friends at one of the many forward operational bases in Afghanistan. As to which one in particular, Lucky wasn't sure since over the course of a decade they had all started to blend together. In fact, the only Thanksgiving dinner from his time in the army that truly stood out was early on in the war. His company had spent several days traipsing through a snowpacked valley near the Pakistani border when they were surprised by a holiday dinner delivered via Blackhawk. There, in the shadow of the Hindu Kush Mountains, he had the best Thanksgiving dinner he'd ever eaten—military issue or not.

But if given the opportunity, he had a feeling Brenda was going to give that memorable meal a run for its money.

Lucky returned his attention to the kitchen where Brenda's daughter Katie appeared with her new baby girl. Her grandmother kissed and cooed over her before Rachel gleefully took the newborn in the cradle of her arms. Then, just as he would have suspected, she fell into that smooth swaying rhythm that people who are naturally good with babies seemed to have.

"You sure do keep an eye on her." When Lucky turned around, his father was standing there with a knowing grin on his face. "And it's not the same as when you were here for your birthday. I take it things have changed?"

"That obvious, huh?"

Duke chuckled. "If it makes you feel any better, I'm a little slow on the uptake." Then he pointed to Brenda, who was currently dropping an entire stick of butter into a steaming bowl of potatoes. "But that one there noticed the minute you walked in the door."

Lucky thought back to when he and Rachel arrived earlier, how he kept his hand placed just above the swell of her ass as they came up the drive and made their way inside. Technically, they hadn't even been together forty-eight hours and already he found it impossible to keep his hands off her. And he couldn't imagine a time would ever come when he wouldn't want to touch her.

"How goes the sleeping arrangements?"

Duke shook his head. "I should've moved home for the week. I'd forgotten what it's like to be around a bunch of mouthy know-it-all teenagers."

"That bad, huh?"

"You have no idea." His father looked around the

room to see if anyone was listening in on their conversation. "This morning at breakfast, Brenda's grandson asked how old I was."

"Nothing wrong with that."

"Absolutely. That's what I thought at first, too." Duke smacked the backs of his fingers against Lucky's shoulder. "Then I found out they did their sex education unit at school last week and they learned that the number of STD cases has risen in the over-fifty age bracket."

Lucky shook his head in disbelief. "What did you say?"

"What could I say?" His father took another long pull from his longneck.

"How much longer are they all here?"

"Last group leaves Sunday morning."

Lucky slapped his hand on the back of his dad's shoulder. "Your room is ready and waiting."

Duke shook his head. "The only way I'd leave now was if Brenda went with me. And that's not going to happen." And then his father took him by surprise when he pulled Lucky into a hug. "It's great to have you here. The both of you." He gave a final pat to Lucky's back, even snuck in a discreet kiss to his cheek before he ventured into the kitchen where he attempted to steal a bite of Brenda's sweet potatoes.

It was nice to see his father finally have someone like Brenda, a woman who valued his kindness and loyalty and fought fiercely to keep him by her side. It would have been so easy for her to let Duke pack his bags and move out for the week while her family was here. They would've easily avoided any awkward conversations if they'd done just that. But he liked that Brenda wasn't willing to pretend their relationship wasn't something serious.

As much as he disliked Rachel's request to downplay their new relationship status, especially at work, he understood it. And he'd go along with it for her. But what he wouldn't give to see her throw caution to the wind and not worry about what everyone else might say or think.

Once again, his eyes met hers across the room. This time, Rachel wove her way through the crowd to him, a soft smile on her face and a baby in her arms.

"Who do you have there?" he asked, reaching out to caress the sleeping baby's head.

"This would be Emma." She smiled down at the baby. "Isn't she precious?"

"You definitely seem to be a natural."

She lifted her face to look up at him with those big blue eyes. "You think?"

He smiled and nodded.

"I've always wondered what it would be like to work in a NICU or a pediatric facility. I think I'd like it." That gentle swaying rhythm made its return as she stood in place. "When I first graduated I tried to find a job in one of the local pediatrician's offices, but ended up at the hospital instead."

They both stared down at the sleeping baby she held in her arms. Jet black hair covered her head and dark eyelashes rested on rounded cheeks. Her rosy heart-shaped lips pursed in her sleep. She was a perfect angel brought into a world filled with people hell-bent on destroying each other.

"I couldn't do it," he said, curling her tiny little fist around his index finger. "Work in a pediatric unit, I mean. One too many times I had to treat one of the local kids that had been injured by an IED or something else and . . ."

She pressed a palm to his cheek, her thumb stroking his chin. "Are you okay? If you want to go we can."

Lucky shook his head. "No. It's fine." His eyes scanned the room. "I've just never been to a Thanksgiving dinner like this. It's . . ."

"Overwhelming?"

"A bit," he said with a shrug.

"You've always been with your friends." He nodded. "And before that it was just you and your dad?"

He covered her hand with his own and pressed a kiss to the inside of her wrist. "What about you? You must have had Thanksgiving dinners."

"Not as many as you'd think. Once my brothers left home they rarely came back, because really, what was the point? And when we were younger, we were too poor to have a meal like this."

"No turkey and mashed potatoes even?"

"Oh, we always had that. Usually a church or some other organization would give us everything to make a meal. But we never cooked it all at once. We had to make it last as long as we could since we never knew when the next meal would come."

And here he'd thought the dinners with just him and his dad were sad. They may not have had much, but his dad was always able to put food on the table. And now he thought about it, Ethan had always followed him back to his house, often having a PB and J since they were both hungry after spending an hour or so shooting hoops. Not once did he ever consider Ethan might not have had much to eat once he got home. Now he felt a stab of guilt for never having invited Rachel or Ethan to their house when he was younger.

With the table set and the turkey carved, the crowd made their way into the dining room. With Brenda sitting at the head of the table, she asked her oldest son to say grace, after which she suggested they go around the table and everyone say something they were thankful for. She, of course, was thankful for his father and her entire family being there to celebrate. Duke was thankful for Brenda and for God watching over his son all those years he was in the army and safely returning him home.

As they worked their way around the table, Lucky stared at the empty plate in front of him. What the hell was he going to say? He knew what he should say. That he was thankful for his father, for Rachel, for this new journey he was taking. That he should be thankful for having survived a decade's worth of deployments to be here with them.

But he didn't feel thankful. He felt guilty.

His thoughts kept drifting to the friends he'd left behind, the friends who were still fighting in that godforsaken war, the friends who were laid up in Walter Reed.

The ones who came home in a box.

He shouldn't be here. In this comfortable house, with enough food to feed an army. He should be over there, with all of them. Not here.

Then he felt Rachel's hand slide into his, palm to palm; she twined her fingers with his and held him tight until he looked over at her. She gave his hand a reassuring squeeze and a sweet smile. Staring into those blue eyes, he felt as if she could read all of his thoughts. That she knew how he really felt.

"I'm thankful for Starbucks Frappuccino and free Wi-Fi," said the teenage girl who sat next to him.

"Mackensie," both her parents chastised in unison.

"What? You want me to be thankful for him?" She pointed across the table at her brother. "I don't think so. Not when he posted that picture of me on Instagram and now everyone in school is making fun of me."

Her parents collectively swung their gazes to the boy sitting near the end of the table. "What picture?" they asked, again in unison.

"The one from the plane. Where she was drooling on herself."

Once the sibling argument began, the rest was forgotten. And while everyone else was annoyed by the disruption, Lucky was silently thankful. Finally, Brenda rose to her feet and grabbed the large platter of turkey. "Why don't we go ahead and eat?"

AFTER A SECOND round of eats, Brenda packed up enough leftovers to feed them for two more days before they said goodnight and headed across town.

Rachel knew Lucky had always been the quiet sort, especially when he was around people he didn't know very well. But today, he was even more so. He seemed distracted, lost in thought, not long after they arrived and even more so when the pregame football broadcast honored the different military branches, even showing live feed of troops gathered in Afghanistan. From that moment on, she could tell he wasn't there in that room with them. He was lost in thought, likely wondering if his friends were okay, if they were having a nice meal of their own. Her gut told her he was thinking he should be there with them instead of here with his father, with her.

In the weeks since his friends were killed and injured, he'd repeatedly claimed to be fine. Why wouldn't he be? After all, it wasn't like his legs had been blown off or his life ended. When he would talk with his injured friend on the phone, or received an email from one of the guys, he seemed lighter for a bit. But afterward, his mood would slowly darken and she feared the pain and frustration he'd felt weeks before was still there below the surface, slowly simmering until one day it would boil over.

He'd been better the past couple of days, at least when he was with her. Probably because when they were together, he was one hundred percent completely focused on her. It was clear she could distract him for the moment. But what would happen if a time came where she couldn't lift him out of his funk?

Only after she climbed into his truck did she bother to check her phone, having left it in her purse for the entire day. She wasn't surprised to see several notifications listed on her lock screen. Several Facebook notifications, a couple from Pinterest. A missed call from her brother

David. A text message from Adam. Another from Dottie. And not one but three from Rich. Wanting to know if she was in town. Another asking if they could get together. Another that simply read **tequila and pumpkin pie** followed by a winking emoji.

Her phone buzzed while she held it in her hand and she practically threw it back into her purse, not even wanting to see the message he sent this time.

"Everything okay?"

For a split second she thought about telling him about the messages, but he'd already had a rough day and the last thing she wanted was to compound it.

"Everything's fine."

When they arrived at his place, she changed into her pajamas and powered off her phone. After she climbed into bed, she rested her head on Lucky's shoulder as he wrapped her up in his arms. As she soaked up his warmth and drifted off to sleep, she feared this would be their last night of solace. Because she knew in her heart, when they returned to work the following night, all hell was going to break loose.

Chapter Seventeen

ON FRIDAY MORNING, Rachel finally went back to her place. Without him. Because later on she'd need to sleep before going in to work her shift. And if they spent the day together, she wouldn't get any rest. And unlike him, she needed more than three or four hours of sleep to survive her shift.

She'd planned on cleaning the house, doing some laundry. The one thing she was not going to do was go to her parents' house. Since she hadn't received any text messages from her mother instructing her to pick up her medicine or stop for groceries, she assumed things were taken care of for the week. And if they weren't . . . well, she wasn't going to invite trouble by texting her and double-checking everything was okay.

After putting her work scrubs in the wash and making her lunch for work, she sat down in one of her hot pink camping chairs and powered up Netflix. Having heard a couple of nurses talking about a show called *The Tudors*, she decided now was as good a time as ever. And by the time Charles Brandon lifted Princess Margaret's skirts and had sex with her on the ship carrying her to Portugal and her husband to be . . . well, she was hooked. Suddenly one episode turned into another, then another. The next thing she knew, she only had time for a three-hour nap before work.

As she climbed into her bed, she couldn't help but notice how empty it felt. How she'd probably have slept better if she'd stayed with Lucky. She tossed and turned for the next hour, her mind spinning as she wondered what he was doing now. If he was sleeping in the bed they'd shared for the past three days or if he was sleeping on the couch. Or maybe he wasn't sleeping at all. Maybe he was lying there awake thinking of her.

She must have fallen asleep at some point in time, because the alarm clock on her phone scared the beje-ezus out of her. As she got ready for work, Rachel caught a glimpse of her reflection in the mirror and noticed she was smiling. Even when she was away from him, she couldn't hide how happy she was.

It was usually in these euphoric, early days of a bud-ding romance she'd get ahead of herself. Not unlike a schoolgirl, she'd test the sound of her first name mixed with a different last name. She'd daydream of an entirely different life, one that began with an elegant wedding and ended with a beautiful home filled with the laughter of children.

"Do not do that this time," she told her reflection. "Not with him."

Because when the day came that he moved on with his life it would most likely be without her. Unless she could somehow convince him to stay here in this town. Odds were he'd leave her brokenhearted, but she would never, ever regret him.

Within minutes of clocking in for work on Friday night, Rich Hamilton was shadowing her. "I texted you a couple of times."

"Yeah. Sorry about that." She'd hoped to avoid this whole confrontation, that he would catch the hint since she wasn't returning his messages. And even now she didn't stop to talk to him or look him in the eye while he spoke to her. "I've been really busy the past few days."

With an ambulance en route, she went into the trauma bay and grabbed a paper gown from the shelf, pulling it on and tying it in back as she walked to the ambulance entrance. But of course, he was the only ER doc working, so he followed right along.

"I was hoping we could pick up where we left off," he said as the ambulance pulled into the drive. "Maybe skip the dinner and go straight for dessert this time."

Ewww.

And really? The cheap bastard wasn't even willing to buy her a lousy dinner again? Not that she'd be caught dead going anywhere with him after the way he behaved last time. Even if she weren't with Lucky, she wouldn't dare go out with Rich again.

The automatic doors opened and the paramedics rushed in with their patient, saving her from a reply. As they made their way to the trauma bay, she noticed Lucky keeping a watchful eye on things while talking on the phone. Just as she began to wonder if he was still upset about keeping things hushed, the one corner of his mouth lifted and he gave a little wink before he disappeared out of sight.

A little after three in the morning, she wandered into the break room, finally ready to take lunch. Much to her surprise she found Lucky sitting hunched over an open book on the table, with a sandwich in one hand and a yellow highlighter in the other. Her ass had been dragging most of the night, but once she saw him, it sparked a sudden burst of energy. Almost immediately she realized the salad she packed to eat wouldn't satisfy her cravings.

"How long have you been on break?"

Lucky glanced at his watch and back up at her. "Five minutes at best. Why?"

"I forgot my lunch in the truck."

Immediately he hopped up from his chair and held out his hand. "Give me your keys and I'll run out and get it. You don't need to be walking out there by yourself at this time of night."

It was exactly what she expected him to do.

"Or you could just walk out there with me instead."

He shrugged his shoulder nonchalantly. "Whatever you want."

She walked at a clipped pace to stay ahead of him, mostly so he wouldn't see her face. Otherwise, he'd see the smile she couldn't contain, the blush in her cheeks, and instantly know what she was up to. He finished his sandwich along the way and was still brushing the crumbs from his hands when they reached her truck. She grabbed his arms and spun him around, pinning him against the side.

"By my count, you've got seventeen minutes. Do your worst."

His eyes widened along with his smile. "Are you serious?"

"Absolutely."

With brisk efficiency, he took the keys from her hand, unlocked the driver's side door, and practically tossed her inside. She was sitting in the middle of the seat when he slammed the door shut and fired up the engine.

"What are you doing?"

"We can't do this right outside the hospital doors, so I'm going to find us someplace a little more private." He was all business as he threw the truck into reverse, stopping just long enough to shift back into drive before he took off through the parking lot. He looked over at her with a smile like that of a cat who'd eaten the canary. "You better have those pants off and any other prep work you might need completed by the time I get this beast parked."

A man on a mission, he raced down the service road and turned out the back entrance, driving less than a block before he reached the darkened parking lot of a small church. If she didn't know any better, she'd think he'd done this before. Or at the very least, the thought had crossed his mind, too.

"Sacrilege," she said with a laugh as she kicked off her tennis shoes and shimmied her pants and underwear down her hips as the truck wildly bounced over the parking lot's ineffective speed bumps.

Lucky drove around to the backside of the building and killed the lights, parking where they wouldn't be seen from the street. "Hopefully there won't be any patrols coming by in the next few minutes."

As he slid across the bench seat from beneath the confines of the steering wheel, Rachel grabbed up the plastic bag from the floorboard. In it were provisions she'd purchased earlier in the day while picking up her father's prescription from the pharmacy. Provisions originally bought for use after work, not during. But they sure came in handy now. She was tearing open the box when he shoved down his pants and his erection sprang free, capturing her attention.

"Someone's ready to go," she said.

"Shortcake, I think you underestimate the male anatomy," he said with a smile so wide it could be seen in the near dark. "When a woman says it's go time, it's go time. That and I'm usually on ready alert whenever you're near these days anyway."

As she straddled his lap she heard herself laugh, a sound that was becoming quite familiar whenever she was around him. She'd never done anything like this in her life. Well, almost. Sure she'd had sex in a car, but she'd never snuck out from work to have a quickie on her lunch break. But being with him made her want to do all kinds of silly and crazy things.

His hand moved between her thighs as she worked at the foil packet, his fingers stroking and teasing her tender flesh. A sigh escaped her lips as he slid two fingers to the hilt inside her. "And you thought *I* was ready to go."

After she rolled on the condom, she knocked his hand out of the way as she lowered herself over him. The position brought them nose to nose and she stared into those deep dark eyes. "Hi."

His smile reached his eyes, crinkling around the corners as he rubbed the tip of his nose against hers. "Hi, yourself."

She kissed him then, her tongue stroking his as he held her hips, helping to match their rhythms, having her ride him harder and faster. Their earlier urgency came rushing back. In the background a maudlin country song played on the radio, but it was lost among the combined sounds of groans and sighs, the creaking of the truck, their shared laughter between kisses and heavy breaths.

Lucky worked a hand between their bodies, pressing his thumb against that small bundle of nerves, giving her just that extra bit of friction her body required. And within seconds, he sent her soaring, only to closely follow.

She collapsed upon his chest as the aftershocks made their way through the both of them. Their chests alternately rising and falling as they each tried to catch their breaths.

He lifted his arm up, bringing his watch to face level so he could read it in the dark. "Ten minutes to spare."

"I wouldn't brag about that."

He retaliated by smacking her bare ass. "You told me to do my worst."

She sat up then, held his face in both of her hands. "If that's your worst," she said, her thumb stroking his lips, "then I'm a very lucky girl."

He leaned forward and kissed her tenderly, once, twice, before he urged her to get up. "Hate to cut this quickie short, but it's time to get dressed."

As she redressed, he took care of the condom, and within minutes they were back in the same parking spot they'd vacated only moments before.

Rachel leaned across and kissed him again, whispering a thank you against his lips.

"Get on inside. I'll be there in a minute." As she opened the passenger door to climb out, he called out to her. "Don't forget your lunch."

She felt her face heat as she turned back to look at him. "I didn't forget it. It's in the break room fridge." Before he could say anything else, she quickly shut the door and ran inside.

LUCKY COULD ONLY shake his head and laugh as he watched her run across the parking lot and disappear through the automatic doors. He rested his head against the seat and closed his eyes for a minute, giving his brain and heart a chance to settle. Otherwise, he'd follow her in there and say something that she was nowhere ready to hear. Like the fact he could no longer imagine a future without her in it.

But for now he would play by her rules, focusing only on today and not worrying about the future.

When he finally made his way inside a few minutes later, Dottie didn't even try to hide the grin on her face. "Did you have a nice lunch?" she asked.

"Can't complain."

"By the way." Dottie waved for Lucky to come closer and he leaned one arm atop the desk so she could keep her voice low. "Hamilton is looking for you. The minute he realized Rachel wasn't in the break room, he went on high alert looking for the two of you."

Lucky shook his head. "I can't believe this guy."

"Now, now," she said, patting his arm. "I told him I thought you went upstairs to check on some labs and that Rachel said something about running down to the convenience store."

"You're a peach. But that wasn't necessary. We didn't do anything wrong."

She chuckled softly at that. "Lord knows that. If anything, you're doing it right."

But this was exactly what Rachel was concerned about, their relationship becoming hospital fodder.

"Can you do me a favor and not mention anything about the two of us to anyone? Rachel's worried about the potential backlash any gossip might cause."

"Darlin', if there's any gossip about the two of you, I can promise it won't start with me," she said with all seriousness before her smile returned. "But I hate to tell you, anyone with eyes will notice simply because you two can't keep your eyes off each other."

Damn. Twice in one week they'd outed themselves. Keeping their relationship a secret might be harder than Rachel thought.

"Well, thanks anyway, Dottie. I owe you."

It didn't matter to him if other people noticed they were a couple. It didn't bother him that Hamilton was looking for the two of them. But it would likely bother Rachel, because she worried about things like that. And the last thing he wanted was for her to be upset.

He stopped at the computer to check on the lab results he'd been waiting on only to find out the system was down for maintenance for the next fifteen minutes or so. Since nothing else was going on, he headed into the break room where he found Rachel eating the last of her salad. The moment she looked up from her plate and her eyes met his, a pretty blush colored her skin.

"I brought your keys," he said, dropping them on the table in front of her.

She ducked her head, trying to hide her smile as she stabbed another bite onto her fork. "Thank you."

He grabbed one of the chairs and spun it around, straddling it so he could rest his arms across the chair back. "Dottie says Hamilton was looking for us." He waited a moment to see if she'd respond, but she just continued on with her meal. "How do you want to handle him? Because I doubt he's going to let this go."

"I've changed my mind," she said, shaking her head. "We've got nothing to hide. Nothing to be ashamed of."

The way she was stabbing her lettuce with her fork, he couldn't help but wonder if she was imagining Hamilton's face as she did so. After all, he'd watched how Doctor Dick followed her around all evening long. And just like he anticipated, good ol' Rich wasn't giving up so easily.

"I went out with him once. Once!" This time she stabbed a cherry tomato and it squirted a seed across the table. "And I'd tell you what he said to me earlier if I didn't think you'd kill him with your bare hands."

The words had barely left her mouth when the break room door swung open and, not surprisingly, Hamilton stood in the doorway. If looks could kill, Lucky would have been dead ten times over within the minute, not that he was scared by a little prick like Doctor Dick.

"I've been looking for you."

At first, Lucky wasn't certain if he was speaking to him or to Rachel, until Hamilton trained his eyes on him specifically. "Don't you have somewhere you need to be?"

Lucky made no move to leave. "Just waiting on a few lab results. They said it'll be another five, ten minutes or so. And it just so happens—" he made a showing of looking at his watch "—I have another five minutes for lunch. So until then . . . nope."

Hamilton took a few more steps into the break room, letting the door swing closed behind him. "I realize you lack a formal education, so let me spell it out for you. I want to talk to Rachel alone."

Immediately Lucky rose to his feet, not to leave but to drill his fist into the arrogant bastard's face. But Rachel was just as quick, wrapping her soft hands around his arm.

"Don't even think about it," she whispered to him.

"I don't know who you think you are," Hamilton bellowed, "but she's spoken for."

"By who? You?" Rachel yelled back.

Lucky took one look at the fire in her eyes and smiled. Doctor Dick didn't have a clue of what was about to hit him. When Rachel looked over at him, he made a sweeping gesture in front of him, letting her know she had the floor and that he literally had her back.

This was, in his opinion, going to be one hell of a show.

"I went out on one lousy date with you. And I do mean lousy," she began. "It was pretty much a pity date at that. I felt sorry for you because you didn't know anyone in this town." She took several steps, bringing herself almost nose to nose with Hamilton. "Let me make this crystal clear for you since you find it impossible to take a hint. Not only do I not want to skip dinner and go straight for dessert, I don't want to go out with you ever again. Don't call me. Don't text me. And if you do, I will report you to Human Resources for sexual harassment."

She waited a moment to see if he would respond, and when he didn't, she gathered her things and tossed them in the trash. And then, much to his surprise, she drove one final nail into the casket when she raised up on her toes and kissed Lucky on the mouth. "I'll see you after work," she whispered, then pushed her way past Hamilton and out of the break room.

"You might have her for now, but it won't last," Hamilton spat. "Trust me. I saw how she looked at me that night in the bar. How she liked taking a ride in my car. Chicks always say they'd choose love over money. But that's bullshit. She'll be back when she realizes you won't amount to anything more than what you are right now."

Lucky shook his head in disbelief. This guy would never get it. "You see her as a piece of ass, when she's so much more than that. And I can promise you, she knows exactly the kind of guy you are. To be honest, I was scared I'd lost her forever when she went out to dinner with you. But you had your chance and fucking blew it. So really, I guess I should thank you for being such an arrogant prick."

"Fuck you, James. I hope you like shit work because I can guarantee that as long as I'm here you'll be seeing a lot of it."

"Do you really think I'm worried about that? I've been dealing with assholes like you my entire life. And one thing is for certain, just because you might rate higher on the flow chart than me at the moment, doesn't mean you know jack shit. Because everyone knows a doctor really worth his salt wouldn't be doing interim work in a Podunk town like this one." Lucky pushed past Hamilton and pulled open the break room door. "After all, you know the joke, right? What do they call the guy who graduates last in medical school?"

Hamilton's face screwed up, taking on a beet red color.

"Yeah. I figured you knew the answer to that one." Lucky laughed as he walked out the door.

As the sun came up and the roller coaster ride of a night shift finally came to an end, Rachel made her way into the employee lounge to gather her jacket and purse from her locker. And there he was, not looking haggard in the way she surely had to look after the night they'd had. Instead, Lucky just stood there with a smile on his face as if none of the drama had even happened.

"I'm starving," he said, taking her jacket from her arms and holding it open so she could put it on. "I've spent the past two hours thinking about a big, fat, juicy steak and an ice cold beer. How does that sound?"

Rachel pulled her ponytail free from her collar. "I'll probably just have a bowl of cereal. I need to throw in some laundry and hit the hay. I'm exhausted." When she turned to look at him he did nothing to hide the surprised look on his face. "What? I really need to do some laundry."

"But you're always saying that."

"And you're always dragging me off to do something else and telling me to do it later. It's reached critical mass now. I've got no choice but to do laundry."

Lucky took her hand in his and laced his fingers through hers as he led her out of the break room. He looked over at her, his expression that of a silent question as if to make sure this public display of affection at their place of employment was okay. She smiled back at him, squeezed his hand, and immediately his expression brightened. As they made their way through the ER and out to the parking lot, the way some of their coworkers smiled at them and others whispered to each other reminded her of high school.

"Are you sure you wouldn't rather have steak instead of cereal?"

Only once they reached her truck did she drop his hand so she could dig her keys out from the bottom of the purse.

"At the moment, I just want to go to bed."

"Alone?" Something about the way he said it made her look at him as he leaned against the side of her truck. "Talk to me, Rach. Is this about Hamilton? Are you worried about him?"

"Aren't you?"

"Hell, no. Screw that asshole." He stood straighter now and crossed his arms over his chest. "And don't you worry about him either. You've worked here how long? Nine years? He's just a temporary guy. If push comes to shove, you tell HR your side of the story, that you went out with him once, but that was it. You aren't obligated to go out with him again. And if he doesn't respect your decision, then that's his problem. Not yours." He stepped closer, invading her personal space while he tucked his hands into his pockets. "But let's not talk about him anymore." He leaned even closer, lowering his voice and speaking directly into her ear. "So . . . about your bed."

His whispered words sent a shiver down her spine. "What about it?"

"Is there room for two?" The look she gave him must have been less than nice since he made some space between them now, holding his hands up in the air like an innocent man. "I'm not suggesting any hanky panky or anything. Because, to tell the truth, there's this crazy woman I work with who took advantage of me last night and now all I really want is to be cuddled."

"Crazy woman, huh?"

He smiled and took hold of her wrists, wrapping them around his neck. "Or should I say I'm crazy for this woman?"

"Lucky . . ."

"Dammit. Sorry. Did I break a rule there? I'm having a hard time keeping them all straight." He pulled her closer and kissed her temple. "If so, let me make it up to you. I'll run to the store and grab a few things. In the meantime, you decide if you want your steak now or later. I can always make it before we go to work tonight. Okay?"

Giving in to the exhaustion for a moment, she leaned into him and rested her cheek on his shoulder. "It'll probably be later, if that's okay."

"Whatever you want."

He loaded her into her truck and sent her home while he ran to the store. She'd showered, changed, and thrown a load of laundry in the wash just as he pulled up in front of her trailer. When she opened the front door, he was climbing the front steps of her deck, grocery bags in one hand and a large bouquet of flowers in the other.

"These are for you," he said with a big grin on his face.

The bouquet was a mixture of roses and lilies and some purple stuff, and large enough she had to use both hands to hold it. She was smelling the different flowers when it hit her. "What did you do?"

"Not a thing. I promise," he said with a laugh. "I saw them, thought of you, so I bought them."

He wrapped an arm around her and led her back inside, whispering something along the lines of "so suspicious" under his breath. Which was probably right. Before Lucky, the only time men had brought her flowers was when they'd spent the night drinking with their buddies when they were supposed to be taking her out on a date. Or when they were trying to convince her to take them back after she'd dumped their butts. Of course, none of them had ever given her a bouquet like this or she might have considered it longer.

"The other guys I dated usually brought me one of those half-dead, cellophane-wrapped, single-stemmed roses from the gas station," she said while adding water to the vase.

Lucky snapped his fingers. "I could've saved, like, forty bucks if I'd bought one of those when I stopped for gas."

Rachel shook her head and left him putting the groceries away as she carried the flowers into her bedroom and placed them on the dresser. Lucky followed along behind, and as he undressed, she pulled the blackout curtains closed and shut off the bathroom light, plummeting the room into darkness despite the bright sun shining outside.

Having already climbed into bed, he held back the covers for her and she placed a soft kiss to his lips. "Thank you for the flowers. They're really beautiful."

"Just so you know, you deserve stuff like this." Lucky cupped her face as he stared at her with those deep, dark eyes. His fingertips tangled in her hair as he brushed his thumb across her cheekbone. "The flowers, the nice dinner. You deserve all of this. Don't ever let anyone convince you any differently. Not even me."

It was probably the single nicest thing anyone had ever said to her. And when she kissed him a second time and then a third, he pulled away and shook his head. "Now, now, Shortcake. I was promised no funny business."

She laughed as he wrapped her in his arms and pulled her close. And as she drifted off to sleep she realized then, despite all of her rules, despite all of her protests, she'd already fallen hard for Lucky James.

Chapter Eighteen

THEY WERE ENJOYING their night off, celebrating the end of college finals with Lucky slowly kissing his way up her inner thigh, when her phone rang. Of course they ignored it, until his phone rang a few seconds later and then both of their phones vibrated with text messages.

The messages were short and to the point.

Mass casualty event.

All available hospital personnel to report immediately.

Within five minutes they were dressed and heading across town.

Although the staff routinely trained for large-scale mass casualty events, they wouldn't know what they were in for until they arrived at the hospital; meanwhile the town had become a sea of flashing lights and sirens. Lucky was flipping through the local radio stations to see if there were any news reports, but all that was on was the same prerecorded stuff the stations played night after night.

By the time he pulled into the parking lot, she was a bundle of nerves. In the nine years she'd worked at the hospital, they'd never had anything more than a drill with fake patients and no real lives on the line. He must have sensed her nervousness, because he took her hand as the automatic sliding doors opened in front of them.

"Don't panic," he said, giving her hand a reassuring squeeze as they headed down the hallway.

The ER was already filled with medical personnel dressed in trauma gowns and gloves as they waited for the patients to arrive. A nursing supervisor armed with the trauma protocol manual called out, asking everyone to gather around for a briefing.

"What we have is an eighteen-wheeler versus charter bus. Life Flight helicopters are en route to the scene. Police and fire estimate fifty to sixty passengers with a variety of injuries. Most patients are assumed to be fifty years and older. We're getting conflicting reports that there may or may not be other vehicles involved."

Rachel's panic level began to rise. There was no way their small regional hospital would be able to handle all the casualties. As a level three trauma center, the ER's main objective was to stabilize critical patients and transport them via helicopter to either Oklahoma City or Dallas. If there were more critical patients than helicopters available, the outcome could be horrific.

"Be prepared for a high number of walking wounded

being transported via private vehicle. The senior nurses will be stationed in the ambulance bay and tagging patients as they come in. Floor nurses will assist with transferring patients into available rooms upstairs. Those patients are ones who do not require surgery but might need further testing or observation."

As they waited on the first casualties to arrive, Lucky and Rachel stocked the trauma rooms and crash carts. "How are we going to handle all of these patients?"

"We won't," he said matter-of-factly. "They won't all survive, Rach. So all you can do is take them one at a time. If you try to save them all at once, you'll end up saving none."

Within a matter of minutes, ambulances, police cars, and small shuttle buses were lined up outside the emergency entrance.

Nothing in her nursing school training could have prepared her for what she saw. An endless sea of patients, battered and bloodied, taking up every available space in the ER. The less emergent cases lay on gurneys in the hall while the walking wounded sat in waiting room chairs. It was a scene she'd only ever seen in the movies.

Tasked with starting IVs and taking vitals of several patients in the hall, Rachel was just about to insert a needle into the vein of an older gentleman when someone grabbed her arm.

"Hey." Rachel yanked her arm free of the person's grip and spun around to see a dark-haired man, his face and shirt covered in blood.

"My wife," he cried, pointing to an area where the less critical patients were seated. "She's stopped breathing. She's not breathing."

She followed him into the waiting room where the woman slumped over in her chair. Rachel sat her up straight, shook her shoulder, and quickly checked for a pulse and a tag, but found neither.

"Where's her tag?" she asked the husband as she moved the woman to the floor. He shook his head. "Her triage tag?"

"She doesn't have one," he answered.

Rachel yelled for a Code Blue as she tipped the patient's head back, opening her airway. She ground her knuckles into her sternum in hopes of waking her. Still no response. "Code Blue," she yelled a second time, hoping someone else would arrive to help her. In the middle of the waiting room, with dozens of eyes focused on her, she began chest compressions. Rachel winced as she heard the crack of her ribs, but knew nothing could be done about it.

Rachel stopped compressions when an orderly appeared and they rolled the woman onto a backboard and lifted her onto a gurney. She then stepped up on the bottom frame of the gurney, giving her enough height and leverage to continue. The orderly, along with the woman's husband, negotiated through the crowd of waiting patients. As Rachel continued chest compressions, she directed them into a smaller exam room that had just opened up.

"Get me some help!"

The orderly darted out of the room, leaving her with

the dark-haired man as he held his wife's hand and begged her to not leave him.

It felt like minutes, although it was likely a matter of seconds, before a nurse she recognized from floor appeared. "Sir, you need to wait outside. There's not enough room in here," she said. When he didn't budge, she took him by the arm and forcibly moved him out the door.

With the patient's husband out of the way, the other nurse pushed in a crash cart.

Rachel's arms and shoulders were burning, but she continued with compressions as the other nurse intubated the patient and began ventilating. They desperately needed more help.

Then from out of nowhere, Lucky appeared in the doorway.

LUCKY WASN'T SURE how long she'd been doing compressions, but judging by the look of strain on her face, he guessed she'd been at it awhile. "Do you need to trade off?" he asked.

"Yes, please."

Immediately she stepped down and back, giving him room to take her place. He looked at the older nurse ventilating the patient, then back to Rachel. "Who's running the code?" he asked while resuming compressions.

Rachel looked to the other woman, then back to him. "You? Me? No one," she said, tossing up her hands.

She was starting to panic, and if this patient was going to survive, he needed her to stay calm.

"Rach, I need you need to start an IV and run it wide open. Then hook her up to the defibrillator so we can shock her." Rachel nodded and immediately went to work removing the patient's clothes and attaching the defibrillator pads. Lucky turned to look at the older woman who was bagging the patient. "How are her breath sounds?"

"You don't really think you're running this, do you?"

Lucky continued the chest compressions. "What? Do you want to run it?"

He knew exactly what was coming next.

The nurse's face pinched, a sure sign she was on the verge of yelling at him. "You're not qualified to run a Code Blue. Someone needs to go get a doctor."

Lucky nodded toward the door. "Have you seen it out there? The docs are dealing with stuff far more difficult than a Code Blue."

The alarms and the crash cart kept beeping as Rachel charged the defibrillator. "It's ready to go."

Lucky, along with the other nurse, stepped back as Rachel pressed the button that delivered two hundred joules. With the patient still in full arrest, Lucky resumed compressions.

The next five minutes were more of the same. Compressions. Vent. Shock. Repeat. The older nurse began yelling at every orderly, tech, and random person who wandered by the exam room door, asking them to get a doctor. And still, none showed.

When Rachel took over the chest compressions, the older woman handed over the vent bag to Lucky, saying she'd go find a doctor herself.

"How long have you been doing compressions?" Lucky asked as he placed his stethoscope in his ears.

Rachel looked at the clock on the wall. "About fifteen minutes or so? She's been in here ten. I'm not sure how long it took to get from the waiting room to here."

He nodded, signaling he heard her answer, then went about listening to the patient's breath sounds as he continued to bag her. Earlier his gut instincts told him something was seriously wrong, but the other nurse wouldn't ever say how the breath sounds were. The patient's trachea hadn't shifted, so either both her lungs were fine, or they both were bad. Lucky listened to the right side, then the left. There were breath sounds on both, but were distant.

Lucky looked up just in time to see a familiar face in the hall. "Howard!" Lucky waited a moment and yelled again. "Howard! Get in here!"

The ER tech rushed in the room and grabbed two gloves from the box on the wall and pulled them on. "What do you need?"

"Can you take over chest compressions for her? Rachel, I need you to bag her."

After they all rotated positions, Lucky pulled a chest tube tray from the crash cart.

"Tension pneumo?" Rachel asked.

"Bilaterally."

He could try a needle aspiration, but really there wouldn't be any point. The patient needed a chest tube and it was a procedure he'd performed dozens of times.

"I know you have a lot of experience, but you can't do this, man."

Lucky glanced up at Howard as he swabbed antiseptic over her skin. "You just keep doing compressions. I can handle this. I've done these for twelve years." He made his incision along the rib, then traded the scalpel for the angled hemostat. "I'm sure as hell not going to stand by and let this woman die because we can't seem to find someone to come do it." Lucky worked the hemostat over the rib and into the chest cavity, then pried it open so he could insert the chest tube. "How does she sound?"

Rachel pressed her stethoscope to the patient's chest. "Better. She's easier to bag, too."

"That's exactly what we wanted to hear." He stitched the tube in place, then grabbed a second tray from the cart and traded places with Howard. Within minutes he had the second chest tube in and was stitching it in place.

"Should we shock her again?" Rachel asked.

"Yeah."

Howard charged the defibrillator and once again they all stepped back as he shocked her. A couple of seconds later, a normal rhythm beeped on the monitor.

"You did it," Rachel said with a smile as she continued to ventilate the patient.

The woman was already pinking up when Hamilton appeared in the doorway and Lucky swore under his breath. "Who authorized you to insert not one but two chest tubes in this patient?"

"No one authorized me."

Hamilton pointed to the hall. "Outside. Now."

Lucky looked at Rachel and Howard, their expressions both one of shock. He then turned and followed

Doctor Dick, who was waiting for him with his hands on his hips, out into the hall. Lucky was determined to speak first. "There are still dozens of patients requiring treatment or haven't you fucking noticed?"

"Fuck you. You performed a procedure you know you are not legally allowed to do."

Lucky crossed his arms over his chest. "The patient had a bilateral tension pneumo and had been down fifteen minutes."

"Then you should have called me immediately."

He took several steps forward, forcing Hamilton to look up at him. "If I had waited, she'd likely be dead."

Hamilton stepped back. "You are hereby dismissed and I will be filing a report with the disciplinary committee."

"Are you fucking kidding me?" Lucky shook his head. "You want me to leave now? We're in the middle of probably the worst casualty event this town has ever seen and you're throwing me out? What the fuck is wrong with you?"

Hamilton turned and gestured to a security officer standing in the hall, and the next thing Lucky knew, he was being escorted from the hospital.

LUCKY WENT BACK to his place, showered, then spent the next several hours staring at the ceiling as he replayed the whole scenario in his head. If he had waited for someone "qualified" to do the procedure, the patient could have died or suffered brain damage at least. And if given the choice to go back in time, he would do the exact same thing. Because saving a life was more important than following hospital policy.

Breaking rules and regulations was not something he did lightly. He understood why protocols were in place. But damn if he was going to stand by and watch a woman die, not when he had the skills and training and experience to help her.

How was it that his training and real-world experience were regarded as nothing in the civilian world? Because he didn't have a piece of paper with the letters MD or PA or RN behind his name? He had more trauma experience than most medical doctors. Had completed trauma rotations in civilian teaching hospitals as part of his program. So why was it the moment he received his discharge papers, all of that training, all those years of experience, didn't mean shit anymore?

He just couldn't wrap his brain around it.

Of course, it wasn't as if this came as a surprise. He'd known the deal when he decided not to re-up with the 75th. But he'd convinced himself he'd be able to tolerate it. He'd survived SOCM and RASP and Ranger School when so many others had failed because they didn't have the iron will and stick-to-it-iveness to graduate. He thought that same mental toughness would help him survive undergrad and then medical school. But being handcuffed by policies and treated as less than qualified was too much for him to bear anymore.

Several hours later he was still fired up about all that happened with Doctor Dick, so he decided to take out his frustrations on the pavement. He was in the process of tying on his shoes when his phone rang and he answered without looking. Within a matter of minutes his carefully crafted plan had gone to hell in a handbasket and his phone lay on the floor in a dozen pieces.

Lucky headed out the front door with no real direction, no plan of how far he'd run or any concern about the cold drizzle that fell. Two hours later he found himself on the two-lane road that led past Rachel's house. He didn't understand much that was going on in his life at the moment, but when he crested the small hill and her place came into view, he knew one thing was certain—she would make everything better.

By the time he climbed the front stairs of her deck, the tips of his fingers were good and numb. He rapped his knuckles against the glass storm door and waited. With no sign of movement, he knocked a little harder the second time, since the woman could sleep like the dead. Finally, he opened the storm door and tried the knob of her front door, and in true small-town fashion, the damn thing was unlocked.

"I swear, woman," he mumbled under his breath.

Just inside the door, he slipped his shoes off on the tile and stripped out of his wet clothes. After throwing his clothes in the dryer, he grabbed a clean towel from the perpetual clean laundry pile waiting to be folded, and dried off as he made his way to her bedroom.

Sure enough, he found Rachel sound asleep in the middle of the bed, her arms wrapped around a pillow. Lucky dropped the towel, lifted the covers, and slid in behind her, already feeling at peace the moment he smelled her skin and felt the warmth radiating from her body. He snuggled up close behind her and she woke with a yelp as he slid his hands beneath her shirt and wrapped his arms around her waist.

"Good gravy, your hands are cold."

And she was unbelievably warm. He pressed a kiss to the tender spot beneath her ear, then trailed his nose along her neck.

"Your nose, too." Rachel rolled over to face him, her hand smoothing over his beard, neck, and chest. "Why do you feel like a block of ice?"

"Because it's cold outside—"

"I get that."

"—and I've been running."

"How far?"

"Not sure. A couple hours at least."

She mumbled something under her breath that sounded an awful lot like "idiot" but didn't move away from him. Instead, she snuggled closer, wrapping her flannel-clad body around his as if she was trying to warm him up. As they laid there in the dark, Lucky played with her hair, letting the long strands slide through his fingers over and over again.

"I tried calling you," she said around a yawn. "It went straight to voice mail."

"What time was that?"

"Eight o'clock. Eight-thirty, maybe?"

"That explains it. My phone suddenly stopped working around 0800."

Rachel pressed one hand against his chest and sat up just enough that she could see his eyes. "Why do I get the feeling there's more to it than your phone died all of a sudden?"

"Probably because there is."

She raised an eyebrow, making it clear she was waiting for further explanation.

"I got a phone call from Human Resources. They've scheduled a disciplinary review for Monday afternoon."

She sat up completely now, crisscrossing her legs beneath her. "Do you want me to go with? I can speak on your behalf."

Lucky shook his head. "I told them not to bother with a review."

"Why? Why would you do that?"

"Because I quit."

"Lucky. No." Rachel shook her head in disbelief. "I don't understand why you'd just quit. They weren't going to fire you. They'd just slap your hand and write a strongly worded letter to be placed in your file. And then when the meeting was officially over, they'd thank you for saving that woman's life."

"It doesn't matter. I can't do it anymore. I don't want to work with assholes like Doctor Dick."

"But he's just there for the interim! You've even said it yourself that he could be gone this time next month."

"Or he might still be there this time next year. How many ER docs are looking for a career in a place like this?" He threw back the covers and sprung out of bed, grabbing the towel he'd discarded only a few minutes earlier and wrapping it around his waist. The last thing he wanted to do was fight with her and the pain in his chest led him to believe this might be a doozy. "That job was more frustration that it was worth. I spent most of my time collecting urine samples and cleaning hospital beds. I can't do it anymore. I can't pretend that's me."

As he headed out the bedroom door, he heard her feet hit the floor as she followed him.

"So don't go back. Maybe you can get a job with the fire department or an ambulance as a paramedic or something."

Lucky reached the laundry room and popped open the dryer door. His clothes hadn't been in there long enough and were still mostly damp.

"That kind of job would just be more of the same."

"Okay, then. It's not as if you needed that job while you were going to school anyway. So do nothing. Just be a student."

Lucky pulled off the towel and stepped into his pants. "Do I seem like the 'sit on my ass and do nothing' type of guy?"

"Considering you like to run fifteen miles in the rain just for the hell of it? Not really. But you went straight from high school to the military to college. I don't think anyone will think you're lazy for taking a few weeks off. Just think about it. You've got a month before spring classes start up. Just relax."

"No. I've decided to go visit Bull," he said, pulling his shirt on over his head as he made his way to the front door.

"At Walter Reed?"

Rachel was right on his heels as he stepped into his wet shoes and laced them up.

"If you want, I can see about getting someone to cover my shifts, and I could go with you."

Lucky shook his head as he opened the front door and twisted the thumb lock. "I think it's better if I go alone," he said, stepping back outside into the rain and pulling her door closed behind him.

Chapter Nineteen

DESPITE RACHEL'S PROTESTS, Lucky stuck to his guns and said to hell with the disciplinary review. There was no way he could go back to that place and work with Doctor Dick, even if he only was there temporarily. Life was too short and he had better things to do with his time.

As a matter of fact, by the time his meeting rolled around Monday afternoon, he was sitting in an east Memphis barbecue joint not far off the interstate, bellied up to a full rack of baby back ribs. The only thing that would have made this day better would have been Rachel sitting beside him.

But this was his journey. His shit to straighten out.

He missed her so much that he did something he swore he'd never do. He took a selfie with his giant plate of barbecue and sent it to her with a message—**Nice rack.**

About ten minutes later he received a simple smiley face in return.

Maybe he should have listened to the other guys in regiment and taken six months, a year, to figure out what he wanted to do with the rest of his life when he separated from the military instead of rushing headfirst into school and work.

Even now, he couldn't imagine doing that. He didn't like being idle. He needed to be busy.

He stopped for the night in Knoxville and spoke with Rachel for about ten minutes before making an excuse to get off the phone. Something about a long day, needing rest, some other shit he couldn't remember. Really, he couldn't stand the guilt of not bringing her along, especially since weeks earlier he'd suggested this as a sight-seeing trip to Maryland in the first place.

Lucky arrived in Bethesda the following day, checked in at his hotel, and immediately went for a run, needing to stretch his legs after two days of driving. By the time he showered and found something to eat, it was fairly late and he decided to wait until the following morning to go see Bull. Of course, when he called Rachel late that night, she questioned why he didn't go straight to the hospital. Then she asked if he was scared to see his friend. He'd laughed when she suggested it, but as he lay in bed and stared at the ceiling, he couldn't help but wonder if she was right.

The following morning he made his way to Walter Reed, successfully negotiated the maze of facilities, and arrived at Bull's room just as an orderly was helping him move from wheelchair to bed. Although he knew Bull had lost both legs and he'd tried to prepare himself for the sight, Lucky found it hard to breathe. The shock of seeing his friend, a man who had been undoubtedly one of the strongest, most powerful men the entire time he served in the 1st/75th, was almost too much.

Once settled in the bed, Bull looked up to see him standing stock-still in the doorway some twenty feet away. The guy women often compared to Thor stretched his massive arms out wide and bellowed, "Lucky James! It's about time your ass showed up. I was about to send out a goddamn search party."

Shock gave way to gratitude as Lucky walked to the bed Bull was sitting in and embraced his friend. They held each other tight, far longer than most men would. But having the lives they'd had and seeing the things they'd seen, they weren't afraid to show their true feelings. They were, for all intents and purposes, brothers.

Bull thumped Lucky's back with his fist one last time before wrapping his huge hands around Lucky's arms and attempting to shake him like a rag doll. Lucky laughed as he shoved away from his grip and took a seat in the chair beside his bed.

His eyes scanned the room and for the first time he noticed nearly identical flower bouquets in blue vases at every bed. "Is this your mother's doing?" Lucky asked, pointing to the one closest to him.

"How did you know?" Bull said with a laugh.

Sylvie Magnusson, called "Mom" by many of their friends, was known in 1st Batt for the many floral bouquets she sent to the barracks their early years in regiment. At first, only Bull received flowers on his birthday or other holidays. Then, after several of the guys teased her during one of her many visits to HAAF about their lack of flowers, she ended up getting a birthday list from someone and started sending flowers to everyone who lived on Bull's floor.

"Where is Mom? I'm surprised she's left your bedside."

Bull shook his head. "God love her, but she's making me crazy. I told her to go shopping, spend some money. Spend *my* money. Anything. Just get the hell out of here for a day. The woman needs to go back home, but that's not happening."

"Well, you can't really blame her. You're all she's got anymore. And Christmas is just around the corner."

"I get that. That's why I'm going easy on her. Thankfully, one of the nurses recommended a hair salon, so she's going to get her hair done, her nails done, all that crap."

That explained where his mother was, but not his wife. Unless they went together. Which would be a miracle in itself because as far as he knew no one liked Bull's wife.

"Where's Charlene?"

"That's over," he said matter-of-factly.

Lucky gestured to his bandaged legs. "Because of . . ."

"No. She actually sent me a handwritten letter. Believe that shit?" Bull folded his arms over his broad chest. "Never sent one in the four deployments before but she mailed me a fucking Dear John letter. Said she was moving out and filing for a divorce. And you know how long it takes us to get stuff. Wouldn't be surprised if she mailed it the day I left."

"Sorry to hear that."

"Don't apologize." Bull leaned far enough to smack his hand on Lucky's shoulder. "Get this, she's pregnant."

"Holy shit. I assume it's not yours?"

"You would assume correctly."

"You're taking this surprisingly well."

"I guess I am," he said with a laugh. "Maybe it's my fucked up sense of humor at this point, but if I hadn't been distracted by that letter, I'd be dead. Because after we swept the compound and we were questioning the men, I wasn't in the mood for any bullshit and the stuff they were telling us wasn't making any sense. Schuler told me he had it under control, told me to take a walk, get my head on straight. Next thing I knew, I was facedown in a fucking ditch and they were all dead." His expression turned solemn. "So in some roundabout, fucked up way, that letter saved me. If she hadn't sent it, I'd likely be dead and she'd be collecting death benefits. Anyhow, Marie went to check out my place, said it looked like Charlene cleared out more than her fair share."

"Are you gonna get it back?"

"She can have the piddly shit. All the furniture and electronics and stuff. What I'm most worried about are my investment accounts and our condo. My lawyer says she'll likely make a play for it, but fucked up by moving out. He doesn't think she knows anything about the other stuff."

Lucky continued to be amazed by this guy. He was definitely one of the smartest men he knew. Before he joined regiment, Bull was a self-made hotshot with a finance degree and an MBA by twenty-three, working as a stockbroker on Wall Street easily making six figures a year. And when the towers came down, he gave it all up and enlisted at the age of twenty-six.

"You won't have to give her half, will you?"

"Since she moved out, she's lost any claim to the place. Truth be told, with the housing market the way it is right now, there's no money to be made there. She was probably hoping to stick me with the loss instead."

"And the other?"

"The way my lawyer sees it, it would look really bad for a judge to award her half when she's moved out, admitted adultery, is pregnant with another man's child, *and* I just had both of my legs blown off." Bull looked down at his bandaged legs for a moment and then back at him, his expression one of sheer determination. "You know me, Lucky. I'm not one to play the sympathy card, but I'll fucking play it all goddamn day to keep her from getting another dime of my money."

AFTER FIFTEEN MINUTES of fighting, Rachel finally made it up the steps and through the front door with her seven-foot fir tree, a trail of needles in its wake. If Lucky had been here, he'd have easily thrown it over one shoulder and taken the steps two at a time.

But he wasn't here and she had no idea when he was coming back.

He'd been gone two days already. Her laundry was all caught up. Even folded and put away. Things even got a little crazy the night before when she took a page from

Lucky's book and broke out her iron and ironing board. While glomming *The Tudors* episodes on Netflix, she starched and ironed her way through the entire pile, impressing even herself.

Which meant when she woke up this morning she had absolutely nothing to do. In need of some festivity, she drove to the Rotary Club's Christmas tree lot on the other side of town and bought the worst-looking tree they had. As she watched the sales guy recut the bottom, attach the tree stand, and load it in the back of the truck, she could practically hear Lucky's voice rumbling in her ear.

"Why the worst-looking tree, Shortcake?"

"Because I want to fulfill its Christmas destiny."

What could she say? *A Charlie Brown Christmas* had made a big impact when she was growing up.

But now that she had it in her living room, the tree wasn't bad looking at all. One side was a little thin, but she just turned it toward the window since no one would see it from outside anyway. Then she spent the next three hours singing whichever Christmas carols came to mind and wrapping her tree in small twinkling lights and ornaments.

She'd considered buying stockings, although she didn't have a fireplace. But as she stood in the middle of the aisle trying to choose the ones she liked best, she decided it was a tad presumptuous to buy him one. And hanging up only one stocking seemed a bit pathetic.

By dinner, the tree was decorated and her living room was wrapped in a soft, warm glow. She slumped into the giant-size bean bag she'd bought the week before and sat in the quiet. She snapped a picture of her tree, then spent the next few minutes debating whether or not she should send it. Was this what their relationship had been reduced to? A few words along with a picture attached?

He should be here with her. Or she should be there with him. She would be lying if she said it didn't hurt, him going to Maryland without her. But she understood why he needed to go alone, why he needed time to figure things out.

Lucky didn't deserve to be escorted out of that ER in front of everyone. He'd been amazing to watch. Calm. Focused. Not the slightest hint of panic. He was a man completely confident in his abilities. And it was very likely that woman wouldn't be alive if it hadn't been for him. But they chased him out of there like he'd killed her, not saved her.

She stared at the screen of her phone and finally decided to send just the picture along with a smiley face. For now, this would have to be enough. She wouldn't call him. Wouldn't dare ask when he was coming home. Instead, she'd remind herself she was giving him the time and space he needed to figure things out, but really it felt like they were nearing the end.

Just a few weeks ago, she thought they'd have at least two years. Now it felt like they wouldn't even last two months.

LUCKY SPENT THE next two days hanging out with Bull and his mom at Walter Reed. The three of them would have lunch and dinner together and he tagged along to Bull's physical therapy sessions. But there were times when Bull needed a little space. So Sylvie would leave to do a little shopping and Lucky would explore the sprawling campus and check out the different facilities.

Over his dozen years in regiment, he'd helped numerous Rangers get to this place, but he'd never really thought much about it. When one of his guys lost one or two, even three, limbs due to an IED blast, Lucky knew their road to recovery would be long and arduous. But his thoughts never progressed past the point of getting them on that medevac or to the closest battalion aid station. He couldn't. Because once that injured Ranger was taken to Landstuhl or Walter Reed or Brooks, he had to put them out of his mind and get back to work.

Not for self-preservation.

Not because his heart had become calloused after more than a dozen deployments.

He put them out of his mind because when one of his Ranger buddies was injured and shipped out, it wasn't long before another took his place. He couldn't spend his time and energy worrying about a guy half a world away. The guys fighting in front of him, alongside him, or watching his back—they were his responsibility. They were his focus. Keeping them alive was his job.

Or at least it used to be.

When Lucky arrived at Walter Reed on Friday morning, Bull's attention was directed at the iPad sitting in his lap. "Are you ready to talk about it yet?" he asked without looking up as Lucky took a seat in the chair beside his bed.

"Talk about what?"

He lifted one shoulder as he continued to type on the touchscreen keyboard. "Whatever shit you came here to talk about."

"I didn't come all this way to talk about my shit."

"Why the fuck not? Personally, I'd love to hear about your shit. Hell, I'd love to hear about anybody else's shit if only to not have to talk about mine for a while." Having finished with whatever he was working on, Bull powered off his iPad and tossed it to the foot of his bed. "So what happened? Girl problems? I should probably tell you Gibby showed everyone your girl, by the way. Very pretty."

"How the hell did he do that?"

"He recorded your Skype conversation."

Lucky felt his blood pressure spike. "He better not be using that video chat as inspiration, if you know what I'm saying."

"You're afraid Gib is jacking off to her face?" Bull laughed. "Sounds like something he'd threaten to do, not that he'd ever really do it."

"Better not. I'll castrate that fucker myself."

Bull adjusted his pillows and reclined his bed a bit. "So is the redhead your problem?"

"Rachel? No." Lucky kicked his feet up on the side of Bull's bed. "She's perfect. It's everything else that's fucked up right now. I quit my job at the hospital." Bull shrugged. "About two seconds before they were going to fire me. Or reprimand me. Doesn't matter."

"Fire you? Mr. Rules and Regs? What the fuck for?"

Lucky spent the next ten minutes giving Bull the rundown on his new life as a college student and an ER tech. Or, to be more precise, former ER tech.

"Well, that's bullshit. But if it was a bullshit job, why does it matter? That won't keep you from getting into med school, right?"

"Probably not. But not doing more than cleaning up piss and vomit for five years? I don't think I can handle it."

Bull folded his arms over his chest and stared at Lucky with a single-focus intensity. "You want back in."

"What?"

"You heard me. Civilian life isn't all it's cracked up to be."

Lucky dropped his feet from the bed rail and started to pace back and forth. "I've planned on being a doctor for as long as I can remember."

"That's a little kid dream, man. Not that there's anything wrong with it. I thought if I made a lot of money it would bring happiness. And it did for a while. But in the end, it wasn't fulfilling. So . . . what do you think will make you happy? What color is your parachute?"

"Are you kidding me?" Lucky stopped in his tracks and laughed. "I can't believe your giving me the 'what do you want out of life' speech."

"You think I'm not going through the same thing right now?" Bull waved a hand in the direction of what was left of his legs. "My military career is over. And as much as I hate that I didn't get to choose when it ended, I'm sure as fuck thankful my mom is putting flowers on my bedside table instead of my grave."

What a self-centered prick he was. Whining about his classes. Whining about quitting a fucking job he didn't need in the first place. Whining to a guy who had one hell of a mountain to climb. He wasn't any better than those snot-nosed college kids after all.

"You were one of the happiest guys I knew in regiment."

"I swear to God, Bull, if you call me 'Happy-Go-Lucky' I'll fucking shove you out of that bed and leave you there."

"Fair enough," Bull said with a laugh before his expression turned serious. "But my point is, you didn't leave the army because you hated it or couldn't physically do it anymore. You left to try something new and you didn't like it. So now the question is whether you continue down a path that you hope leads to happiness or turn around and go back to the path that guarantees it? The answer seems obvious to me."

Chapter Twenty

As much as she hated to admit it, Rachel wasn't in the best of moods when she stopped by her parents' house on Friday morning. But she wanted—no, *needed*—someone to talk to with about her current situation. For better or for worse, Lucky had become her most cherished confidant. And since he was the problem, that left her with only her mother to talk to.

Thankfully, with the weather nice and unseasonably warm for being December, her father was working outside on one of his many cars, leaving her to talk to her mother in peace.

Rachel shouldered through the front door and into the kitchen, where her mother stood at the sink washing a pan so old nearly all the nonstick had worn off of it. As she set the bags on the kitchen counter, she made a mental note to buy her mother some new pots and pans for Christmas. And maybe some new utensils to go along with. Despite how many hours her mother worked, nearly everything she owned was completely worn out.

Rachel took off her coat and hung it on the back of the wooden chair, part of a small set she'd bought for them a few years before. "Why don't you sit down and have a cup of coffee while I put all of this away."

Her mother lifted one brow in suspicion, then reluctantly took a seat at the kitchen table. "You're usually in a hurry to get out of here. Why the sudden need for chit-chat?"

Rachel shook her head as she poured her mother a cup of coffee and placed it on the table in front of her. "Maybe I wanted to spend some time with my mother. Especially since I don't have anywhere I need to be just now, and I don't have to put up with the cold shoulder from Dad."

She went about putting the groceries away as her mother drank her coffee. Although the room was quiet, her mind was whirring away as she second-guessed herself, wondering if she should just leave instead of talking about her love life. After all, her mother was right; she spent as little time as possible with her parents, so maybe this wasn't the best idea.

"Is he married?"

Rachel spun around to her mother, who was nonchalantly blowing across the top of her coffee in order to cool it. "Why would you ask that?"

"You've got that look on your face, so I know it's about a man. And since I can practically see the nervous energy coming off of you, it must be something bad."

Having put away the last of the groceries, Rachel

poured herself some coffee into a worn, chipped mug and took a seat across from her mother. "He's not married. He's very much single. He spent almost twelve years in the military and just got out this past summer. He's working on his degree right now and plans on attending medical school next."

"I don't see the problem, then. Lord knows men with grand ambitions are pretty rare around these parts."

"Well . . ." Rachel spun the mug around between her hands, unable to look her mom in the eyes. "He just quit his job at the hospital and he's been gone a week. And I'm trying to give him time to think things through, but I'm worried . . ."

Her mother shook her head. "And he's not coming back."

"He just went to visit a friend in Washington, D.C. He's coming back. He's not like all the others."

As the words flowed out of her mouth, she wondered who she was trying to convince more—her mother or herself.

"You best just accept that for women like us, men don't feel the need to keep their promises, if they even bother making them in the first place. I've known men who promised to stop drinking, stop smoking, stop cheating. But all men do is lie. Whatever this guy is telling you . . . there is no happily-ever-after. It doesn't get any better than this. Just be thankful this guy didn't knock you up before he left town like your father did to me."

Rachel's thoughts came to a sudden halt as she tried

to replay what her mother just said. "What? What did you say?"

"Doesn't matter." Her mother took another sip of coffee.

Rachel shot up from her chair. "The hell it doesn't! You just said that my father got you pregnant and left town for good. My father is outside working on one of his stupid cars," she said, pointing out the window over the sink.

"No. Your father was a heartless bastard who told me he loved me and your brothers. That he was going to take us away from this place. But he left without us instead."

"You had an affair?"

Her mother simply shrugged her shoulders.

"Does Dad know?"

"He suspects it, although I've never admitted to anything." Her mother pulled a pack of cigarettes from her pocket and lit a fresh cigarette, sucking hard before blowing a stream of smoke across the room. "Hardly makes a difference, does it?"

A wave of nausea washed over Rachel, forcing her to grab hold of the chair back to keep from falling down. Thankfully, the dizziness didn't last long and she grabbed her jacket and headed for the front door, practically running across the front yard to where she was parked. As she climbed into her truck and sped away, her thoughts shuffled through years of rumors and snide comments. Redheaded stepchild. The milkman's daughter.

A middle school science teacher once told her red hair was a quirky recessive trait that sometimes showed up out of nowhere when the gene was passed down from both parents. All of her brothers had blue eyes, just not the same vibrant color as hers. And there were baby pictures of her where she looked almost identical to her mom.

For years that had been her defense whenever someone would ask why she didn't look a thing like her brothers. Or especially her father.

Upset and distracted, her subconscious brain took her to the same place she'd run to for the past several months. Only once she pulled into the drive and threw the truck into park did she realize Lucky wasn't there.

Rachel grabbed her phone from her purse and dialed his number. It was the first time she'd called him all week because she was trying to give him space. But she desperately needed just to hear his voice. To have him tell her everything would be okay.

After dialing his number, she leaned her head on the steering wheel, silently praying he would answer. When her call was sent to voice mail, she couldn't recall a time when she'd ever felt more alone.

SINCE BULL'S APPOINTMENT with the prosthetist would last almost the entire morning, followed by X-rays in the afternoon, Lucky found himself at loose ends for most of the day. He returned to his hotel and considered ordering room service for lunch, but had no desire to stay cooped up in his room. He could go for his second run of the day in the hotel's workout facility but chose instead to take

Sylvie's recommendation and do a little shopping at the outdoor mall across the street.

With Christmas just weeks away, Lucky figured now was as good of a time as any to buy something for Brenda, as well as a gift for Rachel so she'd have something from him to open on Christmas Day. As far as his dad went, he was a small-town guy with small-town tastes. It was highly unlikely Lucky would find anything that would suit his old man here.

As to be expected on a Friday during the holiday season, the stores and sidewalks were crowded with people carrying armloads of shopping bags. Colorful lights were strung from building to building, crisscrossing the open spaces high above the sidewalks. A high school choir sang carols on one of the terraces. A bell ringer dressed as Santa collected donations in a bright red kettle. Lastly, a thirty-foot spruce took center stage, decorated with hundreds of lights and topped with a yellow star.

For a moment he considered taking a picture and sending it to Rachel since she'd sent him a picture of her tree earlier in the week. But he feared sending her a photo of it might be like rubbing salt in the wound.

Sticking with his plan, the first place he stopped was a chocolatier where he loaded up on boxes of truffles. Some were to take back to Walter Reed, others to take back to Oklahoma, and the remainder were for the road trip home. From there he bought a few fancy dessert cookbooks for Brenda and a hand-knitted scarf and gloves for Rachel.

He was on his way into a sandwich place when a familiar logo caught the corner of his eye. Lucky turned to take a second look only to realize he was standing in front of a recruitment office. He stood in the cold for what felt like a lifetime, staring through the plate-glass windows at the uniformed men working inside.

His mind kept circling back to his conversation with Bull earlier in the day. When it came to his career, there was little doubt he was happier all those years he was in the 75th than he was now. He also knew he could make an immediate impact. His skills were far more needed in the military than in the civilian world. But if he did re-enlist, was he just postponing the inevitable? At some point he'd have to leave. He would reach a point that he wouldn't be physically capable of meeting the minimum standards. And then what? He could be forty-five years old and retiring from the military and would find himself in the exact same position as he was now.

The great unknown was whether or not Future Lucky would regret not finishing college and going on to become a doctor or be glad that he didn't.

The door in front of him swung open. "Would you like to come inside?" asked the marine recruiter. "Are you former military?"

Lucky wondered what it was about him that made him ask. As far as he knew, he looked like any other Christmas shopper. And Lord knew he was definitely older than their target enlistment age. And yet . . .

"Army."

"Hey, Sanders. This guy is former army," the marine

recruiter called out to his army counterpart. He was likely sensing they had one on the hook, or at the very least circling the bait. What they wanted to do next was reel him in.

The sergeant dressed in the familiar gray-green ACUs came to the door and extended his hand. "Devon Sanders."

"Lucky James."

"Army, huh? How long were you in?"

"Eleven years, five months. Been out about a hundred sixty days."

The sergeant smiled. "Oof. Not liking civilian life, I take it?"

"Let's just say it's lacking in some ways."

The two men laughed and Lucky couldn't help but wonder how many guys like him came around their office considering reenlistment.

"Well, unfortunately, as you probably know, the army is downsizing in several areas. Depending upon your MOS there might not be anything we can do for you."

Lucky laughed to himself. "I don't think that will be a problem. As a matter of fact, I can pretty much guarantee it won't."

"Well, then, Lucky James. I have to admit I'm intrigued." Sanders folded his arms over his chest. "Just what exactly did you do those eleven years and five months while serving your country?"

He waited a moment, let the suspense build before he dropped it on them. "Sixty-eight whiskey in the 1st/75th."

The sergeant's eyes widened. "Ranger Battalion."

"Yes, sir," Lucky answered.

"I believe you're absolutely right about that. As a matter of fact, there's a pretty good signing bonus for guys like you." Sanders gestured toward the open door. "Want to come inside and see what your options look like?"

His phone buzzed in his pocket, and when he pulled it out to look at the screen, he saw Rachel's face. For a moment he wondered if she had a sixth sense and knew what he was contemplating at this very moment. Lucky looked up at the major, still holding the door open, at the sergeant still waiting for an answer, and then back to his phone as he declined the call.

He'd just get a little information, see what his options were, then call her back later. No big deal.

WHEN SHE COULDN'T get Lucky on the phone, she hopped on the highway and started driving. Two hours later she was staring at the front door of her brother David's home in a suburb south of Tulsa.

She should have called ahead. Should have asked if it was okay for her to show up. Her brother was a lawyer, an extremely busy man, and he likely didn't have time or want to make time for her drama.

The garage door lifted and her niece and nephew came out and climbed into the Suburban parked in the driveway. Her sister-in-law followed them out, car keys in hand, but stopped when she saw the truck parked there along the curb.

"Rachel?" Stacie knocked on the driver's side window. "What's wrong?"

"I shouldn't have come," she said as she lowered the glass. "I just realized David's probably at work and you're busy and I just . . ."

Stacie reached in the window and placed her hand on Rachel's arm. "Come inside," she said. They made their way through the garage and into the family room where she gestured for Rachel to take a seat. Her sister-in-law disappeared into the kitchen, but Rachel could still hear her speaking in hushed whispers on the phone. "I'm not sure what's going on, but I think you need to come home quick," she said.

Stacie returned and pressed a glass of water into Rachel's hand. "I have to take Zach to practice, but David's on his way. Just wait here for him, okay?" When Rachel nodded in agreement, Stacie leaned over and hugged her neck. "Everything will be okay, I promise. I'm really sorry, but—"

Rachel waved off her apology. "Don't. The kids are waiting. I'll be fine."

Having cried most of the way here, she was all wrung out and so very tired. And now the numbness had set in. She sat there in the quiet of her brother's home, in their large leather sectional, and stared at the family photos on the bookshelves, the stockings that hung from the mantel. At the stacks of colorful presents beneath the Christmas tree. This was what she'd wanted her entire life.

A hand touched her shoulder and Rachel jumped. She turned to see her brother standing there, a look of worry on his face. "I didn't mean to scare you," David said. "In my defense, I did say your name, like, three times."

David slipped off his suit jacket and removed his tie, draping both across the back of the reclining chair. The entire time she was watching him, she wondered if he knew. He would've been almost six at the time, Adam nearly eight. They were old enough to remember. But if he didn't know, would he treat her differently afterward? "Want to tell me what's wrong?" he asked while sitting down next to her.

"What do you know about my father?"

"That he's about as worthless and lazy as a man can get. Why are you asking?"

"I don't mean *your* father. I mean *my* father. Mom just admitted she had an affair."

His eyes widened in surprise. "With who?"

"I thought you might know. She said he promised to take you all away, except he left and never came back."

"Holy shit." David rose to his feet and scrubbed a hand over his face. "I'm gonna need a drink for this," he said, immediately heading back into the kitchen.

She sat on his sofa, listening to the cabinets and refrigerator opening and closing, to the clink of ice in a glass. He returned a few minutes later with two very large glasses of what appeared to be Scotch and water. After handing her one, he took a fortifying drink, then collapsed into the sofa next to her. Already having an achy feeling in her head and her stomach, she placed her glass on the coffee table.

"I remember there was a guy that kept coming around for a time." David rested his head on the back of the couch and stared up at the ceiling as he spoke. "I think he might have taken us all to a carnival in Sherman. Adam probably remembers better than I do. But I remember him coming around quite a bit for a while."

"Where was Dad at this time?"

"Where Dad always was. Who knows?"

"Do you remember what he looked like? His name? Anything?"

David shook his head. "Nothing more than a vague recollection, really. He drove a huge pickup truck. A crew cab dually."

Rachel nearly laughed, despite it not really being funny. "You remember his truck but nothing else about the man?"

"He used to take us out into an empty pasture and cut donuts in that beast. It was really fun, especially since Dad never did anything like that or had a truck like that. When you're in first grade that's the kind of stupid stuff that makes a lasting memory, I guess."

"You didn't think it was odd Dad wasn't around when Mom ended up pregnant?"

"Come on." David rolled his eyes. "What did either Adam or I know about the birds and the bees back then?" He chuckled and bumped her shoulder with his. "I mean, I know I'm the smartest kid in the family, but cut me a little slack here."

She offered a halfhearted smile that soon faded and segued into several minutes of silence.

"Did you ask Mom for a name? I have people that can track him down for you."

Rachel shook her head, disgusted with herself. "I

didn't even think to ask. The room started spinning and I couldn't breathe. I had to get out of there."

"How about this?" he said, patting her knee. "Why don't you stay here for the weekend?"

"I didn't bring any clothes or anything."

"Don't worry about that. I'm sure you can borrow something from Stacie. We'll call Adam to see what he remembers, then I'll call Mom and see if I can get some answers out of her." Her brother gave another pat to her knee as he rose to his feet, then disappeared down the hallway to his bedroom.

In a matter of hours, her life had gone topsy-turvy, no way of knowing which way was up or down. While she didn't want to impose on David's family, she didn't really want to go home either. After all, what would she do there? Sit in her bean bag chair and wonder if what her mother said was right? That men didn't keep promises to women like them?

As long as she stayed here, she could focus her energy on finding out what she could about her father. Where he lived. Why he never came back. Whether or not she had other half brothers and sisters out there in the world.

At this point, it would be a very welcome distraction from spending another day wondering whether or not Lucky would be coming home soon or if he was gone for good.

Chapter Twenty-One

Since it was Sunday and Bull didn't have any physical therapy or other treatments scheduled for the day, he and Lucky headed out to one of the many rec centers on the Walter Reed campus. This one, however, was specifically for single military. While it was nice the hospital had made so many spaces family friendly, sometimes guys wanted to be guys. They wanted to be loud and obnoxious and swear at the television without worrying about offending someone's delicate sensibilities.

Just as the broadcast began, Lucky's phone rang and a number with the Durant area code appeared on the screen. It wasn't Rachel's number, or his dad's, or Brenda's. So he sent it to voice mail instead. He looked up from his phone when the National Anthem began to play on the big-screen TV as part of the *Sunday Night Football* pregame ceremonies. He and Bull along with the rest of those in the room sat in rapt silence as a majestic bald eagle was released from the upper deck of the stadium. As the anthem continued to play, the bird filled the frame, its wings spread wide, soaring around the stadium until it finally landed on its handler's glove. Right on cue, the crowd went wild, the anthem ended, and the network cut to commercial.

"I have to say that is fucking fantastic," Bull said with his drier than dry tone. "Because nothing says freedom like a captive bird."

And of course Lucky laughed. It was nice to see that despite all the shit he was going through at the moment— the recovery, the divorce—Bull had somehow managed to hang on to his sense of humor.

His phone buzzed in his pocket, indicating a voice mail had been left. Since the game hadn't yet started, he decided to dial in.

"Hey, Lucky. It's Dottie. I just wanted to check in on Rachel to see if everything's okay. I tried her phone a couple of times but it went straight to voice mail. Anyhoo . . . if there's anything I can do, don't hesitate to call."

Lucky immediately rose from his chair and headed into the hall where it would be easier to hear. He dialed Rachel's number first, and just like Dottie had said, his call went straight to voice mail. Just as it had done the night before. And the night before that. Immediately he dialed the most recent unknown number on his touch screen.

"Hey, sugar," came Dottie's voice on the phone. "How are things?"

"You tell me. I've been in Maryland for the past week

and haven't spoken to Rachel since Thursday." He didn't dare add that he ignored her phone call on Friday.

"Well, I don't really know what's going on. She called in to work Friday afternoon, said she would be out the weekend due to a family emergency. Aside from that, no one really knows anything."

"Is she expected in tonight?"

"Not as far as I know."

Shit. He looked at his watch and calculated what time he'd arrive in Durant if he left now. And the answer was not soon enough.

"Thanks for giving me a call, Dottie. I appreciate it."

"You heading back?"

"Just as soon as I can."

After promising to call or text her just so she'd know he made it back to Durant all right, he ended the call and went back into the rec room where Bull had been keeping watch from a distance.

"Everything okay?" Bull asked.

"Not sure. But I gotta get back to Oklahoma."

"Your girl?"

Lucky nodded.

"Well, I would say the smart thing to do would be wait until the morning before heading out, but if it were me in your situation, nothing would stop me from getting home."

"You got that right. If I leave now and drive straight through, the earliest I'll be there is tomorrow afternoon."

"Well . . . I hope you don't mind if I don't get up to see you off." They both laughed and Bull held out his hand, which Lucky grasped before he leaned down for a farewell hug. After a few seconds and a few final thumps to the back, they let go of each other. "Go take care of your girl instead of babysitting me."

"Tell your mom I said goodbye."

Bull smiled. "Absolutely. Now get the hell out of here."

Lucky ran from the building to the visitor parking lot and within thirty minutes he'd checked out of the hotel and was heading west on the 495. If it had been any other weekend, he would've called his dad and asked him to go by her place and check on her. Unfortunately for him, Duke and Brenda had gone to Kansas City for the weekend and they wouldn't be back until the following night. As a matter of fact, if Lucky could keep the hammer down and not run into any problems, he could beat them home.

Fueled on copious amounts of caffeine and fear, Lucky drove straight through the night. In Nashville, he ran into some bad weather. A little hail, some heavy rains, but thankfully no sleet or snow. He kept his phone on the charger and volume cranked up in the event Rachel called because each time he tried her it was more of the same. Straight to voice mail.

The rest of the time he kept trying to puzzle out what Dottie told him. The fact Rachel had taken off work due to a family emergency. It couldn't possibly be her mom or dad, because if that was the case, they'd most likely have been brought into the ER. So it had to be someone out of town, which meant she could be damn near anywhere in the country since her remaining siblings had scattered to the four winds.

Somewhere around the Mississippi River he'd convinced himself she'd likely lost her phone or she'd killed it somehow and was waiting on a replacement. Either way, the moment he got back in to town, he was going to get Walter's number in case of future emergencies.

A little after five, just as the sun was setting, Lucky arrived in Durant and found himself equal parts relieved and angry when he saw her truck parked out in front of her trailer. Forgetting the chocolates and other gifts in the car, he raced up the steps to her front door. He yanked open the storm door and, in true Rachel fashion, the damn front door was unlocked and he walked right on in.

The first thing he noticed was the new Christmas tree and that the light over the kitchen sink she always left on at night wasn't on. Which meant her whole place was shrouded in darkness. He flipped on the entryway light and made his way to her bedroom, fearful of what he might find. In the dim indirect light from her bathroom, he could see her curled up on the bed, facing away from the door. He didn't know if she was sick or hungover or just dog-assed tired. But if she were sleeping soundly, he'd probably scare the shit out of her if he tried to gently wake her. If he yelled at her, he'd scare the shit out of her. Either way, it was a lose-lose situation.

"Rachel, sweetheart?" She stirred only a bit, so he tried again. "Rachel!"

She shot up in the bed, gasping for breath, her eyes unfocused, her hair wild. He rushed to her bedside. "Hey, Shortcake. It's me. I'm home."

The moment her eyes focused on him, she threw her arms around his neck and clung to him as if her life depended upon it. Lucky pulled her into his lap and held her as tight as he could, not wanting to ever let her go.

IN THE MORNING he opened up her blackout curtains, letting in the bright early morning sun for two reasons: one, so he could get a better look at her since her bedroom lacked an overhead light, and two, so it would hopefully keep her awake long enough that he could get some answers. Within a matter of minutes she woke, climbed out of bed to use the bathroom, and returned just as quickly. That was it. Nothing to drink. Nothing to eat. Obviously if they were going to have any kind of conversation, he would have to be lying down nose to nose with her.

So he climbed back into her bed and pushed the hair off her face. "Dottie called me. Said you had some kind of family emergency. Want to tell me what's going on?"

In the light he could see how dull her eyes were, how they lacked their normal everyday brightness. Her lids were swollen and dark circles shadowed beneath. Her skin was pale, including her lips, which were closer to white around the edges than their normal rosy pink.

She swallowed hard, like she knew it would be a struggle to speak. "I tried calling you Friday."

"I know. I was in the middle of something at that moment." He continued smoothing his hand over her hair, carefully raking his fingers through her tangled strands. "I called you back that evening and it went straight to voice mail. And I've called a bunch of other times since."

Her eyes drifted shut as she gave her head a gentle shake. "My phone died when I was at David's and I didn't have a charger."

"You went to your brother's house? Was that the emergency?"

"There wasn't an emergency."

She drew in a deep breath as if she was about to fall back to sleep, but he couldn't let that happen. He needed to know what was going on with her, because this woman he was talking to was not the same woman he left just nine days before.

"Rach, I'm sorry, but I'm not following." He brushed his thumb across the apple of her cheek. "Can you please just tell me what's going on? Because I drove twenty hours straight to get to you and I don't want to play twenty questions."

When her eyes opened this time, he saw the tears in them.

"It would seem my dad is not my dad."

"What?" If this came out of left field for him, he could only imagine how she must be feeling.

"I was talking to my mom about you and the next thing I know she's telling me that the man who I thought was my dad isn't." For the first time as she spoke, her eyes truly focused on his. "And I was so upset I just drove and ended up at your house and that's when I called you."

Lucky swore under his breath. "I'm so, so sorry that I didn't answer. If I had known—"

"Then, all of a sudden, I couldn't breathe. And I just had to get away from here."

"That's when you went to David's?"

Rachel nodded.

"Did he know about all of this?"

She closed her eyes and shook her head. "No. He's trying to help me find him though. But I wasn't feeling well so he suggested I stay the weekend. By the time I came home on Sunday I felt terrible and all I wanted to do was crawl into bed and never leave."

A couple of tears spilled over onto her cheek and Lucky quickly brushed them away with his hand.

"I don't even know why I'm crying. After all I've put up with from him . . ."

That same anger he felt at Ethan's funeral all those years ago rose to the surface. This time, however, he wouldn't let her suffer all alone. Lucky pulled her into his arms; her head rested on his chested, snuggled beneath his chin. "I'm sorry, Shortcake."

He held her for a long time and she was so still he believed she'd fallen back to sleep. Then her hand drifted across his chest, almost where it was tucked beneath her head. But then he realized she had placed her palm directly over his heart.

"I missed you."

The sadness in her voice, the way it broke around her words, nearly did him in. "I missed you, too."

"I don't want you to ever go away again."

Oh, God. He needed to tell her sooner rather than

later. But it felt like he would be piling on to her misery if he told her now.

She must have sensed his tension because she moved back to her earlier spot in the bed and looked at him, that little crease appearing between her brows. "What is it?"

He ran his palm over her shoulder and down her arm, back and forth, over and over, wanting to soothe her as much for his own sake as it was hers. "Bull and I spent a lot of time talking about what makes me happy. How what seems like a good idea at the time might turn out to be a really bad one. So the better decision might be to go with what I know for sure makes me happy. Then I went to get some lunch near the hotel and ended up talking to a couple of guys who were recruiters."

"You reenlisted," she said matter-of-factly.

Lucky nodded. "I did."

Using what little strength she had, Rachel pushed herself further away from him as she tried to escape his reach, when he wanted nothing more than to drag her back into his arms and give her that minuscule amount of peace she seemed to have only minutes earlier.

"How long?"

"How long is my contract?"

Rachel shook her head. "No. How long before you leave?"

Right then he knew his answer would be the final blow before he even delivered it.

"I have to report to Fort Benning in three weeks."

Chapter Twenty-Two

FOR THE TWO whole days he'd been back, Rachel stayed in bed. She hardly ate, her skin was pale. She was literally wasting away before his eyes. And to know he played a part in this was killing him.

He wanted to fix things so badly, but he just didn't know how. If he stayed here, it'd just be more of the same. Hating college classes. Not having a job or any real sense of purpose. He'd be miserable. And in the long run he'd make her miserable as well.

Not that long ago he thought he had two years to show her there was more to life than this small town. Then he went and blew that timeline straight to hell. Now, he had a little over two weeks before he reported to Fort Benning. Two weeks to convince her she could have the life she wanted beyond the city limits. Two weeks to convince her they were meant to spend a lifetime together.

But first he needed to get her up and out of bed. And

if he really wanted to push the envelope, he'd get her out of the house, too. Even if it was just for an hour or two.

Lucky sat down on the edge of her bed, brushed those fiery strands from her pale cheek. Her eyes drifted open and the look she gave him nearly killed him. Those eyes that were usually so bright and full of sparkle were dull, glassy.

"How are you feeling?"

"Not the best."

He pressed a kiss to her forehead to check her temperature, caressed her cheek with his hand. "I don't think you have a fever. Why don't you get up, take a shower, and then we'll go to my place."

"Why?" she groaned.

"Because you'll be more comfortable there."

She rolled over so she was facing away from him. "You mean you'll be more comfortable there."

"We'll both be more comfortable there." As he threw the covers back she immediately pulled a pillow over her head. "Come on, Shortcake. I'll get the shower running for you."

Lucky went into the bathroom and turned the water to hot. He pulled a fresh towel out of the cabinet and set it on the counter. As he stepped out of the bathroom, he was happy to see she was climbing out of bed. But his heart dropped when she stumbled a little as she went to stand. Immediately he was by her side, steadying her with one hand and wrapping an arm around her waist. "Tell me what's going on?"

"Just a little dizzy. That's all."

"Because you need to eat." She hadn't had more than a few crackers here and there since he'd returned from Maryland. And considering the state he found her in, there was no telling how long it had been since she'd had a real meal.

He guided her to the bathroom, helped her undress and step over the side of the tub. She'd barely pulled the shower curtain closed when he stripped off his own clothes and followed her in.

Rachel only turned halfway around, her arms and hands strategically placed so they covered her front. As if he hadn't spent an ample amount of time in the past month worshiping all those bits and pieces she now hid from view. "Taking your job a little too seriously, don't you think?"

"Says the woman who nearly fell down only a few minutes ago." He backed her into the warm spray of water so it soaked her hair. "The last thing I need is to be hauling you into the ER after you've passed out in the shower and cracked open your head."

There weren't any further protests from her as he worked the shampoo into her long red strands, his fingers easing through tangles and massaging her scalp. If anything, she relaxed more into his touch.

"Where did you learn this kind of bedside manner?" she asked as he rinsed her hair. "Is this one of those differences in military versus civilian medical training you're always talking about?"

Lucky smiled at her jab because it showed there was a little spunk left in her even though she wasn't feeling well.

When they were done, he dried her off and combed her hair, going as far as using a hair dryer for the first time in his life. Afterward, she pulled on plain black yoga pants and an oversize sweatshirt she'd stolen from his closet weeks before. Within the hour, they were headed across town to do a little grocery shopping at Walmart.

Lucky could tell Rachel wasn't thrilled about the idea, but he hoped something would set her stomach to rumbling. Steaks. Popcorn. Donuts. He didn't really care what she ate, only that she ate something. Once they arrived, he decided to forego the shopping cart for a small basket so he could keep one arm around her waist. "What sounds good?"

"I'm not really hungry."

"I know that, sweetheart, but you need to eat."

"I'm sure it's just a bug. It'll pass in a few days."

At the front of the store he grabbed a few honeycrisp apples because those were her favorite along with some blueberry muffins from the bakery. Then they added a few cans of chicken noodle soup. He offered to make her soup from scratch, but she didn't want him to make a fuss and said she preferred the canned kind anyway.

They continued wandering through the store at a snail's pace, up one aisle and down another, until they reached the meat department. He was on the verge of suggesting spaghetti and meatballs when Rachel covered her mouth and raced off toward the back of the store. It was the fastest he'd seen her move since he'd returned, so her darting off took him by surprise. He rushed to catch up with her just outside the bathrooms.

"Are you going to be sick?"

She'd stopped to take a deep breath and shook her head. "I think I'm okay now. It was just the smell of raw meat."

"That bad, huh?"

Rachel looked up at him then, her skin even paler than before. She only nodded, like answering took too much energy. Then, without any prompting, she closed the space between them, leaning heavily against him as she rested her head on his shoulder. They remained that way for a minute or so, his hand drifting up and down her spine as she took slow, measured breaths.

"Have you been nauseous a lot lately?"

"Just the past few days. It comes and goes."

He eased away from her, cupping her cheek with his hand so he could look in her eyes. "Should we get a pregnancy test?"

Her eyes widened in panic. "But I took the Plan B. You watched me take it."

"I'm not suggesting you didn't." Lucky smiled at her, hoping to put her at ease, while he tucked a rogue strand of hair behind her ear. "But come on, Shortcake. Accidents happen. And you know as well as I do that nothing is a hundred percent."

As Rachel made her way across the store to the pharmacy area, she was counting the days in her head. A month had passed since that afternoon she and Lucky had sex on his couch. And that little revelation meant she was definitely late. She should have paid better attention, but the craziness of the last two weeks had distracted her.

Finally, she reached the aisle filled with feminine products and, more importantly, pregnancy tests. Lucky had wanted to come with her, but she worried about drawing unnecessary attention to themselves. If she went down that aisle by herself and someone she knew saw her, they wouldn't think anything of it. But if someone from the hospital saw the two of them go down that aisle together, the gossip would be racing like wildfire.

Even as she stood there staring at boxes, each proclaiming to be the earliest detector or most accurate, she knew she didn't need a damn test. She already knew what the result would be. Not because the possibility of being pregnant had crossed her mind until Lucky suggested it. No, it was because in her entire life she'd never caught a break.

Despite being a relatively good person and doing her best to help others, it seemed the universe had had it out for her since, well, forever. So of course the test would be positive. Of course she'd be pregnant by a man she was not married to. A man who was leaving town in a matter of weeks.

She grabbed a box with two tests in it because false positives happened. And what she wouldn't give for a false positive. Or a positive negative. She didn't care which as long as the stick said she wasn't pregnant.

"Wow. Changing tactics in order to keep a man, Rach?"

Rachel spun around to find her old friend Tamara

standing there with a basket dangling from one hand and a smug grin on her face.

"You've said for years that you wanted to get married, have two point five kids, and the whole white picket fence thing, but I never thought you'd stoop to this level to get a man to marry you."

Rachel's heart pounded in her chest, her head began to throb, and the nausea was trying to make a comeback. She opened her mouth wanting to deny Tamara's accusations, to tell her it wasn't true. But somewhere in the back of her mind a little voice questioned if her former best friend was right.

"Are you ready to go?"

Rachel turned around to find Lucky standing there, despite the fact she'd told him to go away and let her do this on her own. But now that he was there, she couldn't help but think the man had impeccable timing and she'd never been so glad to see anyone in her entire life.

"We haven't met." Tamara pushed her way past Rachel, even knocking her in the hip with the shopping basket as she extended her hand to Lucky. "I'm Tamara. I'm a friend of Rachel's. Best friend actually."

Rachel fought to cover her mouth, suddenly queasy from watching such a gag-worthy display.

"Lucky," he said politely while shaking the hand Tamara offered. "Best friends, you say?"

"Oh, yes." Tamara smiled brightly and batted her eyelashes. "We've been friends since elementary school."

Lucky looked at Rachel, then back to Tamara, who

was now sporting her own shade of bottled blond. "Is that right?"

Tamara was practically twirling right there among the tampons and maxipads because she momentarily had the notice of a man as fine as Lucky.

"As a matter of fact, you and I went to school together, too. We even had an English class together once. But you sure didn't look like this back then." Tamara made a show of looking him up and down and that earlier nausea Rachel had felt came back with a vengeance.

With a smile he took the pregnancy test from Rachel's hand and tossed it in the basket. "Sorry, but we need to be going," he said, wrapping his hand around hers, bringing it to his lips to kiss the back of it as he led her away from Tamara's presence.

But then Lucky surprised her. Stopping short at the end of the aisle, he turned back to face her former friend. "One last thing."

"Yes?" Tamara's eyes were bright with anticipation.

"I need to thank you for being such a great friend to Rachel. You know, for fucking her ex. In their bed. Because if you hadn't made that sacrifice, being her best friend and all, they might still be together. So, thanks again."

This time Rachel covered her mouth, not from nausea, but to keep from laughing right out loud. As Lucky tugged her around the corner, she caught one last glance of Tamara trying to pick her jaw up from the floor.

From there they headed straight to the checkout

where, thankfully, the fifteen items or less lane was empty. "What a piece of work." Lucky placed their items on the conveyor belt and pulled his wallet from his pocket. "What did she say to you?"

"I don't really remember," she lied.

"Well, whatever it was, it mustn't have been nice. I thought you were pale earlier. It didn't hold a candle to when I found you standing there with that—" Lucky stopped himself, choosing to shake his head in disgust rather than say what he was really thinking.

God, he was cute. And polite. And so damn nice.

She loved how he let her fight her own battles, but always had her back. That he was always there, quick to step in and fight on her behalf if she needed him to. She loved so many things about him. Really, she loved everything about him.

After paying, he handed her a chilled bottle of ginger ale. "Drink some of this if you can."

She raised up on her toes and kissed his cheek. "Thank you."

"You're welcome," he said, probably thinking she was talking about the soda.

Then he grabbed the plastic bags in one hand, placed the other at the curve of her back, and walked her out to his Jeep.

The soda helped settle her stomach and by the time they reached his place she'd even managed to choke down a couple more saltine crackers he'd taken from her place and stashed in a Ziploc bag. But despite feeling a bit better, the guilt was still eating her up inside.

What if what Tamara said held some truth? Had she risked getting pregnant intentionally?

When they arrived at his house, Lucky grabbed the food and the small duffel she'd packed earlier. After dropping her bag in his bedroom, he placed the grocery bags on the kitchen island and dug through them until he found what he was looking for.

"No time like the present," he said, handing her the pink and white box. "And since it's a two-pack you might as well do both tests just to make sure."

Rachel looked into those dark brown eyes as she took the box from his hand. She couldn't get a read on him. Calm, cool, and collected Lucky had returned, and while a part of her was dying to know what he was thinking at the moment, the other part felt like she'd be asking for trouble if she asked. He wasn't smiling, but he didn't look upset either. If this had happened with any of the other guys she'd dated, they'd all be ranting and raving right now, telling her that in no way were they gonna marry her. Hell, they would've packed their stuff and hightailed it out the door by now. Or they would've taken her things and tossed them on the front lawn.

Once again, Lucky was proving he was different from all the rest.

She looked down at the box she held in her hands. "I need you to know that I didn't plan for this to—"

Without warning, his mouth covered hers, effectively silencing her with a searing kiss. His hands moved to her face, holding her in place as his tongue stroked hers. She clutched the front of his shirt in her fist, holding on for dear life until his lips softened and they eased to a finish.

"Now then." Taking hold of her shoulders, he spun her around until she faced the hall to the bathroom and gave a little swat on her butt. "Go pee on some sticks, Shortcake. I'm gonna make spaghetti."

Rachel stepped into the bathroom and flipped on the overhead fluorescent light. She stared at her reflection in the bathroom mirror, at the puffy lids and dark circles that shadowed her eyes. At the hair hanging loose from the messy knot on top of her head and her paler than pale skin. It was safe to say she looked the way she felt.

And yet when she narrowed her focus to her lips that were rosy and swollen from his kiss, she felt beautiful. The same way she always felt when Lucky looked at her.

She took care to follow the instructions since that was the number one reason why most pregnancy tests gave the incorrect results. After setting the plastic wands on the back of the toilet, she washed her hands and headed into the kitchen. Just as she expected, he was standing there at the ready, cell phone in hand.

"How long?" he asked, his finger hovering over the timer app.

"No less than three. No more than ten."

"Seven minutes, it is, then," he said, keying the numbers into his phone. "Why don't you go sit down in the living room? Watch some TV. I've got things under control here."

She wandered into the living room and grabbed a throw blanket from the back of the couch before settling into one corner. It took a minute or two before she realized she was sitting in the same place where their lives changed in a matter of minutes.

It wasn't as if her birth control had failed that day since she wasn't taking any at the time. She'd stopped taking her birth control pills months before so she wouldn't have sex with Curtis. By stopping the pills, she effectively cut him off since he refused to wear a condom. Then, even after she moved out, she didn't bother to refill her prescription, telling herself it was a way to prevent herself from falling straight into bed with the next guy that came along.

Only that reasoning didn't work either.

When she closed her eyes and thought back to that afternoon, all she could see was the pain on Lucky's face, hear the anguish in his voice. How he clung to her as if his life depended upon it.

Her whole life, that's what she'd been desperately seeking. Not someone who wanted her. People always wanted and wished for things and after a time they'd tire of whatever or whomever it was only to discard them. Throw them away like yesterday's trash.

She never needed to be wanted. She'd wanted to be needed. And on that day, Lucky had needed her.

His footsteps pounded on the floors as he made his way through the house. Next thing she knew, he was standing there in the doorway, test sticks in hand.

Rachel pulled the blanket up to her chin. "It hasn't been seven minutes."

"So I shortchanged it a bit by a couple of minutes."

"It's positive, isn't it?" One corner of his mouth lifted

as he nodded. "And the other one?" she asked even though she knew what his answer was going to be.

"Same as the first."

She buried her face in her hands as her whole world fell apart.

This was her fault. She did this.

He was drunk and distraught and not thinking clearly. And she took advantage. And now . . .

This was all her fault.

He settled on the couch next to her and she immediately shot to her feet. "I need to go lie down."

"You don't want to talk about this?"

"I can't. Not yet."

She raced from the living room, not wanting to see the look on his face.

"What about dinner?" he called after her.

"Not hungry."

She closed the bedroom door behind her and climbed into his bed, clutching his pillow tight in her arms.

What was she going to do now? She could barely take care of herself, let alone a baby. And to do it all on her own? She didn't even own a couch. How on earth was she going to afford a baby?

Several hours later, with her pillow now damp with her tears, she heard him turn off the TV, lock the doors, and switch off the lights as he made his way through the house. When the low creak of the bedroom door announced his arrival, she feigned sleep, because she wasn't ready to hear what he had to say.

The covers lifted and the bed dipped as he climbed

in beside her. Even though he whispered her name, she didn't open her eyes, didn't move the slightest bit. He waited a moment for a response, then curled his body around hers, wrapping a protective arm around her waist, his hand resting just inches from where their baby grew.

For now, she'd soak up his warmth and the security of his arms, because within a matter of weeks he'd be gone and this would all be over.

Chapter Twenty-Three

Lucky couldn't sleep at all, his mind racing with the possibilities of a future with Rachel. It was selfish to think it, but their unplanned pregnancy might be just the thing to convince her to leave this small town and join him wherever the army sent him after RASP.

He couldn't help but find it funny that what he wanted from life now was so very different than what he imagined just a few months ago. He had never completely ruled out the possibility of a wife and children, but it wasn't a must-have in his book. And now, he couldn't imagine a life without her and a herd of redheaded kids with bright blue eyes.

He'd teach them to ride a bike, to bait a fishing hook no matter if they had boys or girls. They'd spend weekends at the beach building sandcastles and flying kites. And every night he was home, he'd hold her tight and every day he'd thank God for the time she nearly ran him over in the hospital parking lot.

Now that he'd imagined the possibilities, returning to the army and resuming his career as a special ops medic would no longer be enough. He wanted to spend the rest of his life with Rachel. He wanted this baby. And more children. Then grandchildren. Suddenly, he wanted everything.

And to get that, he knew exactly what he needed to do.

But the clock said it was only a little after five in the morning and no respectable jewelry store in a ninety-mile radius opened before ten. For a moment he considered waking her and asking her to marry him right then and there. But he screwed so many things up between them that he was determined to do this one thing right. He wanted to have a ring in hand, maybe even get down on bended knee. Either way, it meant he'd have to wait. So he slid out of bed, changed into his running gear and hit the pavement in the hopes of running off some of his nervous energy.

As his feet pounded the blacktop, he knew in his gut everything would work out right. They'd have to be apart for a little while since she couldn't be with him for the twelve weeks he'd be in RASP. But as soon as he was assigned to a battalion, whether it be in Washington state or Georgia, he'd find a place for them to live off-post, and then, finally, they'd be able to start their life together.

He could hardly wait.

Lucky had run several miles already when he turned

down the two-lane road past Rachel's place. Her trailer had just appeared over the hill when he noticed the familiar silver pickup towing a fishing boat coming to a stop at the end of the drive.

As he got closer, the window eased down and Rachel's landlord waved his hand. "I wondered if that was you. You're about the only person I know who runs out this way. How are you doin' this morning?"

"Not too bad. How about yourself?"

"Can't complain. How's your girl doing?"

Lucky rested his hands on his hips, taking a second to catch his breath. "She hasn't been feeling well, so I loaded her up and took her to my house."

Walter chuckled. "Wanted something more to sit on than those silly camping chairs she's got?"

"That and cable."

"Can't say as I blame ya." Walter shook his head. "I have an old couch in storage that I offered her to use, but she said she's saving up for one she found in a magazine. And that she's more motivated to save her pennies if she's having to use those chairs."

Lucky knew just the couch he was talking about. The page Rachel ripped from a Pottery Barn catalog had been hanging on her refrigerator for weeks. Her plan was to wait until after Christmas to order it and pay cash. Little did she know he'd ordered it a couple of weeks before as her present even though it wouldn't arrive until after Christmas.

They chatted for a few more minutes until Walter slapped his hand on the door frame.

"Well, I better get going. Those fish won't be bitin' forever. Tell Rachel to feel better."

"Will do."

Lucky waved goodbye and continued on with his run with an idiotic grin on his face. This was the happiest he'd been in weeks. Even when he and Rachel had moved forward with their relationship, there still had been something missing. But once he signed that contract to reenlist, he knew that hole had been filled. Now all he needed to do was hang on to her.

She was still asleep when he returned home, sprawled out facedown across the bed, her face hidden from view by all that fiery red hair. The blankets hung off the far side of the bed so he straightened them out and pulled the covers up to her shoulders. She stirred a moment, but thankfully she quickly fell back to sleep. So he showered, dressed, and left a note on the refrigerator that he'd be back by lunch at the latest and if she needed anything to give him a call.

The three hours he spent driving to Dallas and back he tried to work out in his head what he was going to say and do. The older saleslady recommended he just speak from his heart and not worry about rehearsing anything. The younger sales guy told him to just give her the box because " 'nough said." It was safe to say that Lucky wouldn't take his advice. If ever there was a time to talk to one of the married guys from regiment, it was now. They'd give him good advice. But he sure as hell wouldn't ask Gibby his opinion.

As he crossed the Red River back into Oklahoma, his excitement reached epic proportions knowing he'd be home within a matter of minutes. And the closer he got to home, the faster he drove. He'd barely turned off his Jeep when his feet hit the ground and he was jogging up the front steps to his house. As he unlocked the door, the thought crossed his mind he should have brought her flowers. But it was too late now because there was no way he was waiting another minute to ask Rachel to marry him.

The moment he walked through the door he was calling out her name, finally finding her sitting on the edge of his bed as she slipped fuzzy socks on her feet.

"You're up."

She smiled weakly. "Shocking, I know."

It was obvious she didn't feel well. Her blue eyes weren't as bright and her lips were pale. Most of her copper red hair was piled on top of her head and secured with a rubber band and she was wearing the same clothes she did the day before. But she was still the most beautiful woman he'd ever laid eyes on.

"Morning sickness?"

"More like morning, afternoon, and evening sickness."

"Well, maybe this will make you feel better."

And before he knew it, he pulled the ring box from his pocket and dropped to one knee at her feet. "Rachel Dellinger." He eased the box open and looked into those big blue eyes. "Will you marry me?"

How much time over the course of her life had she imagined this very moment? The face of the man kneeling at her feet had changed several times over the years. The setting was usually more romantic with flowers and candlelight. And she sure as hell wasn't wearing yoga pants and a sweatshirt. The ring, however, was far better than anything she'd dared to imagine.

Rachel stared at the diamond solitaire nestled in the black velvet box he held out in front of her. Her eyes drifted up to meet his to see the smile on his face had reached his dark brown eyes. He didn't look like a man who was proposing marriage out of obligation, but deep in the pit of her stomach she felt she'd forced his hand. Because he was a good man. A loyal man.

"You're killing me, Shortcake."

All those times she'd daydreamed about this moment, she'd never imagined it would go down like this.

Rachel covered the small box in his palm with her hand, unable to look at it anymore.

"I can't," she said through tears that sprung up instantaneously. "I'm sorry, Lucky. I'm so, so sorry."

She didn't know how he would react, what he would say. But she definitely didn't expect him to snap the small box shut, stuff it into the front pocket of his jeans, then sit beside her on the edge of the bed. Even more surprising, he pulled her into the warm embrace of his arms and held her tight as she cried.

"There's nothing to be sorry about," he said against her temple. "It's a really big step. One you need to be sure of. I've had more time to consider this. Take your time. There's no rush."

She turned her head, resting her cheek on his shoulder.

"You sure about that? Don't most shotgun weddings occur before the baby's birth?"

Lucky's arms tightened around her, pulling her even closer. "Don't think of it that way. No one has a gun held to my head. No one is forcing me to propose. You of all people should know no one makes me do anything. I go with my gut, my heart. Would you at least try the ring on for me?" he asked while pulling the velvet box from his pocket for the second time. "I had to guess since I have no idea what size you wear."

"Why does it matter? You're only going to return it."

"You don't know me very well if you think one little 'no' will deter me. This way, if it's the wrong size, I can be sure to have it resized before I ask you the next time."

Before she could protest, Lucky plucked the ring from its little nest and slid it on her finger. And of course it fit perfectly. The facets caught the bright sunlight streaming through the window and shot sparks of color around the room.

"It's beautiful."

He tipped her chin upward so she was looking him in the eyes. "I don't want to marry you because some people in this world think it's the right thing to do. I want to marry you because I love you." His hand cupped her face, his thumb caressing her cheek, her lips. "Believe it or not, I've loved you a lot longer than a month." And then he smiled. "So if anyone in this room trapped someone into marriage, it was me and my supersperm. Not even Plan B can stop them."

She laughed then. "Damn your supersperm."

He, of course, smiled proudly.

"So you take all the time you need. I'm willing to give it to you."

Rachel looked down at the ring on her hand as she fiddled with the unfamiliar weight on her finger. "I do have one request."

"Anything you want. Just name it."

She slid the ring off her finger and handed it back to him. "I think it's time for you to take me home."

IGNORING HIS GUT instincts and what he wanted, Lucky did as she asked and drove her home. When they arrived at her place, he followed her inside, carrying the small bag she packed the day before and the few groceries he'd bought. As Rachel disappeared into the bedroom, he remained on the entryway tile, uncertain as to whether she wanted him to stay or to go.

A few minutes later when she emerged with a load of clothes in her arms, he was still standing there.

"What are you doing?" she asked as she breezed through the living room to the small laundry room off the kitchen. He heard the water start, the washer lid slam shut, and then she was back, that little crease between her brows and her arms crossed over her chest. "Why are you just standing there?"

"I wasn't sure I was invited in. And I didn't want to just dump your things and leave."

Her expression softened and her hands fell to her sides. "You're always welcome here, Lucky. Day or night. You have an open invitation."

"Okay, then." He carried her small duffel into her room, then put the grocery bags on the counter. "Just so you know, I'm not giving up on us."

"I didn't expect you would."

She stared at him with those bright blue eyes, the one corner of her mouth hiked up higher than the other. For a moment, as they stood in the silence just staring at each other, he honestly thought she was going to change her mind. He could feel it building between them, just another minute or two . . .

Without any warning she turned and headed into the kitchen, strategically putting the breakfast bar between them. "I thought I should take advantage of the fact I'm feeling a bit better. For now, I'm just going to do some laundry, clean my bathroom, and probably take a nap. Surely, there's something else you'd rather be doing?"

He wanted to spend every minute with her that he could before he left for Benning, but there were other things he needed to do. Like get his fitness back up before he showed up for RASP. "I should probably go work out."

"Didn't you run this morning?"

He nearly laughed. "I did. But a two-hour run won't be enough to get me through a twenty-hour day."

"My God. What all do they make you do there?"

Lucky did laugh then. "Shortcake, you don't want to know."

So he put on his best smile and kissed her goodbye,

promising to return with dinner. With several hours to kill he headed for the gym and put himself through a vigorous workout that would make his Ranger buddies proud. Pull-ups. Push-ups. Flutter kicks. Weights. Another five-mile run.

It distracted him for a while, but the minute he finished, he decided to go talk to the one person he could always count on. And man, did he have a lot of explaining to do.

He drove across town to the house where his dad lived now and rang the doorbell. The look on his face must have said it all, because the moment Brenda laid eyes on him after opening the door, she immediately went to fetch his dad. No rambling small talk. No offering of food or drink. No teasing remarks about how he needed more meat on his bones and a new razor.

His father greeted him with a hug, held him a little tighter and a little longer than usual before they finally took a seat in the living room. Since Lucky had pretty much avoided his father for the past few weeks he didn't even know about his being thrown out of the ER and his subsequent resignation. So he spent the first twenty minutes explaining everything that happened in that emergency room weeks before.

"The woman lived, right? Sounds to me like you did the right thing. I'm sure her family appreciates all that you did."

"But I knowingly violated hospital policy."

"You saved a life."

"I know that . . ."

"Then focus on that. You saved her life," his father said, arm waving as he spoke. "I couldn't do that. Brenda couldn't do that. Ninety-nine percent of the people in this town couldn't do that."

"But that's not all." Lucky winced, knowing his father was far more likely to be upset he'd taken so long to tell him. "When I went to Maryland, to Walter Reed, I kept seeing all these guys who've just come back, and knowing how much medics are needed . . ."

"You reenlisted."

Lucky studied his father's face. He was neither happy nor upset. No indication of any anger or hurt. Just the same neutral expression he often wore. "I did. How did you know?"

"To be perfectly honest, I'm surprised you lasted this long." Duke shrugged. "As much as I love having you home and seeing you every week, you don't belong here. You were destined for far greater things than this small town. Even if you'd gone on to medical school and become a doctor, you still wouldn't have fit here. But I have to wonder what Rachel thinks?"

And he knew this would be the hardest part of this visit. How was he going to explain to his father that not only was he leaving town and the woman he loved, but one who also happened to be pregnant with his child?

"There's something else."

His father didn't say anything, just waited for him to speak.

"Rachel's pregnant."

Still no significant reaction. "And?"

"I don't know. I've messed everything up, Dad." Lucky rose to his feet and began pacing around the living room. "I immediately bought a ring and proposed to her. Not solely because of the baby, but because I love her. And I want to marry her and spend the rest of my life with her."

"And she doesn't want that?"

"It's just like you'd warned me all those weeks ago. That she might never leave this town." Lucky growled and pulled at his hair in frustration. He swore out loud and immediately held up a hand in apology. "Sorry," he said as he resumed his pacing. "It's just that I don't want to be an absentee parent. I don't want to be like Mom. I want to know my kid. I want to teach them to tie their shoes and ride a bicycle. I want to be more than the occasional email or annual birthday phone call."

"Then that's what you'll do."

"Maybe I shouldn't report to Benning. I can get out of it. I can tell them there's extenuating circumstances and that I didn't know she was pregnant at the time I reenlisted. It's not like the army could do anything to me. And if I go back to school here, at least I'd be close to Rachel and the baby. I could help out at least. Maybe I could get my job back at the hospital. Or find an ambulance service I can work at."

His father leaned forward in his recliner and pointed directly at him. "No," he said emphatically. "Whatever you do, do not do that."

Lucky stopped in his tracks. "Why would you say that?"

"Because I know you. You won't be any happier here

for the long term than your mother was. And your child will know it. They'll feel it. It's exactly why I told your mother to go. I know you missed her. I did, too. But if she had stayed, she would have done far more damage in the long run. I wanted you to miss your mother, not resent her."

Lucky made one last trip across the living room before he fell back onto the sofa. He rested his elbows on his knees and scrubbed his face with his hands. "You do realize if I can't convince her to go with me, you'll end up seeing my kid more than I will."

"Have a little faith. That girl loves you. Anyone who sees the two of you together knows it. She's got a lot on her plate at the moment. Let her get it all sorted out. And I bet money she'll come around."

Dear God, how he hoped his father was right.

Chapter Twenty-Four

AS IT TURNED out, two and a half weeks was not enough time to convince Rachel to marry him. And from where he stood, halfway across the country in the barracks in Fort Benning, Georgia, the possibility of her never marrying him looked pretty damn likely. He had no choice but to leave the decision in her hands along with the ring he bought her. He could only hope and pray that the three months she'd have to think about it while he was in RASP would be enough.

Not much about RASP had really changed since he went through it a decade earlier—except for the name. The same Ranger hopefuls who talked the biggest game before things got started were usually the first ones to quit. And while many of the recruits were the same age as Brittany and her crowd of giggling friends, these guys didn't spend their time talking about *The Real Housewives* or One Direction. Many of them did, however, spend a great deal of time talking about how much they kicked ass at *HALO* or *Call of Duty* and arguing over which video game was better.

The Ranger instructors were still assholes when they wanted to be, making them do stupid, useless shit like clutching a wooden telephone pole like a koala—upside down. The days still started early and ended late, if they ended at all. And Cole Range during the winter months was still cold, still wet, and continued to be the absolute worst, soul-sucking part of the assessment program and the most likely place to break even the most mentally tough men.

For the most part, the RIs didn't give him a lot of grief since his paperwork said it all. Thirteen deployments in eleven years earned him more than a modicum of respect.

The few hours they spent in the barracks, his room became another first aid station. He even had to go as far as setting office hours of sorts, because although he'd survived this life for a lot of years, he still needed at the very least a couple hours of sleep if his brain was going to function. But when he didn't have his makeshift "closed" sign hanging up, he spent a lot of time checking guys' feet, taping blisters, taping wrists, taping ankles, and reinforcing the fact they needed to learn how to take care of not only themselves, but their Ranger buddies. And those few who came to him with injuries beyond athletic tape's treating capabilities, he sent them off to the aid station, reassuring those who had the grit and heart to become a Ranger that it was more than likely they'd be recycled into the next class once they healed instead of being summarily dismissed from RASP and returned to the general army.

Their phones were confiscated the first eight weeks of RASP as a way of removing unnecessary distractions. After completing phase one, the RIs returned them to the recruits who still remained and Lucky found himself hoping for a slew of text messages, voice mails, and emails from Rachel. Instead, there was only one.

One lousy text message that was a picture of the couch he'd bought her as a Christmas present. Only five words accompanied the picture.

I love it! Thank you.

"Just great," he mumbled under his breath as he shoved his phone in his pocket. He'd been gone two whole months and all she had to say was she loved her new couch. Not him. Her new fucking couch.

At this point, he'd be better off volunteering as a shooting target on the live fire range. He could dress all in black and draw concentric ovals on his chest with a small X in the center. At least that way he'd be put out of his fucking misery.

Finally he pulled his head out of his whining ass and sent a series of messages to his dad, to Bull, and then to Rachel, letting them know he'd survived phase one just fine and was looking forward to graduating in a month.

Bull replied within seconds, which quickly segued into a long back and forth as they both reminisced about their adventures in the Ranger Indoctrination Program the first time around. Messages which just reinforced

Lucky's assessment that while many things had changed, a lot had stayed exactly the same.

His father replied a few hours later with the standard **I'm very proud of you** parent message.

Much to his disappointment, he didn't receive a reply from Rachel before he mustered the following morning.

During the course of phase two, those who remained were asked which battalion they preferred. No way in hell would he request 3rd Batt because Fort Benning was a place better seen in your rearview mirror. For a moment he considered requesting 2nd Batt for a change of pace since it was located in Fort Lewis, just a few miles from Tacoma, Washington. Plus, as much as he hated to admit it, his curiosity had been piqued by the 2nd Batt stories of supposed Big Foot sightings and part of him wanted to know if there was any truth of the matter.

But really, why reinvent the wheel? He loved Savannah. The sunny weather. The great fishing. Not to mention the fact all his friends were there.

And the last thing he wanted was to be on the other side of the continent, surrounded by strangers, especially if his future didn't include Rachel.

IT WAS THE middle of March when David showed up on her doorstep, offering to buy lunch. He'd taken the week off from his law practice since it was spring break for his kids, but after doing the family thing for five solid days, the togetherness became too much and things were getting a little chippy. His wife decided it was best to divide and conquer and strongly suggested he drive down to Durant and spend the day with Rachel instead.

That was how she came to be at the same diner, sitting at the same booth she and Lucky used to share, eating a club sandwich and French fries with David. As much as she loved her brother and appreciated him taking the time to visit, it just wasn't the same. It would never be the same.

Rachel shoved her food to one side and made a small puddle of ketchup. Then she added more. And more still. Because she missed watching Lucky pour half a bottle onto his plate.

"Adam and I have been talking a lot lately and we both owe you an apology," David said as he added a more than healthy amount of salt to his fries.

Her head shot up to meet her brother's eyes. "For what? It's not your fault you didn't know about my real father. Or the fact that he's dead."

It took a month before any of them could get a name from her mother. Then it took another few weeks for David's private investigators to find her real father had died in a single vehicle accident less than two years later in Missouri. No known marriages. No known children. No known living relatives. A part of her life had been firmly sealed shut before she ever knew anything about it.

"I'm not talking about your dad," David said as he wiped his fingers on his napkin. "I'm talking about how Adam and I left you to handle all of Mom and Dad's crap. We both kept telling ourselves it only made sense for you to take care of it because you live here. And because you're a woman and a nurse only added to our bullshit excuses. And I'm sorry for that."

"It's okay."

"It's not," he said, shaking his head. "And from here on out, they aren't your responsibility. If there's something they need, Adam and I will take care of it. If it's not something they need, too bad. You've provided far better for them than they ever have for you. So focus on yourself from here on out. If we need help, we'll call you. Got it?"

Rachel smiled and nodded, immediately feeling as if a heavy weight had been lifted from her shoulders. Now, she had the freedom to focus on what would be best for her and her baby.

After lunch, she drove the two of them to the outskirts of town where Ethan was laid to rest. The last time she hadn't come alone was the day before Lucky left for Fort Benning. On that day he was there as she cleared away the fake poinsettias she'd placed in front of his grave. Since then, it had been too cold to give his headstone a proper cleaning. So today was the day.

Just as she'd done hundreds of times in the past, she followed the single lane road along the perimeter and stopped at the back. She grabbed the bucket and cleaning supplies from the bed of the truck, taking them straight to a nearby tap. As the bucket filled with soapy water, one of the groundskeepers called out her name and waved.

After waving back she turned off the tap and was about to pick up the bucket and brushes when her brother knocked her hand out of the way. Clearly that was his way of saying he'd carry it.

"How often do you come here?" he asked as they made their way across the cemetery to Ethan's grave site.

"Quite a bit. I always come here to talk to him when I'm confused about stuff. Especially since he always seems to give me the right answers. But I've been coming here a lot lately and . . . nothing."

David placed the bucket on the ground and laughed.

"Why are you laughing?"

"Are you listening to yourself?" He shook his head while simultaneously dipping the scrub brush in the soapy water. "Ethan gives you the right answers? That's funny. And I'd bet money even Ethan would think it's funny. You of all people coming to him for advice."

"Why is that?"

"Because Ethan was never more than a kid," David said, now scrubbing the backside of the white granite. "What did he know about life that *you* didn't teach him?"

"I assumed he had a better perspective."

Rachel followed suit, dipping her brush in the cold water, her fingertips already going numb as she started at the bottom and scrubbed her way up, taking extra care to clean the black letters engraved on the front. They worked in silence for several minutes, she on the front, him on the back and sides.

"So maybe you can talk to me instead of him. Tell me what's going on."

"Well, for starters . . . I'm pregnant."

David rose to his feet so that the headstone didn't obstruct his view. "Okay. That's not something a guy likes to hear from his baby sister. Especially when she's not married."

"Wasn't Stacie pregnant with Zach when you two got married?"

"That was different." The scrub brush he'd been using went flying into the bucket, splashing brown, soapy water up and over the sides.

"How so? Doesn't she have an older brother? Did he get all upset?"

David laughed. "As a matter of fact, he did. Took me out for drinks under the guise of wanting to get to know his brother-in-law better, and before the evening was over, he was threatening to drown me in the Illinois River if I ever hurt his sister."

"Wow. That's . . . not nice."

He took the brush she had been using and tossed it in the bucket as well, carrying it back to the tap where he dumped the dirty water out and refilled it with clean.

"It was an idle threat," he said while carrying the bucket back to her. "It's not like there's ever that much water in the river. Whereas Lake Texoma is just a ten-minute drive away and happens to have way more water and be far deeper. So where do I find the asshole who knocked up my baby sister?"

"Fort Benning, Georgia. And he's not an asshole."

"But does he know you're pregnant?"

"We found out together before he left for training."

"And he still left?"

"He asked me to marry him. And I said no."

Using one hand David backed her away from the headstone before pouring the water over top, rinsing away the remaining soap and grime. "Why did you say no?"

"Because I was afraid he was only asking because I was pregnant. I was afraid of moving halfway across the country to a place where I didn't know anyone. I was afraid that something could happen to him and then I'd be left all alone."

David lifted one brow. "And what are you now?"

Dammit. He had a point.

"What should I do?"

Her brother slung one arm around her shoulders. "No. I'm not going to tell you what to do. You need to figure it out for yourself. Or maybe," he said, gesturing to the headstone with the bucket he held in his hand, "I should ask what do *you* think Ethan would say?"

Rachel sucked in a lungful of air and let it all out. "He'd probably say it's time for me to let go of him and this town and move on with my life."

David smiled. "I think that's exactly what Ethan would say."

He pulled her closer to his side and kissed her temple. "Don't tell the others, but you've always been my favorite sister."

"Why am I not your favorite sibling, period?" she asked as they made their way back to her truck.

"Because Adam has this great little house in the Florida Keys and he lets us use it for two weeks every summer. Rent free, I might add."

"So let's say I marry Lucky and move away. Ethan's truck really isn't conducive to infant car seats. Won't Zach be getting his driver's license soon?"

"Okay. I like the way this is going."

"If I give Ethan's truck to Zach, would I be your favorite sibling then?"

David smiled at her. "There's only one way to find out."

Chapter Twenty-Five

LUCKY CHECKED HIS reflection in the mirror one last time, still finding it odd to see a clean-shaven face staring back at him. Over the past twelve weeks he'd been at Fort Benning, he hadn't heard much from Rachel. They exchanged text messages here and there, but never really finding the rhythm of conversation since their schedules kept them from replying. And now a part of him regretted reenlisting.

How did he end up in this place, so very lost and alone?

He'd never been a guy who questioned his decisions before. He made life and death decisions all the time and never once second-guessed himself. And yet, that was all he seemed to do lately.

Six months ago he believed the right thing to do was follow his dreams to become a doctor and leave the military. And then when everything went to hell in a handbasket back home, he was certain returning to regiment was the right decision. But the more he thought about it, the more he realized that Rachel was the thing missing from his life all along.

And now she was carrying his baby but choosing to stay there. And he was here. He was going to end up like his mother, an absentee parent who only saw his kid on birthdays or holidays.

The thought twisted in his gut.

"That's it," he said to himself. "No more fucking around."

He had to do whatever was absolutely necessary to win Rachel over. After graduation finished, he had a four-day leave and he intended to make the most of it. It was a twelve-hour drive to Durant with a twelve-hour return trip to catch the bus to Hunter Army Airfield first thing Monday morning. Which meant if he went with a minimum amount of sleep over the next four days, he had about sixty hours to convince that stubborn redhead he was madly in love with to marry him.

So no more Mister Nice Guy. No more waiting for her to come around to the idea. This time, if he needed to, he'd pack her bags, duct tape her into the front seat of his Jeep, and drive her back to Georgia kicking and screaming. Because one thing was for certain, he would not leave Oklahoma without her this time.

An hour later Lucky was standing on the stage of Marshall Auditorium with sixty-four of his fellow RASP graduates, most of them the same age as the kids he attended college with. Partway through the ceremony, even though he told his dad not to come, he realized he was searching the crowd for a familiar face. More specifically, a flash of fiery red hair. But if his dad wasn't here, it was likely she wouldn't be either, because he couldn't imagine she'd get on a plane and fly here all by herself.

Once they donned their tan berets and the ceremony was complete, they filed offstage, in line but out of step. He was itching to get out of there in a hurry, but a few of his classmates wanted to introduce him to their families. Finally, having made his way out of the auditorium, through the large crowds of friends and family gathered outside, he reached the main road and broke into a trot, headed for Oklahoma and her.

THIRTEEN MILES BETWEEN the Columbus, Georgia, airport and Fort Benning and Rachel managed to get lost along the way, arriving just before the ceremony started. Which meant she was seated all the way in the back. Which was good because she was close to the bathrooms. It was also bad because she couldn't make out any of the faces onstage.

She made it through most of the ceremony until the baby started tap-dancing on her bladder. But when she returned from the bathroom, the Rangers were scattering in every direction and she worried she'd never find him. They all looked the same with their camouflaged uniforms and tan berets and clean-cut faces. Not one scruffy beard in the bunch.

Immediately, she made her way out to the sidewalk

where the crowds were thinner, hoping he'd pass by her or at least she'd be able to spot him easier. She was holding up one hand, shading her eyes from the afternoon sun, when she noticed what looked to be a uniformed man in a sea of kids. She watched as he pushed his way through the crowd before he broke into a jog headed in the opposite direction. And the moment she saw him in motion, she knew without a doubt it was Lucky.

Okay, so she was like seventy-five percent certain because it'd been a while. But either way, she'd never be able to catch up to him.

"Lucky!" She didn't think anything of it when she yelled his name, but now a hundred sets of eyes were trained on her. Of course the man whose attention she was trying to get didn't turn around, so she was forced to yell again. And louder this time. "Lucky James!"

This time the man in question slowed, then stopped and cautiously turned around. He was far enough away she still wasn't one hundred percent sure, but he was walking toward her now. That had to be a good sign. So she walked toward him and they met somewhere in the middle.

He looked so different, but the same. His hair was definitely shorter. And the heavy scruff that used to tickle her skin was gone.

"Sorry I missed you when you came offstage. I had to use the restroom."

She smiled as she said it, but Lucky stared at her, a blank expression on his face. She felt her smile slipping and suddenly she wondered why she'd come all this way. Because he certainly did not look happy to see her. "Congratulations on your graduation."

Still not even a hint of a smile.

"How did you get here?" he finally asked.

"I flew. Your dad was nice enough to drive me to Dallas." He nodded as if it all made sense. "I caught a plane to Atlanta and then to Columbus. Which is really crazy when you think about it because we flew over Columbus only to backtrack to it. What I don't understand is why we didn't just stop along the way. Anyhoo, I rode my first plane today. Two planes actually. And then I rented a car at the airport and drove here. I got a little lost and tried to turn in at one gate but they had barricades and stuff and they told me I couldn't enter there so I had to turn around and go over to this other . . ."

He looked at her like she'd lost her damn mind. Having heard the rambling explanation that just came out of her mouth and the way her hands were flapping in midair, she couldn't really blame him for looking at her that way. She blamed pregnancy brain. And nerves.

"So . . . you must be wondering what I'm doing here."

Lucky still didn't say anything. Just folded his arms over his chest and the stance made him look more imposing, bigger somehow.

"Did you grow?" The words flew out of her mouth before she could stop them. Dammit. She was really losing it now. "You look taller . . . than I . . . remember."

At least that made him smile. Not that panty-melting

grin she'd fallen for, but at least one corner of his mouth raised up a bit revealing, much to her surprise, a hint of dimple in his clean-shaven cheek.

"It's the boots. And the beret."

God, she'd missed the sound of his voice.

"But it's not just the uniform." He was leaner, stronger. She could see it in his face, his hands. She stepped closer to him now, unable to keep from touching him. "You've lost weight." She placed her hand on one of his and was surprised when he turned his hand over and curled his fingers around hers.

"About twenty pounds or so."

No wonder. He didn't have twenty pounds to lose when he left eight weeks ago. "Brenda wouldn't like to hear that. You better not tell her or she'll send you a dozen lasagnas."

His smile was bigger now as he lifted his hand to touch her hair, running a long strand between his fingers. "Your hair is longer."

"It's the prenatal vitamins."

Just as he'd done so many times before, he skimmed his palm across her jaw, cradling her cheek, his fingertips tangling in the hair around her ear. He tipped her face upward to meet his gaze. "How are you feeling? How's everything with the baby?"

"I'm good. We're both good."

She'd be happy to just stand here and look at him, and have him look at her and touch her.

"Are you going to tell me why you're here?"

He dropped his hand from her face, released her fingers from his other hand, and took a step back.

She was too late. He'd changed his mind.

Her stomach twisted into knots, fearing her mother's words were coming to fruition, that men didn't keep their promises to women like them. But she'd come this far. She refused to give up without a fight. Her baby deserved better. She deserved better.

Rachel cleared her throat as she tried to find the words she'd spent the past eight hours rehearsing. "I'm here because I wanted to see you and I hoped you wanted to see me, too. I got used to you being around all the time and then you were just gone. And I missed you."

He folded his arms over his chest a second time and added a little scowl to his face for good measure. "I emailed. I texted. I called when I could."

"I know. I guess it's safe to assume you're mad at me."

"Twelve weeks of radio silence from you, Rachel."

"I thanked you for the couch."

"Oh, yes, that's right. You sent a picture of the couch and said how much you loved it."

She'd wanted to say she loved *him*, but she didn't think telling him in a text message or email was the right way to do it.

"Okay. I get why that would upset you." She stared down at his booted feet, unable to look him in the eyes. "But I wasn't sure what to say to you. Everything happened so fast between us. It feels like we went from arguing about who hit who in the hospital parking lot to having a baby in the blink of an eye. I was trying to straighten my life out. And I almost made it. I was standing on my own two feet, living on my own, paying my own bills, and next thing I know, my dad isn't my dad, you've reenlisted, and I'm pregnant." She looked back up at those dark eyes staring back at her. "Then you're standing in front of me with a ring proposing marriage and I panicked.

"I got your messages. And emails. And texts. I've saved them all and read or listened to them a hundred times a day." She held her hands in front of her belly in an attempt to keep them contained and not flailing about. "And before you left you said you probably wouldn't have time to talk and I didn't want to bother you. Because I knew this was important and I didn't want to do anything to screw it all up and get you in trouble with your CO."

He raised a brow and for a moment she thought he was amused, but then she blinked and his face was back to that same unreadable expression. "My CO?"

"Your commanding officer? Is that not what they call it?" One of her hands broke free and started waving madly in the air. "I've been reading up on these army wives blogs and trying to learn the lingo and everything in case I decided to come with you. But now I'm here and you don't look happy at all to see me and maybe it's for the best anyway, because I don't think I'd make a very good army wife.

"Oh, hell," she said, throwing both hands in the air. "I probably won't be a very good mother either considering the job my parents did. But I'd hoped to be a good mother. And I thought I might not be the most terrible of wives, but I see that you're not happy and I've completely and totally screwed up everything."

Lucky shook his head. "That still doesn't explain why you're here."

She couldn't stand this space between them, so she took a step closer to him. "Because I wanted to know if you still loved me. If you still wanted me to be your wife."

"Why does that matter?"

She took another step and then another, until her hands rested on his arms and she was looking into those deep dark eyes. "Because I love you, okay? I love you so much it hurts. I thought if you went away, the feeling would go away. But it didn't. It just got worse and worse. And I've realized I want to be with you wherever you are."

His hands came up to cradle her face. "Say it again."

She couldn't help but smile, and when she did, he smiled back at her. Not the little half smile, but the full-blown panty-melting smile. She raised up on her toes and whispered against his lips, "I love you."

Lucky wrapped his arms around her waist and lifted her off the ground. "It's about damn time, Shortcake."

FOR A MOMENT, Lucky had forgotten where they were as he kissed Rachel right there in front of God, his fellow Rangers, and everybody. At least until the loud whistles and clapping began.

"Where's your rental car?" he asked as he lowered her

to the ground and tried to ignore the fact that several cell phones had been pointed in their direction.

"I'm in the visitors' lot."

Lucky took her by the hand and began towing her down the street. "Have you booked a hotel room?"

"Your dad reserved me a room at the Holiday Inn. The directions are in my car."

Earlier he thought he'd be on the road to Oklahoma by now. And that he'd be fortunate to spend sixty hours with her. But now . . . oh . . . the possibilities.

"Lucky."

Admittedly, he ignored her pleas, knowing they were walking at a pretty good clip. But there would be no stopping. His central focus was to get her to that hotel room where they could have four full days together. He wouldn't be able to make up for the twelve weeks they were apart, but he'd give it a good, solid effort.

"Lucky!" Rachel tugged her hand free from his.

Now he turned around to see her standing there with one hand low on her belly, the other on her chest.

Shit.

"What's the matter? Are you okay?"

"You take one step for every two of mine," she said, waving one hand in the air. "I'm practically at a full sprint here and I can't keep up."

He placed both hands on her waist and bent at the knees, bringing his face level to hers. "You're okay, then? No pain?"

"I'm fine. It's just . . ." That little crease appeared between her brows and she balled up her delicate hand into a fist and punched him in the shoulder. "You know how much I hate running!" Lucky laughed and she punched him a second time. "It's not funny!"

But it *was* funny. And it only reinforced how much he had missed her.

"Well, then, I've got an easy fix."

Rachel squealed as Lucky scooped her up in his arms and started jogging through the parking lot, much to the delight of his fellow Rangers and their families. Once again, the cell phones were up and capturing the entire scene. He wouldn't be surprised if the video was uploaded to YouTube by the time they reached the hotel.

Within the half hour, they were checked in. It wasn't anything fancy, but it would suffice, because it had a bed, it had delivery menus, and most importantly it had her. And he didn't plan on them going anywhere for the next four days if he could help it.

Lucky swiped the key card in the lock and had barely shoved the door open when Rachel pushed past him to get to the bathroom. The door closed behind him as he tossed his beret on the dresser and set her small suitcase on the floor at the end of the bed.

"Do you need me to go get you some ginger ale and crackers?"

The toilet flushed but she didn't answer. He waited a few seconds, then decided to get comfortable, taking a seat on the end of the bed. He unzipped his ACU jacket and unlaced his boots. Then, much to his surprise, the bathroom door opened and Rachel appeared with a smile on her face.

"I take it you weren't sick."

"Nope. The morning sickness has passed. I just really, really needed to pee." She dropped her purse on the bed beside him and straddled his lap. "So, Mr. James? What did you have in mind for this weekend?"

"Plenty, Shortcake."

The next few seconds was a flurry of hands and arms as she pulled and tugged off first his jacket, then the gray-green T-shirt he wore beneath and tossed them in the direction of a nearby chair. Her bright blue eyes widened as her soft hands smoothed over his shoulders, his arms, and chest. "Wow. RASP really does a body good."

"Glad you approve," he said with a laugh. He grasped the hem of her soft cotton dress. "Can I have a turn now?"

Rachel raised her arms above her head. "Sure thing, baby. Knock yourself out."

"Well, well. What do we have here?" Lucky trailed a finger across her collarbone and down her sternum, admiring the heavy swells of her breasts. "I have to say these are amazing."

"I know, right?" Rachel cupped her breasts over her bra and arched her back, lifting them higher and giving him one hell of a look. "I've never had boobs this great in my life."

He pushed her hands out of the way, wanting to cup and caress her breasts himself. "Do we get to keep these?" he asked before leaning over to place a kiss to the soft skin that swelled above the lace.

"That all depends."

Rachel leaned over to grab her purse and pulled a familiar-looking box from the side pocket. "I wanted you to put it on me," she said, handing him the small velvet box. "Of course, I feel like I should be the one asking you since it took me forever to make up my mind."

Lucky cupped her cheek with his hand. "So ask me."

Rachel took his left hand in both of hers and pressed a kiss to his knuckles. Then those bright blue eyes lifted to meet his as she took a shaky breath. "I love you and I want to spend the rest of my life with you. From here on out, wherever you go, I'll go. Because I'm not scared anymore as long as I have you." She took a fortifying breath. "So . . . Lucky James—"

He silenced her with a kiss, not really wanting her to ask because he was old-fashioned. And proposing was his job.

"Why didn't you let me finish?"

"Because I asked first. And I've been waiting a long time to hear you say yes." He lifted her hand to his mouth, kissed the tender skin of her wrist before he wrapped his hand around hers. "You've been a lot of things to me in these past few months. Friend. Coworker. Fishing buddy. Mother of my child. But what I really want is 'wife' added to that list." The tears that had been building in her eyes finally spilled over onto her cheeks. He caught each one with his fingertip, brushing them away. "Rachel Louise Dellinger, will you marry me?"

She said "yes" several times, her voice never raising above a whisper. Lucky slipped the ring on her finger, happy to see it finally freed from its velvet confines and on her hand where it was supposed to be. He kissed her lips, her cheek, her neck, and shoulder before he wrapped his arms around her and held her tight against him. Now that he finally had her, he intended to never let her go.

Chapter Twenty-Six

May

Lucky stood in the middle of their new condo looking at all the work that still needed to be done before Rachel arrived in forty-eight hours. The living room alone was filled with paint cans and drop cloths, unassembled baby furniture, and beer coolers. But if he and the guys could finish painting within the next day, that would leave the following day for him to put everything together and clean up the house. That way, when that U-Haul truck pulled in the drive, he and the guys could move everything in right away and make this cold empty space feel like a home.

When his post-RASP graduation leave ended, Rachel returned to Oklahoma and Lucky reported to Hunter Army Airfield. If he'd had his way, she would have moved with him to Savannah that very day. But he was temporarily assigned to the barracks and she didn't feel comfortable staying with people she'd never met before. She was also being practical not wanting to move multiple times. Rachel wanted to line up an OB/GYN before moving, give two weeks' notice at work, and take another week to pack. When he reminded her they'd moved all of her things in a day, she was sure to point out she hardly had furniture then and she'd only been moving across town, not across the country.

For a time, it felt like she'd never get here, and he'd be lying if he said he worried more than once that she might change her mind.

So for four weeks he was here and she was there until their new place was ready to go. Luckily for them, he didn't have to look very far since Bull offered to rent them the three-bedroom condominium he had been awarded in his divorce proceedings. A condo he would lose money on if he tried to sell. So leasing it to him and Rachel was a win-win for everyone.

Two weekends earlier, the C-Co guys packed up what remained of Bull's things and moved them into a storage locker per his instructions. Then, under the strict supervision of Ben's interior-designing wife, Marie, the guys spent the following weekend rolling on a fresh coat of builder's beige paint on all of the walls. The only exception was the upstairs bedroom that would become the nursery, complete with an eastern exposure that would flood the room with early morning light and a scenic view of the marsh.

While Lucky and Ben taped off the trim, and Danny

covered the wide plank floors with drop cloths, Gibby pried the lid off the first gallon of paint.

"You're having a boy?" Gibby shouted.

Lucky, Danny, and Ben all turned to see Gibby holding up the can lid, the underside coated in light gray-blue paint. Within an instant, three pairs of eyes were staring back at him.

His eyes went back to the can lid held in Gibby's hand. "We don't know what we're having. Rachel wanted it to be a surprise."

"Maybe she found out and this is her way of surprising you with the news?" Ben suggested.

"Like those cake reveals!" Gibby added. "Where they cut into a frosted cake and the inside is either pink or blue."

All eyes now landed on Gibby.

"First of all . . ." Danny started. "That's weird. People do stuff like that? And how the hell would you know about it?"

Gibby shook his head. "I have three sisters, man. I know way too much about shit like that."

Hearing the commotion, Marie appeared in the doorway. "Is everything okay?"

When Lucky, Danny, and Gibby dared to question Marie's color choice, wondering out loud whether or not blue would be appropriate for a little girl, Ben quickly abandoned his post and ran for the hills, leaving his little Italian wife standing in the doorway and blocking their exit. She proceeded to give them a thirty-minute dressing down about the art of interior design and explaining that in this scenario she was the commanding officer. Questioning her expertise was akin to insubordination, especially since their idea of stylish colors began with cinder block gray and ended with desert sand.

There were no further questions.

Over the next two days the four of them taped, painted, and assembled furniture, with Ben being the only one authorized to hang the plantation shutters and curtain rods. According to Marie, he had been properly trained and possessed the installation experience the others lacked.

No one dared question her.

Finally, with the draperies hung and the new furniture moved in, assembling the crib was the only major item left.

"You have to insert the tenon of the Crib Ends Top A into the slot of Crib Ends Bottom B before you insert the bolts through the legs and the threaded inserts." Gibby flipped to the next page of instructions, shook his head, and took another drink of his beer.

Lucky held up a wooden piece in one hand and a bolt in the other. "Is this a Top A?"

"No," Ben answered from where he sat in the window seat. "That's a Bottom Stretcher Bar."

"What the hell is a Top A?" Lucky asked.

Danny held up another crib piece. "This has an 'A' sticker on it."

Lucky took it from Danny's hand and held it up against the other. "But it looks just like this one."

HERE AND NOW   329

Much to everyone's amusement and surprise, the exception being Ben who'd been down this momentous path more than once, it took Lucky two hours to finally win the battle of Tab As and Slot Bs. Once the crib assembly was complete and standing on its own, Ben grabbed hold of one side and gave it a violent shake.

"What the hell are you doing?" Lucky asked, fearing he was going to undo the last two hours of hard work.

"Stress test." Ben moved to the opposite side and repeated the action. "Have to make certain this thing is structurally sound. Trust me when I say that while toddlers might be small, they're mighty. And those little terrors will give this crib a run for its money."

Lucky shook his head, silently praying his kid wouldn't be anything like the mini-monster that Ben described.

Just as he heard the rumble of a large truck, his phone chimed in his pocket. After a quick glance at the screen he took off down the stairs and out the front door as his father backed the large U-Haul truck into the driveway while Brenda parked her SUV along the curb. Rachel must have been as excited as he was, because she flung open the car door and hopped out the moment Brenda came to a stop.

He met her in the middle of the front yard and wrapped her up in his embrace, her belly noticeably larger than the last time he saw her in person. "God, I've missed you," he whispered in her ear. He buried his face in her hair, soaked up her warmth, breathed in her scent, his heart and mind at ease for the first time since he'd arrived in Savannah because she was finally here with him.

Lucky held her face in his hands and pressed a gentle kiss to her lips, before he knelt down and placed another to her belly. "Hi, baby," he whispered, and when he rose to his feet he noticed the shimmer of tears in her bright blue eyes.

Her fingers skimmed over the light stubble on his face. "It's still so strange to see you without your beard. And your hair, it's so short."

"Having a change of heart?"

She ran her hand over the top of his head. "Absolutely not."

IT WAS HOURS before she had him all to herself. His friends stood on the front steps, anxious to meet her the moment she climbed out of the car. They were able to steal a few minutes alone while Lucky gave her a quick tour of the condo but then he and the guys went right to work unloading the U-Haul. They spent the next hour carrying in boxes and mattresses and the new couch Lucky had bought her. Brenda and Duke helped unpack a few things, but left to check in at the bed-and-breakfast Lucky booked for them as a thank you for helping them move and driving her across country.

By the time they were done, it was well past dinnertime so it was only right to feed them. Then they spent the next three hours eating pizza, drinking beer, and telling Ranger stories. Ben and Danny were just as Lucky had described them. And Gibby was just as she remembered. Together the three of them were funny and loud and had a million and one stories. Most of the time Lucky was content to sit back and listen, unless he thought he was portrayed incorrectly. Then he was quick to lean over and whisper loud enough they could all hear that he thought they were full of shit.

Around midnight, with the guys finally gone, Lucky led her upstairs to their bedroom, laid her down on cool sheets, and did his absolute best to make up for the past eight weeks apart. The time away from each other wasn't easy, but Rachel considered it good preparation, an army wives boot camp of sorts to prepare her for a military marriage. As they laid there in the darkness, the moonlight streaming in through the plantation shutters, she imagined this is how it would always be when he returned after a long training session or even longer deployment. How all that time apart would fade away into the background as they lay in each other's arms, sharing stories about things the other missed.

She still couldn't get over the shape of his body now. How much harder, leaner, his muscles were. The first time she saw him in the ER she'd thought he was the best-looking thing she'd ever seen in person. And now he'd gone and made himself look ten times better. She could hardly believe he was hers.

Even more surprising, how he completely changed her life for the better. By showing her there was so much more to life outside her little bubble. Because of him she'd quit her job, given away her brother's truck, and moved halfway across the country to a city she'd never been to. And soon she'd be a wife and a mom. Her life was a lot like this house he'd found for them to live in—far better than she ever could have imagined.

She smoothed her hand over his face and lightly scratched the chin covered in a day's worth of stubble. He smiled at her, and despite video chatting almost every day they were apart, she was still surprised by the dimple in his cheek no longer hidden beneath his beard.

"You look happy," she said.

"I am." His hand smoothed idly over her belly, alternating between sweeping side-to-side movements and lazy circles. The baby was still for the moment, but Lucky was trying his best to jump-start a kicking session. "In some ways it's like I never left the army. The training is the same. The places are the same. For the most part, the people are all the same. But when I'd get back to the barracks and things were quiet, like now, that's when I missed you the most."

Lucky smoothed his hand across her arm and shoulder, finally reaching her jaw, his fingertips curling around her ear as his thumb brushed across her cheek. "So yeah, I'm very happy."

And then, without any warning, he threw back the covers and sat up in bed. "You need to get dressed."

Rachel looked at the alarm clock on the bedside table. "It's not even five in the morning. I'm pretty sure there's nowhere I need to be right now."

But he didn't relent, taking hold of her wrists and tugging her into a sitting position. His eyes and smile conveyed his excitement as he leaned over to kiss her forehead, the tip of her nose and then to her lips. "Come on, Shortcake," he whispered against her lips. "There's something I want to show you."

LUCKY MADE HIS way around to the passenger door where he helped Rachel out of his Jeep. Instantly her head tipped back, her gaze traveling upward, to the bright light at the top of the lighthouse.

"I didn't know places still used lighthouses."

"They don't, really. Not with all the navigational equipment that's available these days. I think it's more for the history and charm than anything else." He took hold of her hand as they made their way across the boardwalk. "Just so you know, they do a lot of weddings here."

He looked to see what her reaction might be, but she was too busy looking at the sand oats and the dunes and everything else.

"Is that right?" she replied.

Just as he anticipated, Rachel didn't take the bait. As long as it took her to say yes to his marriage proposal, he could only imagine how long it would be before she set a wedding date. He didn't care where or when they had it. Or if they invited two hundred people or kept it to the two of them. None of that mattered. He just wanted Rachel to be his wife. The sooner, the better.

When they reached the end of the boardwalk, she sucked in a breath.

"What do you think?"

Rachel shook her head as if she couldn't find the words.

Lucky wrapped his arm around her waist and pulled her to his side as she looked out at the ocean for the very first time. The sun was just breaking over the horizon, adding streaks of pink and orange to the dark blue sky.

"It's amazing. Beautiful." She turned to look at him with a bright smile on her face. "And definitely bigger than the farm pond."

Lucky chuckled. "Just a little bit."

They made their way onto the sand to the water's edge, walking along where the tide slid up and over their feet before retreating back into the ocean. He liked listening to her talk about how soft the sand was. How white it was. He loved watching her discover this place, seeing her smile, hearing her laugh as she wriggled her toes in the sand and the foam tickled her feet. She kept stopping every few feet to gather another shell until the pockets in both her jacket and his were stuffed full.

"I found another one of those pink ones," she said, leaning over and plucking a half-buried shell from the sand. She was rinsing it clean when the tide receded and a tiny crab scuttled across her toes. Rachel panicked, screaming and jumping around as if the crab was the size of a dog instead of the size of a pink eraser. In all of the excitement, she threw the pink shell she'd found at it, and the tide came in and swept it away.

Rachel held her hands up in surrender. "You know what? I'm done."

"No more shells?"

"Not after that." Rachel brushed her hands together,

knocking off the sand and grit from her fingers. "Besides, I'm hungry."

"Say no more." He held out his hand and she twined her chilled fingers with his as they made their way back to the Jeep.

Much to his surprise, they'd had the beach all to themselves the entire time they'd been there. As they started the mile walk back to the lighthouse, their hands swung between them as they walked hand in hand. Lucky could easily picture their future, how one day there would be a child between them, holding on to each of their hands as they swung back and forth.

"Have you given any thought to baby names?"

Her smile was sweet and a little shy. "I have."

"And?" He prompted her with a squeeze of her hand.

"I only have one name so far."

"Ethan?"

"Am I that predictable?"

"Not really." After all, it was pretty easy for him to guess what the one name would be. If they had a boy, it would be the perfect way to honor her brother. Plus it only seemed right that when she finally let go of one Ethan that she'd gain another.

But as much as he'd love a little boy, he really wanted a little girl. One with fiery red hair and bright blue eyes just like her mother. "Maybe we should buy a baby name book to help with the girl names."

"Do you really think we need one? It shouldn't be that hard to come up with one."

So they continued walking hand in hand, listing girls' names off the top of their heads. Anna. Emma. Laura. Elizabeth. Many of the names were quickly scratched off the list because they either reminded them of a girl they once knew and didn't like or someone in their families already had it.

Rachel dropped his hand and stopped in her tracks. "I've got it!" She flung her hands in the air like a cheerleader. "Brittany!"

"No. Absolutely not."

Rachel laughed hysterically. To the point of tears even. She only stopped once he pointed out the likelihood of her peeing her pants.

"By the way . . . your little Brittany joke?" He wrapped one arm around her shoulders, pulling her against his side. "Still not funny." With the brainstorming of names effectively finished for the day, they walked in silence the rest of the way, the only sound that of the waves crashing on the shore.

"What's your schedule next week?" she asked.

"Nothing special. At HAAF all week. Three-day weekend."

"Well, then, if you aren't busy next Friday, I thought we could elope."

Lucky rounded in front of her, needing to see her face. "I thought you wanted your brothers to be there. You said they wanted to come to the wedding."

"I changed my mind." She shrugged one shoulder. "On the drive here I was getting information on marriage licenses. There's no waiting. No witnesses required."

A breeze kicked up off the ocean, sending those red strands in every direction. Using both of his hands, he smoothed them back from her face, burying his fingers in her hair. "You want it to be just the two of us."

She wrapped her hands around his wrists and smiled up at him. "I want it to be just like this. Here. At sunrise. With no one else around. Is that okay?"

"It's perfect." Lucky sealed their wedding plans with a gentle kiss to her lips, and another to her belly. Then he wrapped his arms around her waist and pulled her as close as their baby would allow. "And afterward, I'll take the two of you to breakfast."

Acknowledgments

IN THE PAST few months, I have definitely learned it takes a village to produce a book and I have the best village out there. Thank you to my editor, Rebecca Lucash, and her figurative mighty red pen. Many thanks to the art department for making my fiery redheaded heroine look simply amazing on the front. I cannot show off this cover enough. Thank you to my agent, Stephany Evans, for her cheerleading, her feedback, and her well-timed emails.

Thank you to Edith Lalonde for reading an early version and not pulling any punches when I knew something was wrong and desperately needed brutal honesty. Many thanks to Liz Kerrick for labeling Lucky a unicorn as well as listening to me go on and on and on about this series and not once telling me to shut up. Special thanks to Eric Leisering for providing a wealth of one-liners and insight into the single man's mind. I find myself appreciative and scared all at the same time. Once again, many thanks to

George Kohrman, MD, who doesn't run screaming from my messages and tells me all I need to know about hospital protocol and medical procedures. Any medical mistakes in this book are the fault of the student, not the teacher. And a special shout out to the crew at Red Horn Coffee House and Brewing for keeping me fed and caffeinated.

Last but certainly not least, thank you to my husband and three girls. I love you all more than you will ever know.

About the Author

CHERYL ETCHISON graduated from the University of Oklahoma's School of Journalism and began her career as an oil and gas reporter. Bored to tears and broke as hell, it wasn't long before she headed for the promised land of public relations. But that was nearly a lifetime ago and she's since traded in reporting the facts for making it all up. Currently, she lives in Austin, Texas, with her husband and three daughters.

www.cheryletchison.com

Discover great authors, exclusive offers, and more at hc.com.

About the Author

CHERYL ETCHISON graduated from the University of Oklahoma School of journalism and began her career as an oil and gas reporter bored to tears and broke at left. It wasn't long before she headed for the promised land of public relations. But that was nearly a lifetime ago and she's since traded in reporting the facts for making it all up. Currently, she lives in Austin, Texas, with her husband and three daughters.

www.cheryletchison.com

Give in to your Impulses . . .
Continue reading for excerpts from
our newest Avon Impulse books.
Available now wherever ebooks are sold.

ONE LUCKY HERO
THE MEN IN UNIFORM SERIES
by Codi Gary

STIRRING ATTRACTION
A SECOND SHOT NOVEL
by Sara Jane Stone

SIGNS OF ATTRACTION
by Laura Brown

SMOLDER
THE WILDWOOD SERIES
by Karen Erickson

An Excerpt from

ONE LUCKY HERO
The Men in Uniform Series
By Codi Gary

Violet Douglas wants one night where she can be normal. Where she can do something for herself and not be just her siblings' guardian. So when she spies a tall, dark, and sexy stranger, she's ready to let her wild side roar. The last thing she expects is to see her one night stand one week later, when she drags her delinquent kid brother to the Alpha Dog Training Program.

"You done throwing a tantrum?" he asked.

As his hard body moved into hers, tension hummed around them. "I was not—"

"Yeah, you're revved up into a full-on hissy fit, but I'm going to overlook that while I . . . clarify a few things."

The way his voice softened on those last four words made her body tighten, especially when she realized one of his legs was pressed between hers. His wide shoulders blocked her view of who might be watching them, and his hands were braced flat just above her shoulders. If she moved a fraction higher, he could graze her bare skin with his thumb, and just the thought of it made her nipples perk up against the sheer lace of her bra.

"First of all, yes, I was rude to you, but not because I wasn't attracted to you."

Violet held her breath at this, her eyes riveted to his lips.

"I was trying to save you."

Huh? Save her? She could hardly concentrate on what he was talking about, his proximity casting a spell of confusion over her. Maybe she'd been binge watching too much

Charmed, but she was too caught up in the obsidian flecks in his brown eyes to fully process.

"From what?" Was that her voice? It was soft, dreamy, and not at all normal.

And good God, but were his lips inching closer? "From me."

"Are you dangerous?" Silly question. *If he was really dangerous, you wouldn't be putty in his hands.*

His right hand moved, and he began trailing one of his fingers along her temple and cheek, until the very tip smoothed over her bottom lip. "I would never mean to hurt you, but I'm not looking for anything serious."

That woke her up a little, and she frowned. "Neither am I."

His finger dropped, and he stared down at her grimly. "You say that now, but—"

"Okay, you know what, that's enough." The balls on him, getting her all revved up and then acting like she was just a soft piece of feminine fluff who didn't know her own mind. Putting her hands up against the wall of his chest, she pushed hard, but he wouldn't budge, so she settled for pointing her finger up between them, wagging it in his face. "Don't act like you know me or what I want. Don't just assume that I'm looking for a relationship because I have ovaries. I have too much going on in my life to handle anyone else's wants and needs, so the last thing I'm looking for is a boyfriend. And you might have learned that if you had bothered to spend more than ten minutes at a time talking to me tonight, instead of running away like a big wimpy asshat."

He leaned back but still didn't let her escape. "Big wimpy asshat, huh?"

Lifting her chin up, she didn't back down. "Yeah, that's right."

For several moments, he did nothing but stare at her, and the intensity in his eyes made her twitch. Finally, he nodded, as if coming to terms with his new title. "Fine, I made an assumption. I'm an asshat."

"Happy we agree on something," she said.

"But I didn't come here today looking to hook up. I planned to drink some beer, chill with my friend, and eventually head home to bed—alone."

Violet flushed. "Well, it's not like I was trolling for just anybody. If that were the case, I would be dragging Robert off to have my way with him in the parking lot."

"Are you saying I'm special?" he asked.

It was a loaded question, and her answer could be taken a hundred wrong ways. Why was it that the first guy she'd actually actively pursued had to be so complicated?

"Nope, you're absolutely right. Nothing special about you. There are still a few hours left for me to meet someone who doesn't make snap judgments and would love to make out with an attractive single woman who hasn't been kissed in six months, so if you'll—"

Dean's mouth closed over hers, stopping her tirade with the sheer heat of his soft, deep kiss. Violet melted on impact, her eyes rolling back as her lids closed. She opened her lips to the thrust of his tongue and felt a pool of joy bubbling up in her lower abdomen.

Holy shit. And you thought the sunshine was hot.

An Excerpt from

STIRRING ATTRACTION
A Second Shot Novel
By Sara Jane Stone

When Dominic Fairmore left Oregon to be all
he could be as an Army Ranger, he always knew
he'd come back to claim Lily Greene. But after
six years away and three career-ending bullets,
Dominic is battered, broken, and nobody's
hero—so he stays away. Until he learns Lily has
been the victim of a seemingly random attack.

Lily is starting to find a life without Dominic
when suddenly her wounded warrior is home
and playing bodyguard—though all she really
wants is for him to take her. But she refuses to
play the part of a damsel in distress, no matter
how much she misses his tempting touch.

The door swung open and a large figure filled the doorway. The light from the parking lot made it difficult to identify his features. But she knew him. She'd know him anywhere.

"Now?" she cried as fury rose up partly driven by the pinot noir. But after all this time, how could Dominic Fairmore walk in holding a freaking key in the middle of the night?

Beside her, the dishwasher moved as if Lily's one-word cry had been a directive. Out of the corner of her eye, she saw Caroline reach for the pie dish. And then it was hurling through the empty bar. The pie collided with the target, covering Lily's ex with a mixture of berries, sugar, and home-made crust. The tin dish dropped to the floor.

"What the hell?" the man roared, whipping the pie from his face.

A year ago, Lily would have laughed at the sight of Dominic covered in dessert. She would have smiled and offered to help clean him up. She would have been happy he'd returned home. And she would have set aside all of the lingering heartache from their last and supposedly final breakup.

But too much time had slipped past. Too much had changed. And for him to show up now? In the middle of the night when her fear rose to fever pitch? For him to waltz in here without even knocking?

She felt Caroline's hand close around her arm and pull as if trying to drag her away. Lily grabbed her wine glass and hurled it at the door. She missed and the glass fell to the ground three feet in front of her and shattered.

"Turn around and leave, Dominic," she snapped as she allowed Caroline to pull her behind the bar, into relative safety. Only she'd never be safe from the man she'd loved for so long, because he didn't aim for her face or her arms.

He went for the heart.

"You had your chance to come back," she added as Caroline released her.

"Lily, please calm down," Dominic called.

From their position behind the bar, she heard the door close. Caroline glanced at her. "You know him."

She nodded. Caroline pushed off the ground without a word. And Lily followed her, turning to face the former love of her life, who had stepped just inside the door.

"Ryan dragged me back," he said. "At Noah and Josie's request. How do you think I got the key? Or does your friend here throw food at everyone who walks into the bar?"

"It was the only thing I had," Caroline said simply. "Noah locked up my gun."

"Remind me to thank Noah in the morning," Dominic said dryly.

His hands dropped to his side, abandoning the attempts to wipe away the pie that had hit its target with near-perfect aim. Lily glanced at Caroline. She wasn't sure she wanted to see the dishwasher with a firearm.

Then she glanced back at Dominic. Marionberries clung to his beard. He'd always been clean-shaven. But now, his dark hair was long and it looked like he'd lost his razor around the same time he'd kissed the rangers goodbye. She'd loved the hard lines of his jaw and the feel of his skin against her when they kissed. But this look . . .

She ached to touch and explore. He looked wild and unrestrained, as if he didn't give a damn, as if he didn't hold anything back. Her gaze headed south to the muscles she'd wanted to memorize before he left. He appeared bigger, more powerful.

Impossible.

He'd always been strong, able to lift her up and press her against the wall. He'd held her with ease while she fell apart . . .

And with that memory, her fury and her fear opened the door to another entirely unwelcome emotion—desire. It was as if they were forming a club determined to barricade her heart, mind, and soul against the feelings that might help her return to her calm, steady life. But no, her unruly emotions took one look at the bearded, buff man in the bar and thought: *touch him!*

An Excerpt from

SIGNS OF ATTRACTION

By Laura Brown

From debut author Laura Brown comes a heart-
poundingly sexy and wildly emotional New
Adult novel about a Hard of Hearing woman,
struggling to accept her "imperfections,"
and the gorgeous Deaf man who helps
her see that she is perfect for him.

You know those corny movies where the love interest walks in and a halo of light flashes behind them? Yeah, that happened. Not because this guy was hot, which he was, but because the faulty hall light had been flickering since before I walked into the room. His chestnut hair—the kind that flopped over his forehead and covered his strong jaw in two to three weeks' worth of growth—complimented his rich brown eyes and dark olive skin, which was either a tan or damn good genetics.

Not that I paid much attention. I was just bored.

And warm. Was it warm in here? I repositioned my hair; thankful it not only covered my aids but also the sudden burning in my ears.

Dr. Ashen stopped talking as Hot New Guy walked over to the two women, shifted his backpack, and began moving his hands in a flurry of activity I assumed was American Sign Language. Chic Glasses Lady moved her hands in response while Perfect Ringlets addressed our teacher.

"Sorry. My car broke down and I had to jump on the Green line," Ringlets said, speaking for Hot New Guy.

Car? In the middle of Boston, was this guy crazy?

Dr. Ashen spit out an intense reply. Chic Glasses signed to Hot New Guy, who nodded and took a seat in the back of the room.

For the next two hours—the joy of a once-a-week part-grad class—I watched the two interpreters. Every half-hour or so they switched, with one standing next to Dr. Ashen. They held eye contact with one spot near the back of the room, where Hot New Deaf Guy sat. I'd never seen ASL up close and personal before. My ears, faulty as they were, had never failed me, at least not to this degree.

From the notes the students around me took, pages of it according to the girl on my left, this class was a bust. I needed this to graduate. Maybe my advisor could work something out? Maybe—

Beep. Beep. Beep.

Dammit. To add insult to injury, my hearing aid, the right one, traitorous bitch, announced she needed her battery changed. Right. This. Second. And if—

Beep. Beep. Beep.

I reached into my purse, rummaged past lip-gloss, tampons, tissues, and searched for the slim package of batteries. I had no choice. If I ignored the beeping it'd just—

Beep. Beep. Beep.

Silence.

Fuck. My left ear still worked, but now the world was half-silent. And Dr. Ashen was a mere mumble of incomprehension.

I pulled out my battery packet only to find the eight little tabs empty.

Double fuck. No time to be discrete. I tossed the packet onto my desk and stuck my head in my bag, shifted my wallet, and moved my calendar. I always had extra batteries on hand. Where were they?

A hand tapped my shoulder. I nearly shrieked and jumped out of my skin. Hot New Deaf Guy stood over me. It was then I noticed student chatter and my peers moving about. Dr. Ashen sat at his desk, reviewing his notes. All signs I had missed the beginning of a break.

Hot New Deaf Guy moved his fingers in front of his face and pointed to the empty battery packet I had forgotten on my desk.

"What color battery?" asked Perfect Ringlets who stood next to him.

"I... Uh..." The burning in my ears migrated to my cheeks. I glanced around. No one paid us any attention. Meanwhile I felt like a spotlight landed on my malfunctioning ears. Hot New Deaf Guy waited for my response. I could tell him to get lost, but that would be rude. Why did my invisibility cloak have to fail me today? And why did he have to be so damn sexy standing there, all broad shoulders and a face that said, "Let me help you"?

He oozed confidence in his own skin. Mine itched. Heck, his ears didn't have anything in them, unless he had those fancy shmancy hearing aids that were next to invisible. The kind of hearing aids I assumed old dudes wore when their days of rock concerts gave them late onset loss. Not the kind of aids someone who had an interpreter at his side would wear.

At a loss for words on how I was supposed to communicate, or where my jumbled thoughts headed, I waved the white flag and showed him the empty packet like a moron.

He nodded, twisted his bag around, and found the batteries I needed.

I glanced around the room again. No one looked at us. No one cared that a hot guy holding out a packet of hearing aid batteries threw my world off kilter.

This class was going on The List of Horrible Classes. Current standing? Worst class ever.

He tapped the packet and signed. A few movements later, much like a speech delay on a bad broadcast, the interpreter beside him spoke.

"Go ahead. Sharon says this guy has a thick accent, must be hard to hear."

This could not get any more humiliating. I glanced at Perfect Ringlets, who I hoped was Sharon, and she nodded.

"Thank you." I took out one battery, pulled off the orange tab, and popped it into the small door on my hearing aid before shoving it back in my ear. Hot New Deaf Guy still hovered over me, wearing an infectious smile, a smile that made my knees weak. I handed the packet back. "You don't wear hearing aids, why do you have batteries?"

He watched Sharon as she signed my words while putting the batteries away. "I work at a deaf school. Most of my students have hearing aids and someone always needs a battery. I keep a stash on hand," he said via the interpreter.

"That's nice of you."

He smiled again. I wished he would stop. The smiling thing, I mean. Every time he did, I lost a brain cell. "My name's Reed." He stuck out a hand when he finished signing.

I looked at his hand, a bit amazed at how well he could communicate with it.

Not an excuse to be rude. I reached for his outstretched hand. "Carli."

Sharon asked me how I spelled my name. Reed looked at her instead of me. When I touched him, a spark of some kind ignited and dashed straight up my arm. A tingling that had nothing to do with my ears, or his ears. His eyes shot to mine and I froze. Unable to move or do anything human, like pull my hand back. All I could think of was the fact I'd never kissed a guy with a beard before.

An Excerpt from

SMOLDER
The Wildwood Series
By Karen Erickson

In the second book in *USA Today* bestselling
author Karen Erickson's Wildwood series
stoic sheriff's deputy Lane Gallagher has
lusted after his brother's ex for years . . .
but will he ever let himself have her?

The man was a complete idiot.

Like straight-up ignorant, ridiculous, gorgeous, stubborn, infuriating, sexy, elusive, and arrogant . . . yet sweet at the oddest times.

Delilah Moore frowned, tapping her fingers against her desk. She was at the dance studio trying to get some work done and failing miserably. And she definitely didn't like that bit about him being sweet intruding on her mental hissy fit. She wanted to hate Lane Gallagher right now. Hate him with the built-up anger of a million frustrated women because that's exactly what she was. A frustrated woman who was sick to death of being rejected by the only man who had ever given her true, real butterflies fluttering in her stomach.

Well, not *real* butterflies. Just that fluttery sensation one had when one saw the person she had feelings for. Not lust, not infatuation, not any of that shallow crap she'd experienced time and again as a way to try to rid her system of Lane once and for all. That stuff never lasted.

Nope, irritatingly sexy, aloof Lane Gallagher was the only one who ever made her feel something *real*.

No one else had ever done it. Not Weston—Lane's younger brother—when they were briefly together. They'd been in high school and in lust; that was it. None of the other guys she'd gone out with had ever made her feel much either—and she'd gone out with more than a few. She wasn't a celibate nun. She was a woman with needs, damn it. Had even had a couple of steady boyfriends over the years. Though for the past two years, she'd been so consumed with running her own business she'd sort of forgotten all about her own needs.

And she was too damn young for that sort of thing. She should be living it up! Having the time of her life! Look at West and Harper. Those two were up to no good in the best possible way. Harper glowed. That's what regular bouts of sex with the man you're madly, passionately in love with did for a girl.

Delilah, on the other hand, had thrown herself at Lane time and again. She'd barely escaped a horrific fire three weeks ago. Lane had seemed so relieved to find her, had held her so close and whispered comforting words in her ear while she'd practically trembled with nerves and adrenaline and fear. She'd savored the sensation of his thick, muscled arms around her. The way his lips had moved against her temple when he spoke and how he'd stroked her back with his big, capable hands. She'd melted into him, closing her eyes on a sigh, imagining all the delicious ways he might kiss her. Lips she'd never touched before but that she knew would taste like heaven . . .

And then he'd set her away from him, offered up a gruff,

"Glad you're all right," and practically ran away from her, never once looking back.

Jerk.

That had been the final straw. She hadn't really seen him since. And she was glad for it. So incredibly glad. Maybe she could finally purge him from her thoughts for good. She'd been kicked to the curb for the last time. The very last time . . .

The bell above the front door chimed, letting her know someone had entered the studio, and she sat up straighter at her desk, pretending she was actually getting work done versus daydreaming—more like day *scheming*—about Lane. She figured it was Wren, her best friend and business partner, coming in to work.

"Did you bring coffee with you?" Delilah yelled when Wren still hadn't made an appearance in the back office that they shared.

There was no reply.

Weird.

She rose to her feet, tucking a stray hair behind her ear as she made her way out of the office, down a tiny hall to emerge into the waiting area. All the breath expelled from her lungs when she saw who stood there with his back to her, eating up all the space with his mere six-foot-two presence.

Stupid Lane Gallagher, Wildwood County deputy sheriff, at her service. Ha, like he'd ever *service* her.